The AURATOR
DEADLY SECRETS

The AURATOR
DEADLY SECRETS

M.A. KROPF

To order additional copies of this book, contact:
Xlibris
844-714-8691
www.Xlibris.com
Orders@Xlibris.com
852147

Acknowledgments

This book is dedicated to my children for being my love and inspiration. I want to thank my family for being so patient while I spent countless hours on the computer. To Denise for pushing me through every instance of writer's block and whose input helped to shape major story lines. To Dad, for being a constant support; no matter what harebrained idea I came up with you have always been in my corner. To Mom, for sending countless emails with research and follow-up phone conversations to bounce ideas off another set of ears. To my father-in-law Frank, who read for me and encouraged me along the way. Lane S-B, whose professional feedback on my very first draft was difficult to hear but helped to make the story better. To Uncle Larry, a well-published author, for encouraging me to rewrite when I didn't want to, whose wisdom said I wouldn't regret it— you were right. To Anita Todd, my editor, and Chuck Todd, the book cover artist, for their professional guidance and advice to help make the project complete. These two gave so much of their time and energy toward this project because they believed in it and I am extremely grateful to them. To my readers who read one, two, and sometimes three drafts and gave feedback: Claire W., Bill K., Larry L., Rae Jean E., Valerie L., Nanette M., Larry B., Carole L., Sam Y., Diana K. , Carlee S., and Char M. for reading and lending her name for the detective character. Special thanks to my musical inspiration: Evanescence, Creed, and Machine Head for setting the mood. Thanks to Kathy Weires, photographer, for making the process of taking the author photo relatively painless and making me look good.

Reflection

This is it . . . the resolve . . . this is who I am. I never asked for this. As a nurse . . . as a mother . . . I always tried to be a good person, someone for my kids to look up to. Yet here I am doing the unthinkable . . . deciding who lives and who dies. Who am I to think that I should hold such control? Yet, as I stand here viewing the surreal scene in front of me, I struggle to fight the fear and the nausea . . . the excitement. I become acutely aware of every muscle in my body. One by one, flexing and extending as the blood pulses hard to supply the oxygen my muscles need to stay satisfied. My heart is pounding and racing . . . aching. A sudden chill vibrates through me as I become aware of a slight sweat band spread above my brow line. The back of my neck feels moist as a drop slowly trickles down my back. I take in a deep breath and, noticing the raggedness of my breathing, I steady myself. I smell the aroma of victory as the scene overtakes me, making me shudder as I feel the high. I can taste it on my tongue, which makes my mouth water and I have to swallow hard. I feel my saliva moving downward, a bit cold in my overheated body, only to land in my now quivering stomach. I sigh, realizing that the nausea has finally passed.

I stand and look at him, my victim, with contempt but also with a deep sadness that it had to come to this. He never saw it coming. His lifeless body is twisted into an unnatural position on the ground, still, but not dead . . . not yet . . . and a smirk spreads across my face.

But as the breeze of reality kisses my cheek, my face drops ever so slightly. The others . . . they were right . . . I have been created for this. I close my eyes for a moment as I feel a strange sensation. A need to do something, but what? Is this what they were talking about? I was drawn here and it felt right, but could I really finish it? Could I really end a person's life? Even if someone deserved to die, was I really to be judge and jury? I feel lightheaded as the faces of so many victims who were dead because of this person swirl in front of me. Resolve overwhelms my senses as I realize that he cannot live to repeat these acts. My eyes close, and as I take a deep breath I feel a sense of calm wash over my body. At this moment I understand who I am meant to be and how far I have come to get here. In front of me I see my past, present, and future. I was born to complete a purpose . . . *my purpose.* I suddenly see flashes of my past as I feel myself slipping into the memories of my youth . . . and the path that led me here.

1. The Pain

Everyone has a destiny, and whether it is predetermined or not, reaching it is up to each one of us.

Growing up I had always been . . . well *felt* different. I'm not sure why. I was a moderately attractive girl, sleek athletic build from all the years of soccer and running, long dark hair which I had been told had the perfect wave and body, although I was constantly at odds with it. I was good at sports, and academically I was in the top ten percent of my class. Still I never felt like I fit in. Friends, or the lack thereof, were a difficult subject for me to talk about. Many tried to be friends with me, but I was never able to let anyone close enough.

"Megan," my father would say to me, "why don't you call one of your friends and go to a movie or something?" But there was no one to call. It's hard to explain, but I *see* things that other people don't. A sort of a light or dark essence around a person. I remember my first experience with this when I was six years old.

The Catholic church that my family went to had a priest who always looked angry to me. But whenever he was around certain young boys in the congregation his shape took on an eerie dark hue. It was almost as if someone had taken a thick black marker and drawn a perfect outline of him, careful not to draw into the lines of his body but also not too far away. At least this is how my six-year-old eyes saw it. Everyone at the church loved him. He was, after all, one of the chosen ones . . . chosen by God. However, he disappeared one day, and neither I nor anyone in our church ever saw him again. It was much later, well into my twenties, that I heard he had been molesting the boys in the church.

The next time I noticed the strange outline, as I called it then, was not until my teenage years, when I was sixteen and a junior in high school. I hated high school. This time the outline was around a boy at school, and

I remember it was much darker, more pronounced, and had a feeling of impending doom to it. Since I didn't have a lot of friends, no one noticed when I became obsessed with following him around. I watched his every move, waiting for . . . well, I don't know what I was waiting for. I was always intrigued by others and felt as if people wandered around with blinders on, not watching their actions, others' reactions, or quite frankly even where they were going. I felt very aware of *everyone,* as if I was waiting, looking for . . . or about to miss . . . something.

The boy's name was John Steele, and I followed him around for two months the way an obsessed stalker follows his or her intended, watching his ever-changing outline. Sometimes it was jet black and very defined, moving with him. Other times it was a faded gray, less defined, more see-through and not very snug to his figure. But always there. By all accounts, John should have been a very popular boy since he was attractive and played on the lacrosse team. I saw that girls were definitely attracted to him because they would stare at him when he wasn't looking. He seemed completely oblivious to this. He was an attractive boy with short brown hair, blue eyes, and a strong build. The lacrosse team had to work out in the weight room every day so most of the boys on the team were fairly muscular. We were similar in one respect . . . he did not appear to have a lot of friends either. While I did not find myself attracted to John in *that way*, I was drawn to him. Why? I didn't know.

One night, two months after first noticing John, I had an extremely vivid and terrifying dream. Little did I know then that what I saw was more than just a dream. The dream started in a classroom, not one that I regularly attended, when something dark walked into the room. There was a loud noise . . . many loud noises. I saw three specific faces, kids that I recognized from school but didn't take classes with, twisted in terror and screaming. Everyone was screaming.

The screen in my head went red and I heard loud noises. It was more than noise, the screaming started to take shape. Words began to pierce the red screen . . . NO . . . HELP . . . MOM . . . PLEASE. The words were prefaced by and ended with more terrified sounding screams.

I wanted to wake up. I wanted out. I couldn't take it anymore. LET ME OUT!

I woke up screaming, unable to breathe, my eyes wide with terror. *The pain . . . so painful . . . in my chest . . . in my head . . . so painful . . . more screaming . . . make it stop.* Still today I can recall this and remember the pain with complete clarity.

My mom ran into the room and looked at me with worry and fear in her eyes. She grabbed my arms and pulled me close as her voice shook with uncertainty, "What's wrong, what hurts?"

I couldn't stop screaming, the pain was intense and wasn't like anything I'd ever felt before. My mom yelled for my dad to call 911 and I found myself writhing in pain. My next conscious memory was of paramedics holding me down, then strapping me to a gurney. Why weren't they stopping the pain, the pain, the pain? "MAKE IT STOP!" I screamed. At least I thought I had said it out loud.

I missed the ambulance ride and more in the cloud of pain. I then recall people working over me, poking, prodding, and testing in the emergency room. They finally gave me pain medicine, which coursed through my veins causing my fear and panic to slip through the welcomed shade of rest. The pain dulled and I was able to fall into a fitful sleep. I didn't dream. Through a fog I could hear things in the room. I heard the doctor come in to speak with my mother, who was hanging on by her last thread of sanity. I heard him say they couldn't find anything medically wrong with me that would have explained my symptoms. He suggested I see a psychiatrist. My mother broke down crying but reluctantly agreed . . . anything to help me, and I fell back into the haze.

By the next morning my pain had subsided and I was released to my mother's care pending an appointment with a shrink. I was exhausted, I just wanted to go home but was afraid to go back to sleep and . . . no, I couldn't think about what I had seen anymore.

Thankfully no more dreams. My mom called the school, explaining, "She's . . . *sick.*" I heard the confusion in her voice.

I went to the psychiatrist that day, explained what had happened, that I woke from a dream in extreme pain that I truly felt physically. My head . . . my chest . . . I shuddered when my memory of the pain flooded my consciousness again. I was not in pain today.

He asked if anything else had been going on, boyfriends (ha!), family, school? Well I couldn't tell him about the outline I saw around John because that was just crazy. So I said no. He spoke with my mom, chalked it up to normal teenage stress, hormones, possibly some attention-seeking . . . *quack* . . . but he didn't think anything was seriously wrong. I was starting to wonder if I *was* crazy, or, if not already there then at least on my way.

As we drove home my mom listened to the radio, we didn't talk, and I stared blankly out the window. *What the hell was that,* I thought. The pain was *real,* I think, but then I wasn't so sure.

Suddenly my concentration was broken, my heart sped up, my breathing was shallow and ragged. I felt dizzy. On the radio . . . my school . . . a shooting . . . a lot of kids dead . . . and the shooter . . . *a student*. Dizzy . . . and then everything went blank.

I woke up a few minutes later to find that my mom had stopped the car and was calling out my name. I had fainted or maybe hyperventilated myself into unconsciousness. Was it a dream?

Then she started crying. "I'm sorry honey, your friends . . ." she said.

"What? What, what happened?" I tried to slow my breathing and concentrate. I didn't want to pass out again.

"There was a shooting at your school, a student, I don't know the details. Oh my God . . . if you had been there!" Her words were difficult to understand as she buried her head in her hands to sob.

"How many? Did they die? Who did it?" A sudden pain in my stomach, and I knew who but was trying to grasp at reality and put the pieces together. The outline around John, the feeling of impending doom, the dream . . . kids . . . faces . . . red . . . loud noises. Then the pain, and I shuddered once more.

"We need to go to the school mom. My friends." I really didn't have friends to worry about but I wanted to see the aftermath myself.

"No!" she exclaimed, "Haven't you been through enough? No! I'm taking you home."

We went home and I immediately turned on the news. "Breaking news, less than one hour ago a student opened fire on fellow classmates in a massive shooting . . . ." The words trailed off as I tried to think this through, feeling more aware and more in control. "The student suspected of being responsible for the shooting is a senior attending the school . . . the student's name is being withheld until the investigation has been completed . . . ." Again they trailed off but my breathing had become ragged, shallow, dizzy. No, I can't faint, I thought, not now, get ahold of yourself. "Reports coming in," I tuned back in, "three students shot and killed, one in the head and two others in the chest." Was this what my pain was about?

"The identities of the victims will be withheld until the families can be notified," the reporter continued. But didn't I already know who they were? Didn't I see their faces . . . feel their pain? What do I do with this? Do I tell someone? Am I right or am I crazy?

Then they showed him, John, on camera, his head tucked between two police officers . . . in shame? Hands were behind his back in cuffs.

Then I saw it again, even on TV . . . the darkness that encircled him was wider and darker than it had ever been before. Had I seen this coming? Okay, that *is* crazy.

I ran out the front door, not bothering to say good-bye to my mom. But she heard me and screamed after me, "Stop!" But I couldn't. I needed to see what had happened for myself.

I jumped into my car, sort of a heap but it was all I could afford. I had just gotten my driver's license and bought a stick shift . . . ugh. I was still so slow at this. I was able to get it going, shifting and grinding the gears, and lunging forward just to get up to the speed limit. I made it to the school as some of the families arrived, the families of the children, my classmates. Would they be the faces from my dream?

My brother, Tim, a San Francisco police officer for four years already, was there. He saw me and his eyes were wide with concern. "Go home," he hollered at me. I saw the worry on his face but shook my head at him and looked away . . . *moron*. He needed to focus, he was not a very good cop. I moved through the crowds of onlookers, some of them staring in bewilderment and others crying for the kids they knew and those they didn't. I knew the back entrance to the building well, since that was how I often slipped out of class to avoid talking to anyone. It was unguarded and I let myself in. I knew where to go.

I felt the heat inside me rise as I got closer. "It's the same room," I murmured to myself. My breathing quickened and I peeked around the corner waiting for one of the officers to step away from the entrance. I saw my opening as a mother came running in, pushing past the police screaming, "My baby, my baby!" My heart ached and tears welled up in my eyes. I tried to shake it off, I needed to focus . . . to see.

The officers rushed to hold back the grieving mother and I snuck into the room. I stopped suddenly, unable to breathe.

There it was, just as I had seen it. All of it. The three faces, the three classmates . . . Gayle Alexander . . . Tori Cunningham . . . Jeff Whiten. All of them, just as I had seen their faces in the dream. I clutched my chest and, suddenly feeling dizzy, I fell against the wall, trying to brace myself and not look away. I needed to know this. Gayle, shot in the head twice, maybe three times? She lay in a large pool of blood on the floor. Tori, shot in the chest, maybe once. Blood was splattered like a Rorschach behind her on the wall and she was slumped in a heap in the corner. Jeff was the worst. He must have put up a fight. Several obvious wounds, his t-shirt shredded in pieces. He had left a trail of blood behind him as it looked like he was trying to get out of the room. *How could this be? How could I have known this? Could I have done anything? What would . . . ?*

"Hey!" an officer yelled at me. I tried to turn my head but the room was spinning . . . had I stopped breathing?

He rushed over, grabbed me before I fell, and carried me out to the ambulances. "Keep her out!" he ordered.

Ambulances? Oh no, not again. I tried to take deep breaths and recover so that I could avoid yet another ride to the hospital, where surely this time they would lock me away.

I stood up carefully. Good, my feet were working, my legs still a little wobbly, but I convinced the EMTs that I was all right. They were too busy to worry much more about me. I walked slowly back to my car, past the onlookers, crossing the caution tape. *Odd . . . caution tape . . . could it really keep anyone out?*

I got to my car and broke down. I cried so hard that I wasn't sure I was making sound anymore. By the time I looked up, the parking lot was half empty and I was drained. I drove home, the car grinding and lurching most of the way. As I walked in, my mom and dad ran to me with a mixture of sadness and concern in their eyes.

"I'm sorry you lost friends, honey. It's not fair," my mom said. Friends? Funny, that hadn't been what I was so shaken about. Sure I'd known them all since kindergarten and was sad anyone died. But friends? No.

"Honey, can I do anything for you?" my dad asked.

"No," I replied looking at both of them. Fear and sadness covered their faces, and I had a sudden rush of shame welling up inside. Should I say that I had known, that I could have done something?

My parents . . . Diane and Russ Alcosta. I've been told my whole life how our last name means *the one who walks along the coast.* "The coast being San Francisco," my dad would always add. Having heard this story about a hundred times, I would roll my eyes . . . again. My family has been here since the beginning, my father always told us. "We built this city and won't leave 'til they've burned the whole thing down."

They are the epitome of a Beaver Cleaver family. My dad, an attorney with the San Francisco District Attorney's office. I wondered calmly if he would be prosecuting John. My mom, the stay-at-home mom, PTA all the way.

It hadn't always been like this for them. My parents used to be very active alcoholics, throwing parties almost every night and passed out late at night . . . *every* night. They were Monday through Saturday atheist alcoholics and Sunday withdrawing Catholics. They both got help right before they had me and have been sober, Alcoholics Anonymous, model parents ever since.

I knew the story very well, they retold it to me hundreds of times when I was growing up, as if trying to make sure I wouldn't choose the same rocky path. They were . . . are loving and good parents. But how would they respond to me telling them my truths? Ugh . . . more psychiatrists.

I hugged them both and walked to my room. I just wanted to sleep.

I woke up feeling a little weak and sore. I got dressed for school and wandered to the kitchen. Dad had gone to work and mom walked in as I was eating breakfast.

I looked up to say good morning and stopped suddenly. My mom had a white outline. She paused in the doorway and looked at me, a little stunned, even nervous and asked, "You okay honey?"

"Yeah mom," I finally got out. Come on Megan, pull yourself together. "I'm fine." Then I looked back down at my Cheerios. My mom paused for a minute, as if waiting for something. Then she turned and walked out. I glanced up to watch her walk away, white light and all.

School was equally painful, everyone walking around me with various shades of light and dark, everyone with their own marker. But for what? Good or bad?

I couldn't look. I didn't want to know.

I hung my head, not making eye contact, wishing I was blind. It would be years before anything, or anyone, would make me want to look up to greet society again.

2. Warmth

I survived high school and started college. I was terrified to move away from home. Over the next few years, I had unwillingly developed, no perfected, seeing the outlines on people. I felt as if I could sense a dark outline near. Maybe I was crazy. But I would turn away, walk away, do whatever I could to avoid seeing . . . knowing.

Occasionally I had to look up and was awe-struck by the fact that *everyone* had this kind of aura around them. They were different shades, sometimes switching between light and dark. I had no idea what that meant, but I didn't really want to analyze it.

I hadn't had another dream since high school and prayed I never would again. I went to college, did my homework, and just like high school . . . no friends.

I was in my senior year and about to graduate as a nurse. I had always wanted to be a nurse. My dream job was to work in an emergency room, saving lives.

As I passed by my favorite old building on the campus, a beautiful red brick building, worn, but loved by weather and time, I saw it . . . him. An amazingly bright aura that stopped me in my tracks. I had never seen anything like it before and it shimmered like bits of colored sunlight dancing on the water.

I felt myself pulled toward it, my heart racing, breath quickening, palms sweating. I got within twenty feet of him and it hit me like a gust of hot wind and I closed my eyes. My breathing stopped.

As I regained my composure, I slowly started breathing and opened my eyes. He was a rugged looking guy, but somehow soft. He looked at me with the bluest eyes I'd ever seen. My breath quickened as he smiled a smile that could melt any ice-cold heart . . . even mine. I noticed one crooked tooth, a smile just shy of perfect. I took a deep breath and felt the flush on my checks. My heart sped as he put something down and started walking toward me. His blonde hair ruffled slightly in the breeze as he approached. I watched as he drew closer and closer, stopping just in front of me, easily eight inches taller as me and at least twice as wide, all muscle.

Just then I felt it . . . a wave of heat, smacking me in the face, forcing me to gasp. He chuckled, probably drawing his own conclusions from this. I quickly thought the heat must be connected to this very different aura. Different . . . but beautiful. For the first time in my life I felt safe and at ease. And very warm. I had a sudden urge to remove my sweater. My distraction caused by the aura and heat quickly dissipated as he spoke.

"Hi," he said with the sweetest smile. He held out his hand.

What was I just thinking about? Doesn't matter.

"Hi," I was barely able to utter and I reached out to shake his hand. My hand warmed and softened in his as he reached with his left and grasped my hand in his.

He looked curiously at me, or confused, trying to figure out if I was nothing short of a moron, and chuckled, "I'm Luke. You a student here?"

"Uh, yeah. You?" My IQ was dropping by the second.

He smiled bigger and chuckled. I became aware that he was still holding my hand, "No, maintenance department. I work here."

I wish I could say it took more than that, but it didn't. We spent every day after that together. I couldn't get enough of him . . . in any way. The way he looked at me . . . touched me . . . but more so how I felt with him. I had never felt so at ease or comfortable in my surroundings. I also noticed that I still had the same anxious, nervous, "don't fit in" feeling when I wasn't with him.

We married the following year after graduation. I got my first nursing job working in an emergency room. Night shift, but it was worth it. Life was amazing. Three children came . . . all girls . . . over the years. First Alexandra, or Alex, now fourteen and a brunette like me. It took us many years to have our next child but then came Trina, now eleven and a redhead—we don't know how that happened. Then right away Abigail, seven and a blonde, the spitting image of my husband. My life was perfect. I finally fit somewhere. But always, the minute I was away from my family the same angst hit. Work was good but I was always edgy there too. A lot of commendations for good work. I was . . . I am a good nurse.

My daughters were everything to me. When I wasn't sleeping, trying to catch up from the night shift, I was working in their classrooms, shuttling to and from school or some blur of soccer/violin/volleyball practice/concerts/

games. Each of my girls had the same colored shimmering aura that their dad had. Only Trina's had a slight pink hue to hers, probably some odd reflection of her gorgeous hair.

I still saw auras around everyone and mostly avoided looking too closely or paying too much attention. I had learned to become numb to it, to look at someone and tune out the light around them, almost as if lifting them out of it. I noticed that if I touched them—like while I was at work—the aura dimmed and the person became more prominent . . . more comfortable for me to work with. This is the way life went on for me, day in and day out. Until . . .

One month ago . . . the dream

Women writhing in pain
screaming
many very clear distinct faces
all screaming and begging for mercy
screaming
laid out, twisted in different positions
everything covered in red
screaming
the agony of each face moving in and out of view
one by one
screaming . . . screaming . . . screaming
the pain on each face
red everywhere . . . too much red . . .

I pleaded with my sleeping self . . . wake up . . .
screaming
wake up . . .
screaming

OH GOD, WAKE UP!!!!

I woke up crying out in pain. It hurt so bad, the intensity of it. *Not again,* I thought . . . My family!

My husband was the first in the room. It was still dark outside, not yet morning, and he was getting ready for work. My daughters ran in after him, but he reassured them, telling them to go back to bed. "Mommy's okay," he kept trying to say.

I could hear the hesitation in his voice as if he didn't believe the words himself. I could barely focus on him because of the blinding pain. My head, my body, between my legs. I had to hold myself. I brought my knees up to my chest, wrapping my arms around my legs, trying to squeeze the pain, trying to suffocate it. My husband wrapped his arms around me, enveloping me in his warmth. I gasped . . . the pain was gone. But my visions . . . the nightmare . . . had returned and I started to cry. "Don't let go of me, please," I begged.

He rocked me, speaking slowly, fear in his voice, "I have you. I'll hold you as long as you want."

He held me for a while, occasionally kissing my forehead, although I'm not sure how much time had passed. I tried to clear my throat as the crying stopped, trying to speak, but all that came out was a raspy noise.

My husband noticed my dry throat and went to get me a glass of water. When he let go all the pain returned, just as intense. Crippling me. He reached out again and clutched me toward him. The pain disappeared again. Now I really thought I was crazy.

I looked at my husband's wide, terrified eyes. Yeah, he thought so too. "What do I do?" he finally asked.

"I don't know, just hold me, it seems to be better when you're holding me." I couldn't tell him what I was thinking. *You married a crazy person . . . run while you can . . . run . . . I had a vision . . . maybe a dream . . . no wait I need you . . . no, run!!!* How do you say that to someone without them calling a psychiatrist. Too bad for my husband that when we took our vows, we hadn't added for better or worse *or crazy.*

The sun came up and my pain subsided. Every time my husband got up to help one of the girls, make lunches, or get ready himself, the pain returned. But each time it was a little better.

By the time my husband had to leave to take the girls to school, the pain was a dull ache and I could bear it. As he left, he made me promise to get rest and call him if anything else happened. He urged me to call the doctor but I said I was fine.

3. Chaos

Finally alone, I tried to put the pieces together . . . another dream. I hadn't had one since I was sixteen. I shuddered. That one didn't go so well. Would this one be better? I hadn't noticed anyone with a black aura like the one I'd seen on John Steele in high school.

Okay, I'm nuts . . . I need a break. *Shopping!* I thought. That will help. I need to forget the faces, push them away . . . besides, we need milk.

Driving around, I couldn't help but notice. *Everyone* was lit up . . . light and dark . . . as if trying to get my attention. I tried to look away, but it haunted me . . . taunted me wherever I looked. Why? Is it getting stronger? But why now?

I turned the music up in the car . . . I forgot I'd put this CD in. It was a metal band that a friend from high school was in and they were having some much-deserved success. I suddenly remembered my old '80s big-hair Scorpion and Van Halen days. Ugh. I shuddered at the image of myself. That did it, I was better. I'm sure the guy sitting in his way-too-expensive-now-I-don't-have-a-college-fund-for-my-kids BMW next to me thought I had completely lost my mind as I started singing at the top of my lungs, bellowing out words that I knew didn't match the lyrics and throwing my head forward and back like I was at some absurd rock concert. I didn't care. I felt better.

I got to the store, and as I walked in I felt the familiar rush of cooler air from inside. I loved these all-you-need stores with their clothes, electronics, and food all under one roof. As I negotiated up and down the aisles, paying attention to the auras around me, I became aware of a temperature sensation attached to each one. The darker the aura, the colder the temperature as I got close to them. Conversely, the lighter the aura, the warmer the temperature.

How had I missed this before? I looked at one shopper with a white aura. He was African American, short and a little on the stocky side, middle-aged, with just the beginnings of a thinning hairline. He had on a pair of dark slacks with a white button-up shirt. There wasn't anything particularly distinct about this man. So why such a bright white aura? Was he that good?

I then looked around and found a fairly dark aura. Not black like John's had been but definitely dark. She was a tall Caucasian woman with smartly styled hair and expensive-looking jewelry. Her suit was clearly tailored for her and her shoes looked Italian. She was talking on a cell phone about some *idiot* in some merger and that she would take care of it when she got back to the office. I watched her cut in line at the checkout and decided that I'd seen enough.

I then focused on something that I had noticed before but had never taken the time to investigate. I saw a young boy walking through the clothing section whose aura apparently shifted back and forth between light and dark, sliding through all the shades in between. He was a very strong and handsome high-school football type. Could a person switch between good and bad, or rather *decide* to be good or bad and have it reflected around him?

I found myself a bit distracted for a second, wondering why this kid wasn't in school. He walked between the racks with his white aura neatly attached and then approached a shirt rack. He shifted darker as he held a particular shirt and then shifted back to light. I found myself squinting to see his face, but his shoulder-length wavy red hair covered his face like a curtain. He then moved on to another rack, sliding back to a darker shade as he stood there. What was he thinking? Ah, maybe he was deciding which way to go.

I tried to shake it off, actually shaking my head. I walked down the cereal aisle toward the milk, concluding that I really didn't want to know this much about the auras. Out of the corner of my eye I saw someone looking at me and I turned to meet his eyes. A man stood holding a box of cereal, seemingly struck by something and looking at *me*. He smiled and nodded at me, then turned to look back at the boxes on the shelves. I didn't stop looking, however, because his aura was different. Unlike anything I'd ever seen before. It was red.

I examined him for a moment. He was maybe in his late fifties and tall with a muscular build, slightly olive skin and dark wavy hair that looked like he wouldn't have to brush it and it would still fall effortlessly into place.

He had a beautiful face and was striking to look at with deep green eyes that seemed to stand out against his skin. He was very attractive and well dressed in casual clothes that were clean and pressed with a blue button-up shirt. So why a red aura?

I turned away, not really wanting the answer to this question in my head. As if I didn't have enough to worry about! As I walked I thought I should go to the girl's clothing section. My girls were growing so fast, it was hard to keep up with . . . .

"Excuse me," said a voice behind me. I turned and it was the same man I had been looking at, except now his aura was right in front of me, almost blinding me. I was caught off guard and I staggered back.

"Yes," I barely got the word out, my voice cracking as if I had just awakened out of a deep sleep. His eyes bore down on me in an awed, almost bewildered gaze that I'm sure mirrored my own.

"I'm sorry to bother you," he said. "My name is Aaron. I wanted to introduce myself."

Oh great, I thought, he's coming on to me. I'm sure he could surmise my distaste by my expression. I was never one to have a poker face.

"I know this seems odd, and you don't know me, but we have something in common," he said. He smiled warmly, making it seem I should trust him. There was something familiar about him that I couldn't put my finger on. Had I worked with him? A patient? Hopefully not one of the ones we had to put on a psych hold.

I thought it would be better for me to let him tell me who he was before I started throwing out guesses and giving away unnecessary information to this stranger.

"What?" I blurted out almost rudely. I could feel my walls going up. Caution. But I still couldn't fight the familiar feeling I had.

"Well," he started again, still smiling with excitement in his eyes, "it's hard to explain, especially here in the middle of the store. Let's just say that I know what you see, what you are . . . we share this. Does that make sense to you?"

I suddenly felt my breathing speed past me as if I were trying to catch it. My heart was hammering so fast that I was sure it would burst out of my chest. I felt dizzy. My words spilled out, making no sense, "What? . . . Who? . . . What? . . . I don't understand."

I sat down on one of the displays and tried to compose myself. What could this stranger know about what I see? I don't even know what I see. He stood next to me waiting for me to collect myself.

"What do you mean you know what I see?" I squeezed my eyes shut hoping to keep out an answer I wasn't sure I wanted.

I was momentarily distracted as I heard a scuffle and watched the store security escort the young red-haired boy past us while using a walkie-talkie to call the police. The boy had been caught shoplifting. The boy's aura was white now . . . and I wondered to myself if this experience had made his decision for him.

Aaron looked toward the boy and then back at me. He knelt down next to me and said in a barely audible voice, "Your dreams, the auras."

He stopped suddenly as he noticed my wide, deer-in-the-headlights eyes and moved back cautiously from me. As if trying not to frighten me any more than I was. "I'm sorry . . . I shouldn't have . . . I just wasn't expecting . . . you . . . ." He shook his head and reached into his pocket.

I could feel my lungs laboring to move in and out with any sort of fluidity.

"This wasn't the best way to do this. I'm sorry, but I was surprised to see . . . *you*," he continued, still looking at me, confused now.

What did that mean? *You.* As if he knew me. He handed me a business card that he had removed from his pocket and smiled apologetically.

"Call me if you want answers."

And then he walked away rubbing his forehead and running his fingers through his hair as if he had a headache.

Answers? What the hell! What was that? I didn't ask for this. I didn't want this. I watched his red aura move away . . . fading. I could feel the tears welling up. I dropped the items I was holding and moved quickly out of the store, breaking into a run as I hit the doors to the outside. I barely made it into my car before the waterworks started. I was sobbing, and the pain in my chest was sharp with every breath.

I don't know how much time had passed, but when I finally pulled my head up from the steering wheel I felt as if I could burst. I drove home on autopilot, not paying much attention to cars around me. Who was he, and what did he know about what I could see?

As I pulled in the driveway, I called my husband. It would be time to pick the girls up from school soon and I was in no condition to do it.

"Honey?" I said as he answered on the other end.

"What's the matter?" Luke could always tell when something was wrong. He was the only one in my life with whom I was transparent . . . until now.

"I'm fine, better than earlier. But I don't think I'll make it to pick the girls up. Can you?" I tried to sound sane . . . put together. I don't think I was successful.

"Sure, love. I'll leave now. Do you want to talk about anything?" Always so reasonable, so calm.

"Not now. I think I just need some time. Okay? I love you." I hung my head. He was always more open than me. So patient and willing to be there for me, but I'd always been so closed off.

"Okay, just let me know." I could hear him wanting to ask for more information. "And honey . . . whatever it is . . . it will be okay."

I was choking back tears. I did want to tell him. "Okay, I love you."

"I love you, too."

I hung up and continued crying. I was able to regain enough composure to get out of the car and walk inside the house. I walked into the kitchen, got a glass of water and tried to breathe. Visions of my dream came flooding in, and I was struck by a sudden wave of rage. I started thinking of this stranger I met. *What did he know?*

I'm not sure what happened next but my vision changed. I saw flashing lights in front of my eyes, a strong sensation shot through my body and I reacted. It was involuntary. I started grabbing everything off the counters, out of the cabinets, throwing them with more force and strength than I even knew I was capable of. Dishes and glasses smashed against the walls and floor. I could hear them breaking yet somehow felt disconnected from the reality shattering around me.

The thought flittered through my head, *Who's doing this?* Flashes again of my dream, not just this last one but also the one from high school. I saw red, lots of red. The screaming in my head was so loud I almost couldn't hear the crashing around me. As I was losing control I had a strange sensation of a different kind of awareness.

A sudden shudder went through my body and my state was broken. I felt immediately conscious of my surroundings. And of course, the mess. What had I done? I sat on the floor among the shards of glass and porcelain dishes in ruins.

I was filled with remorse. I wasn't used to losing control. I'm a wife, a mother, a nurse. I'm supposed to be the one *in* control. My head dropped into my hands. Maybe I finally do need that shrink, I thought. What's wrong with me? I remembered something from earlier in the day and reached into my pocket.

I pulled out the business card. It was white linen paper, classy, but with very little writing on it. Just a name and a phone number.

I picked up the phone and dialed. It rang just once.

"Hello?" said the familiar voice from earlier.

"Aaron?"

4. The Meeting

After cleaning up my mess, and myself as well, I wrote a note to my husband apologizing for the lack of dishes, writing that I needed to go out tonight and I would explain later. I placed a stack of paper plates alongside plastic forks on the counter, considering they would need some way to eat dinner.

Aaron had agreed to meet me at a nearby cafe. I wasn't sure what I was walking into and felt horrible for not telling my husband where I was going. If this person actually had answers then I wanted them . . . didn't I? I wasn't sure how he could have the answers or know what was going on in my head, the things that I saw, that I dreamed.

I started to panic. Was I going to meet some crazy guy who noticed a woman in a store on the verge of a nervous breakdown and saw an opportunity? Maybe he was just very perceptive. I got into my car and tried to distract myself with other random thoughts and with the things around me. As I shifted my car from second to third gear smoothly, I chuckled, thinking about learning to drive a stick shift when I was sixteen. Life seemed so much simpler then. But even that didn't seem to help, as my mind flashed to the classroom scene from high school and I could feel my heart take a sudden gallop forward. I tried to shake it off. *Think of something else, Megan.*

I turned into the parking lot of the cafe, not really remembering how I got there. After parking I took a minute to collect myself. I got out and looked into the cafe. There were a lot of people in there . . . safe.

I walked in and glanced around. There was a woman behind the counter . . . white aura . . . good, I'll talk to her. What do I say, *Hey, have you seen some guy come in with a red aura?* Instead I told her I was meeting someone and would just take a look around. As I scanned the tables I saw a blur of white, black, gray. Then in the back corner I saw it, a red glow, like a beacon in the middle of an ocean. Our eyes met and he smiled at me. His eyes seemed warm and inviting, and a little curious.

I made my way across the room, noticing cold blasts or warm waves hitting me as I walked through the room. As I had noticed earlier, the cold corresponded with the darker auras and the warmth with the lighter. I had never "felt" so many auras before. As I got to the table, he stood, still smiling, and motioned for me to sit.

"I'm glad you called," he said as I tried to size up this strange red aura. Oddly, I noticed as I sat down that there was no temperature change around him.

"You said you know what I *see?*" I left it at that. I had a sudden surge of confidence that it was all a mistake. This guy didn't know anything. He couldn't know what I had to deal with, and I was nuts to come meet him.

"How long have you seen light and dark auras?" he asked.

"What do you mean light and dark?" Better to seem aloof. I wanted to know what *he* knew.

He smiled, seeming to sense my hesitation. "Maybe I'm going about this the wrong way. Forgive me, but seeing you really piqued my curiosity. You probably want some proof to be sure you can talk openly with me."

Okay, he's good. "Go on."

"Again, my name is Aaron. I'm an Aurator, just like you. I can see light and dark auras around individuals. Simply put, light is good and dark is, well . . . not so good."

I could feel my heart speeding and my breath quickening. I had a sudden urge to run out of the building, but an intense curiosity kept me here.

He continued, "I have dreams that show me . . . *things* and I connect them to the aura and . . . well," he leaned toward me and lowered his voice, "I fix it." He leaned back and smiled again, acting like he sensed my anxiety.

I swallowed loudly and tried to steady my voice. "What does this have to do with me?"

He looked as if he knew my doubts. "Do you see my red aura?"

My breath caught. "Yes."

He smiled wider, again leaned forward, and said in such a hushed voice that I had to concentrate to hear him, "I see your red aura too."

My head was spinning. My words came out so fast I could barely keep up, "What do you mean? I don't have . . . I mean I've never seen . . .

everyone else has . . . but me . . . no." I put my hands over my face and tried to fight the spinning.

"It's okay, I can't see my own either. It's the only aura we can't see." I'd never thought about this before. Of course I had never considered that I actually *had* an aura that could or couldn't be seen. Far less that I simply couldn't see it for myself.

"Why?" I asked.

"We're not exactly sure. But none of us can. There may . . ."

"Wait," I cut him off. "Us? How many of you are there?"

"How many of *us* are there," he corrected me. "Not many." He shook his head, "Not enough."

"Enough for what?" I didn't feel like I was getting information very quickly from this man.

"To take care of the *others*." He stared at me as if waiting for a reaction. I didn't have one.

"Who are the others?" I asked. His eyebrows furrowed at this question and he looked deep into my eyes as if trying to dig for information.

"Others who are completing *their purpose*," Aaron said carefully without answering me.

Now I was confused. Not only was I sitting in a cafe with a complete stranger, someone whose sanity I was starting to question along with my own, but now he's speaking in some sort of code.

"What's a *purpose*?" I glared back into his eyes.

He sat back in his chair, his face going white, his eyes wide with surprise.

"What?" I asked.

"I'm not sure what to say. I think I've already assumed too much." He shook his head as if trying to discount something.

I was losing my patience. "You're the one who asked me here. If you know something that is going to save my sanity, I need to know what it is. Or . . . if you're just some lunatic, then I'm calling the police."

He put his hand up as if asking me to wait. Taking a deep breath he asked, "Have you had a dream that has come true . . . in a way? Saw victims of a crime?"

Now it was my turn to sit back. I took a deep breath. "Yes, why?"

"When?" he asked.

"When I was sixteen in high school." I tried to shake the memory out of my head.

His eyes were wide and he was breathing fast. "What happened?"

I decided to take a leap of faith and began to tell him about my experiences, my vision of the kids at school and how I had found the bloody scene afterward. As my story unfolded, Aaron's expression grew more and more confused. When I ended, he was shaking his head in disbelief, and I found myself beginning to wonder if I had been right to confide in him.

"That's impossible," Aaron finally struggled to say. "I don't understand how this could have happened."

"Now I've told you enough, I want some answers," I said under my breath to him. You *clearly* know something, or *think* you know something about me that I don't."

"I do."

"Well?"

He took a couple of deep breaths and then began telling me more than I ever wanted to know.

"I'm an Aurator. I'm designed at my most basic genetic structure to right the wrongs in this world. I have dreams or visions that show me people who are going to be victims . . . unnecessarily. Then I connect those visions with an aura . . . the essence around the person who *will be* responsible for these crimes. When I see the aura of my purpose, the visions show like a slide show around the person. It is clear to me in that moment that I have the right person. I then eliminate them to protect the potential victims."

It's settled, I thought, this guy is crazier than me.

He continued, "I've run into others of our kind, but never one like you. First off, our purpose usually does not begin for us until well into our twenties when our psyche is strong enough to handle it. Second, we don't develop the red aura until we've completed our first purpose, something you say you haven't done yet. And third, there has never been a woman." He looked at me, waiting for a reaction.

I paused, thinking about which of the points I wanted to clarify. "What do you mean completed our first purpose?"

"Elimination of the person."

"Elimination? You mean *kill?*" I asked, almost shocking myself with the bluntness. I looked around to be sure no one was listening.

He paused, thinking over his response, "Yes, that's one way to look at it."

I snickered sarcastically, "Is the person's heart beating when you're done? I'm a nurse. If it's not beating, that's called DEAD." I couldn't believe I was having this conversation.

He grimaced, "Well then, I guess I would have to agree."

"So what does that make me?" I raised one eyebrow at him.

"One of us . . . I think."

"What do you mean *you think*?"

"I'm not sure I'm the right person to answer your questions," he said. This was becoming maddening and I was losing patience.

One thing I knew for sure. I am a nurse. I save people, I don't kill them. On this point I was perfectly clear.

"If you can't answer questions about me, can you tell me more about you? Why do you do it?" Keep him talking was all I could think to do in the moment.

"Well . . . I don't just *do* it. I'm born this way. It's hard to explain."

"Try," I said curtly.

He took another breath, "Do you believe in creation or evolution?"

My eyes widened. I hadn't expected this question. "I was raised in the Catholic Church, so, creation to a point. However, as a nurse, being science-based I also believe in evolution. Why?"

"That's good. The truth is that it's both. Life is a delicate balance between creation and evolution. We are all fragile threads of DNA teetering on the fence between these two truths. Created by one and being changed by the other. Mistakes happen. Our DNA change relative to evolution or environment, maybe both, we're not sure. But like everything in life, when there is an action, there is an equal and opposite reaction."

I was pretty sure I wasn't breathing.

He took a drink of his water and continued. "While some people change and do bad things, we change to counter this. We like to think of ourselves as God's clean-up crew, not that God makes mistakes. It's just that we can help keep the balance and effect change, positively, for many people."

I found myself flashing back to church, to the priest who had been molesting boys. I remembered that the only thing I got out of the Bible was that those thin pages, when torn out, wadded up, and sucked on for an appropriate amount of time made the best spit wads. Shaking my head, I said, "This is hocus-pocus, fiction. This doesn't really happen."

"It does, and you are a part of it. Although," he paused and looked curiously at me again, "I'm honestly not sure how."

"What do you mean?"

"Well, like I said, there's never been a woman. Additionally, you shouldn't have a red aura if you haven't yet, as you say, *killed* someone. I'm not sure what to make of it."

"Okay," I said, "I've heard just about enough. How do I find out why I have this red aura you're talking about, since you don't know?"

"We need to talk to Max."

"Who's Max?"

"Well, Max has been around a lot longer than I have. He's our local historian."

Okay, I thought, I'll bite. "How long does this go back?"

"Centuries." He turned away and shook his head. There was a hint of sadness in his face. I pressed on.

"So, if I am who you say I am, do I have a choice?"

"What do you mean by choice?" he asked.

"Can I choose not to complete a *purpose*?"

His eyebrows furrowed, "I don't know if anyone's tried."

"What was it like for you?"

He thought about this for a moment. "It was 1974, and I was twenty-two. While in college, I was living in the Noe Valley area of San Francisco. I loved that area, so diverse and so many beautiful views of the city. It was during this time that I had my first vision. The images in my vision, which was more like a dream to me at the time, were so vivid, and the terrifying depictions of blood and death . . . well . . . they shook me to my core. What was worse was the pain I felt once I woke up, and I had to spend the whole day in bed. It was the next day while I was walking around that I suddenly noticed everyone had these lights around them. Different shades of white light and others with a dark shadow-like cloak. It was the early '70s, and while I had done my fair share of drugs in the late '60s, I hadn't done any for a while. I thought I was having some sort of flashback. However, over the next few days the lights kept getting stronger, and eventually I felt temperature changes around the lights."

I wondered if he could possibly know that this was how it was for me.

He took a drink of water and continued. "A week or so later I was out walking around Coit Tower on a date. I'll never forget it because it was so foggy we couldn't see the top of the building while standing at the bottom. We were remarking on it when what felt like a cold knife stabbed into my back. I turned, half expecting to see a mugger trying to rob me, but saw that no one was there. I looked around and saw the darkest aura I had ever seen hugging tightly around a man's shape as he moved swiftly away. I felt drawn to him somehow. I wanted to watch him. I *needed* to watch him. I didn't want to leave my date so I asked her to walk with me, but the man was too quick and I lost him.

"Two days later, walking down by the wharf after dinner with friends, I passed by an alley—you know, the ones that are one-way only?"

I nodded my head, eyes wide.

"I felt it again, the cold blast slamming against me, and this time it nearly knocked me over. I followed the feeling of cold down the alley, scared and not sure what I was doing. When I got to the end of the alley, standing under a streetlamp was the same man I had seen two days earlier. Medium build, brown hair, glasses, nothing special, except for this eerie black aura. I felt myself drawn toward him again and he turned to walk away. I felt something boiling inside me, almost controlling me. A feeling of strength that I had never felt before. A need to do something, but I didn't know what. As I got closer, he turned as if to say something to me, and without thinking I lunged at him, took him down. He wrestled with me, but I had a new strength—call it adrenaline, fear, whatever, but I knew I had a job to do. I saw the images of women he had hurt and would hurt flashing around him and I knew he was the one connected to my dream. I learned later that this is called my 'purpose' or my reason for being an Aurator, if you will.

"He begged me to let him go. I couldn't. I asked him who he was and if he had killed people. I needed to know this was the right person. It *felt* right but I needed to know for sure. At first he said nothing, so I twisted his body like a pretzel. I felt bones crack under my hands. His mouth opened with a scream, and confessions flowed like a river. When he was done I grabbed his head between my hands and twisted his neck until it broke. He died almost instantly. The feeling that came over me afterwards was . . . well . . ." and then he paused looking at me thoughtfully, trying to gauge what I was thinking.

What was I thinking? I wasn't sure myself and I couldn't feel most of my body.

He took a breath to start talking again, but I put a hand up. "Wait a minute, you killed him just like that?"

"I had to." He looked calm, confident as he said the words.

"Why? What had he done to you?" I glared at this self-righteous man sitting across the table from me.

Then he smiled and very matter-of-factly said, "He was the Zodiac Killer."

My jaw dropped. I remembered hearing about the serial killer when I was just a kid. I knew he had disappeared, but this guy was saying *he* was responsible? Many people had claimed they knew the killer, even claimed to be relatives. But this was absurd.

I couldn't take any more. I grabbed my purse, took out two dollar bills and threw them on the table. "Thanks for meeting me. I have a lot to think about." I looked at my watch. It would be dinner time at home, and I was ready to go.

"Wait," he tried to say.

I raised my hand again. "Really, I've had enough today. I'll call you." *Not,* I thought to myself. He stood, looking a little worried as I got out of my seat and left.

As I drove home I felt numb. I reviewed the events of the day and shuddered. I was glad I didn't have to work that night and I couldn't wait to see my family, I thought as I hit the gas pedal.

5. Home

As I walked through the door I felt an immediate wave of affection. Down the hall I could see my three girls and my husband at the dining room table, laughing about their day. The parade started as they emptied from the table to run to me.

"Hi, Mom."

"Hi, Mom."

"Hi, Mommy," said my youngest.

I hugged the girls with more intensity than normal, eliciting probing, confused looks from them. After a moment, my husband scooted them all back to the dining table and came over to me. He wrapped his large arms around me. He whispered in my ear, "Are you okay?"

His voice was warm and sultry, with just a hint of concern. His words seared through my body. I suddenly felt warm . . . everywhere. I pulled back a little so that I could see his face, and noticed my heart pounding in my chest. I loved this man. He wrapped one hand around the back of my neck, cradling it. I could feel my breathing getting faster.

He chuckled softly. "Hmmm, nice that I still have this effect on you," and smiled at me.

I smiled back wrapping my arms around him, "Always will."

He leaned in and gently kissed my forehead, then he moved slowly down to kiss both eyes before pulling back. "You've been crying." I wasn't sure if it was a question or observation.

"Yes," but here in his arms it was a little hard to remember why.

He leaned forward again, this time also having to shift lower because he was so much taller than me, and kissed me. He'd kissed me like this many times before, but there was something different in it. I needed him right now. My entire body was responding to his kiss. Moving slowly closer together, our lips stirred every emotion in me. He made a small groan through his lips against mine and said in a soft but urgent tone, "Later."

I groaned. Then I realized that our girls were still within earshot. I could hear them talking in the background but knew that the ache for him that my body was feeling would have to wait. We wandered back into the dining room where I sat down and joined them to eat. Simple, uncomplicated conversation flooded the space between all of us as I switched back and forth in my head between the conversation I had just had in the cafe and the goings-on in little girls' lives. I couldn't be one of the people Aaron was talking about, I just couldn't. Just then my oldest daughter's comment caught my attention.

"I told Haley today that we live in a magical house." This was Alexandra, or Alex as she preferred to be called, the fourteen-year-old, who spoke the words with a hint of sarcasm.

Trina, now eleven, asked, "What do you mean magic?"

"I'm a princess!" shouted Abigail . . . Abi, the seven-year-old.

We all laughed.

"No," said Alex. "I told her it was magical because I put my dirty clothes on the floor at night and they show up in my dresser clean and folded a couple of days later." She turned to me with wide eyes, laughing hysterically. Her laugh was infectious and the whole table roared. She was right.

"Ahhh, the kids are asleep," I heard my husband say as he came up behind me while I was making the girls' lunches.

I smiled without turning, knowing what his tone of voice meant. "Go ahead. I'll be done in a minute and then I'll be up."

I felt him move closer to me from behind. He reached both of his hands out and rubbed the top of my shoulders. I shuddered. Slowly he moved both hands onto my back and down my sides. Stopping at my hips, he slowly started to massage the small of my back with his thumbs. I could hear his breathing, slow and steady until I shivered under his hands, then his breath caught and he let out a low chuckle. I realized that I had just put mayonnaise on the peanut butter sandwich, so I decided that making the lunches could wait until I could think more clearly.

He leaned against me gently, urging me forward until I was slightly against the counter. He wrapped one arm around my waist, pushed up against me. My breathing was fast and I could feel my heart pounding in my throat. My body was aching for him. He reached with his other arm and, sliding down my hip, he reached around my thigh and I felt what I needed. His breath quickened with the occasional moan, and I was unsure if each breath was his or mine.

As I turned to face him, he kissed me with an urgency, the same need as my own. Both of us, breathing fast and desperate, as if our obsession was realized and we were achieving our fix, like addicts. Our bodies moved together, our hands removing clothes, almost without thinking from years of practice.

He lowered me to the floor, and with the heat of his body and my own I didn't mind the cold floor. He had a way of touching me. I couldn't get close enough, my body needed more. He held himself above me for a moment, looking at me, his eyes filled with my same desire. He pushed softly down on me, moving rhythmically over me. Our bodies performed the dance we had perfected. In that moment I was able to let go of my day, my worries, and my fears. In that moment I was lost . . . in my soul mate . . . I was able to release all fear.

The next few days passed without incident. I was working the next four nights in a row and I welcomed the busy schedule. I loved my job and could easily get lost in taking care of people, forgetting all the problems in my life . . . real or fantasy. If it weren't for the auras around me and the corresponding blasts of heat or cold, I could almost forget that something was not right with me.

My days blurred together, and I was content in my mundane household duties of cleaning the house and attending to, as my daughter referred to it, the "magic" laundry before heading to my last shift.

Everyone was already in bed as I got ready for work. I loved to look in on my girls before going to work. It grounded me in what was important and why I was *really* here. Then I walked to our bedroom where my husband was reading in bed. As I leaned over to kiss him good-bye, he wrapped his arms around my waist and pulled me on top of him. He kissed me the way he usually kisses me when he's looking for more. My body was responding before I could think about being late. He chuckled and pulled my face gently from his. His eyes were warm and a little excited. I heard his quickened breath, but as the moments passed it slowed. I giggled and blushed. "I love you," I whispered.

He squeezed me close to him and whispered in my ear, "Always have, always will." One more quick kiss and I was gone. I hated leaving my family. My little corner of sanity where everything felt normal.

6. Vision Realized

Work passed quickly that night and it was a fairly normal shift . . . busy. Lots of patients left over from the evening shift. Slowly but surely we got everyone out, discharged or admitted, dealt with the few who came in, and around two in the morning we actually got to sit for a few minutes. I enjoyed most of the nurses I worked with—good people with good hearts and all with white auras. It definitely made it more comfortable to work. We caught up on family, took a few bites of food and then heard a call come in. "Ambulance coming in with a female, 37, multiple trauma." I took a last couple of bites of my sandwich and got up. This patient would be coming to my room tonight.

I watched as the paramedics wheeled the gurney in, and I saw that she was covered in blood. Her arm was wrapped where reportedly there was a compound fracture. I could see the bump in the bandage from the bone protruding through the skin. Not too much bleeding at the break . . . good . . . maybe there were no arteries damaged. The report was given by the lead paramedic, and I listened as he read off his notes. "Found in the park by a pedestrian passing by, he called 911. Appears she was attacked, beaten, possibly raped. Naked from the waist down, top torn. Multiple contusions all over abdomen and extremities. Police are still on the scene and a detective is on her way here."

They transferred her to our gurney as she hollered out in pain and I began to check her lines as I yelled for someone to grab pain medication, and maybe a sedative. I was pleased to see all the IVs the paramedics put in seemed to be working well. The doctor was there listening to her lungs as he called out orders for labs and an x-ray, while I drew blood.

As I filled the last vial I looked at her face for the first time. My breath caught and I clutched my chest, which suddenly felt tight and painful. I had seen her before. I would know her face anywhere, as it, along with others, haunted me daily. She was one of the women in my dream, and I could see her face in my mind moving in and out of focus. The image was burned in my memory, the shoulder-length curly brown hair and large green eyes that stared at me, full of fear and pain. There she lay with the same hair and face, eyes wide open, and I stared at the same green eyes that looked at me in the vision. The memory of her face was so vivid and sharp, mirrored by the bruised one that lay before me, that I had to close my eyes. I stood and staggered back from the bed in obvious distress. My coworkers took this as a reaction to the situation, not knowing what I was truly reacting to, and sent me outside for some air as one of them gave her medication to help relieve her pain.

I ran outside, I couldn't breathe. How could this be? Leaning against the wall to steady myself, I screamed, "NO!" and dropped to my knees. People were walking around me but I didn't care. Unfortunately a scene like this outside of our hospital was not terribly uncommon, and nobody seemed distressed by my behavior.

"Are you okay?" came an obviously concerned voice behind me.

I turned and felt pushed over by the wave of heat that crashed into me. There in front of me was a police detective, judging by the uniform and badge, with the hottest, whitest aura I had encountered since Luke. It hurt me to look at her. I wondered what this meant about me: if it hurt me, did that mean I was bad?

"Are you okay?" This time she spoke a little more slowly.

She offered her hand to me, and I took it. She had strong hands, warm to my touch, and I noticed her carefully manicured short nails.

"I'm fine, thanks. I was just caught off guard by a patient they just brought in." I stood with her help and looked at her. She had short, wavy brown hair, and deep brown eyes that seemed to bore directly into my soul. She was taller than me but just as slender, although she looked like she worked out a lot more than I did.

"Well, as long as you're okay. I need to go in and check on someone who came in." She smiled, turned, flashed a form of identification and was let into the emergency entrance by security.

I brushed myself off and realized that I had a job to do and couldn't let whatever insanity was going on right now get in my way. I put my key card up against the sensor and walked through the doors. Back in the trauma room, my charge nurse walked up. "You all right?"

"Yeah, just needed a moment." I need an eternity to process this, I thought, but I can't say that without ending up strapped to a gurney myself.

"Good," she said and walked out of the room. "Let me know if you need anything. I've got a chest pain coming into room two."

I waved her off without looking at her, as if I was fine, and walked back over to the bed. I looked at my patient's face again and noticed she seemed more comfortable now, probably due to pain medication and sedation. I started to feel a strong urge building in me, anger . . . almost painful. My breathing sped and I felt my face getting hot. *This has to stop*, I thought to myself. My fists clenched, and then it all stopped as I felt a wave of heat smack me from behind. I turned quickly, eyes still intense, jaw tight, and stepped toward the heat.

"Whoa," she said, holding her hands up in defense. It was the same woman from outside and I now saw the identification she flashed earlier. A police detective, probably the one coming for this woman.

I closed my eyes and took a deep breath. "I'm sorry, this case . . . well, I'm a little upset."

"I can understand that. I'm here to investigate. Are you the nurse taking care of her?"

"Yes."

"Okay, we'll need a rape kit and pictures of the injuries." She said this so matter-of-factly that I took a step back. Then I remembered that only I knew this woman . . . sort of . . . before she came in here.

"I'll take care of it." I tried to go back to work, not looking too much at the patient's face. Images kept racing through my head. The faces . . . the screaming . . . I remembered every detail of the dream. I turned to the detective who was sitting now, writing, and asked, "There are other victims, aren't there?"

She raised an eyebrow and looked at me over her glasses. "Maybe, why?" Her look was too intense. I looked back at the patient.

"No reason, just wondering." Now I was wishing I had phrased my question a little differently, rather than trying to confirm what I already knew.

The detective got up and walked toward me. I had finished assessing the patient and was washing my hands. She extended her right hand. "I should have introduced myself to you. I'm Charlene McGuire. Detective McGuire. And you are . . . ?"

Drying my hands, I turned to face her. "Megan Hales." I shook her hand but said nothing else. I tried to pull my hand back but she held on. It was a firm handshake, not one of those limp ones you sometimes get from women. We locked eyes for a moment, and then she let go of my hand.

I moved away from her, partly because I was uncomfortable with her questioning eyes, but also because her heat was too much.

She sat down and started writing again. I sighed. *Good*, I thought, maybe she missed my saying too much.

"So, have you seen any other victims?" She asked suddenly without looking up from her paperwork.

Damn. "No," I tried to say nonchalantly, although I didn't think I pulled it off.

She chuckled, "No?"

"No." Good, I was much more resolved in my answer that time.

"Okay," she said in a conceding tone. "If you do think of someone or something that would help the case, here's my card. I'm going out to make a phone call." With that she walked closer to me, handed me her card, smiled a very knowing smile that really pissed me off, and walked out.

I continued to care for my patient. I couldn't believe it. How could this happen? I couldn't ignore this terrible urge, a drive to do something. I couldn't place the feeling I was having. I knew who I needed to call to help me. Damn.

I got home from work just as the kids were ready for school. My husband was leaving with the oldest and I would be dropping the other two off. They all came running, just as they always do, and we were out the door. I stopped at the grocery store, did the usual shopping and headed home. I knew what I needed to do today but part of me was delaying. I didn't want to admit that I needed his help.

Back at home, I started putting the groceries away and reluctantly dialed the number.

"Aaron?" I asked as he picked up the phone.

"Hello, Megan."

"Aaron, I need your help. I guess I need some answers. Can you meet with me today?"

"Of course I can. I can get out of work in about two hours. Want to meet at the cafe?"

"Sure. Umm, Aaron?"

"Yes?"

"Thanks."

"Of course."

I finished putting away the groceries, cleaned up, and had time to take a quick nap. I lay down, but my mind was racing. I had seen her in the dream but she wasn't dead . . . nobody had killed her. I didn't know what to think about this. Clearly I was out of my league here. One thing I knew—I didn't want to admit that maybe he was right about who I was.

7. Truth

I showed up at the cafe. Right away I saw his red aura all the way across the cafe and shook my head. He smiled and stood to greet me. He motioned for me to sit. I had barely sat down when he asked, "What's wrong?"

Still not very trusting, I said, "What makes you think something is wrong?"

He furrowed his brow, looked at me for a moment, and said, "You look different . . . ." He trailed off and then, as if he were going to ask something else but changed his mind, he continued, "So, what can I do for you?"

"What do you mean I look different?" I know that this was not the reason for calling him originally but, well, I couldn't see me the way he could. My curiosity was piqued.

He took an exasperated breath, probably wishing he hadn't said anything in the first place. "Is that why you called me?"

I shook my head annoyed, "Look, I called about something else but I want to know what you see."

He sighed, "Your aura, well, it's more red than before."

"What does that mean?" I asked.

"Usually the aura deepens as our, well, our acceptance of purpose deepens. But have you?"

"Nothing's changed. I mean . . ." I took a deep breath and spoke the words quickly so I wouldn't lose my nerve. "I was at work and a patient came in who was a woman from my dream . . ."

"Vision," he corrected me, then motioned for me to continue.

I was always so irritated when I was interrupted. I tried to shake it off now so as not to lose my rhythm and continued. "I had a sudden surge of anger and had to focus to be able to care for her. She didn't die, so I'm not sure what to make of that. If what you told me is true then she should have died, and then I would be going after her killer, right? I guess I need answers. I feel like I'm losing my mind." I stopped to catch my breath.

He sat back and smiled, took a breath in and out and spoke slowly. "You are not crazy, you are exactly who you are supposed to be."

Ugh, I thought, that tells me nothing. I rolled my eyes and shook my head.

He held one hand up and continued, "Wait, listen. You had a vision of what *will* be. If you don't intercede . . . well . . . those people could die. The fact that she didn't die is good, it could have been affected by a number of factors. Have you seen the person responsible yet?"

"How would I know who it is?" This question made sense to me, but it seemed to send Aaron a different message.

"If you don't know, then you haven't because you'd be unable to stop yourself, the urge would be too much."

I put my head into my hands and fought the urge to cry. "I can't . . . can't be . . . this."

He spoke in a soft, almost tender voice. "I'm sorry, it's not your fault. It does take some time to adjust."

"I don't understand," I finally got out. "When I was in high school and I saw John, the boy who killed the students at my school, I didn't kill him. So, it can't be true."

After a minute I looked up because he didn't answer me. He was sitting back, eyes wide.

"What? What did I say?" I was confused. I wondered what I could have said that would have caused him to react this way.

He almost whispered, "You knew who the killer was? That person is still alive? The kid from high school?"

I leaned forward in response to his whispering, "Yes, I guess, I don't know. I think he went to jail when I was in high school. That was the last I heard of him."

He shook his head, "No, let me rephrase. Then from what you're saying, you saw him, but you did not complete your purpose?"

"Well, your definition of *completion of purpose* is to kill someone, right?"

He nodded in agreement.

"Then no, obviously, he went to jail. I did *not* kill him. Why?"

He sat there for a moment as his expression changed into one of confusion. Then, again shaking his head side to side, he said, "This is beyond me. We need to call Max."

I was confused. But then, I seemed to be spending most of my time this way lately. Was it beyond him because he didn't know what to say or felt he couldn't say anything? I got the feeling there were a lot of secrets. Many of which I was probably not privy to and maybe didn't want to know.

"What's beyond you?" It was a simple question, should have been easy to answer.

"There's nothing in our history that comes close to this. No one that I know of has ever NOT completed a purpose. I don't know what it means. I didn't even know that it was possible. Then again, you're the first woman that I know of."

"Okay then, can we call this Max?" I felt anxious to find out answers but nervous at the same time.

He smiled, "You're starting to accept who you are?"

I scoffed at that, "Well, I don't know about that. I'd just like answers."

Smiling wider, he reached into his pocket and pulled out his cell phone. After dialing a number he said, "Your aura shows that you're starting to accept. The aura doesn't lie."

My breath caught at his comment. He began to talk into his phone.

"Hello Max, this is Aaron . . . . good, good . . . and how are you? . . . Great . . ."

Pleasantries, I thought to myself.

He continued, "Well, I'm here with Megan . . . yes, that's right . . . well, she actually has some questions for you. Can you meet? . . . Tomorrow?"

I nodded yes.

"Okay, sure. What time? . . . Ten in the morning?"

Again I nodded yes, but added, "Where?"

"UCSF," he whispered.

"Okay," I responded. They exchanged a few more words and then hung up.

I spoke first, "So this . . . Max . . . he's going to have answers for me?"

"I don't know. I told him about you last time we saw each other and he just nodded as if he understood. Then he told me to call him if you contacted me again. Why don't we meet here at nine-thirty and go over together?"

"Why UCSF?" I asked. "Does he work there?"

"Yes, he's a professor."

"And he's . . ." I trailed off, trying to lead him to answer.

"Yes, he's one of us . . . an Aurator."

I took a deep breath, becoming more resolved. "Okay, I'll meet you here tomorrow."

We said our good-byes and I left. I had enough time to go home and take a nap before picking up my kids. As I drove home, I kept thinking back to when I started seeing auras, first the priest, then high school. Now what am I up against?

8. Max

The next day after dropping the girls off I went to meet Aaron. Normally I was not thankful for the year-round schools my daughters went to, but lately I seemed to need the extra time for myself. Aaron and I drove over to the University of California, San Francisco campus. I had never asked what Max taught but didn't bother now because I knew I was about to find out. We parked a few blocks away, lucky to find a spot there, and walked up to the Parnassus Building at the School of Medicine.

We walked down the long hallway and I had flashbacks to nursing school. I shuddered, grateful that I completed it but sure that my time there had created some post-traumatic stress disorder. We reached a door that read,

Max Reibolt, MD
Medical History, Medical Anthropology

I wondered, what kind of medicine is that? Aaron knocked on the door and I heard a muffled, "Come in."

As we walked through the door I was amazed at how large the office was. My nursing instructors had small closet-like offices or they all shared one big room sectioned off into cubicles. This room was very large with high ceilings. Every square inch of wall space was covered with shelving littered with books, papers, and what looked like various artifacts from all over the world. There was a massive wooden desk under the far window, covered with stacks of papers that, while a little disheveled, looked somewhat organized. The floor had an expensive imported rug with a beautiful red woven design that peeked out from among stacks of books and papers. Along the fringe of the carpet lay what looked like a long row of Big Little Books on the floor. These were something I knew well, but it was surprising nonetheless—my uncle was proud of being the only person in the world with a complete collection of these same books. I smiled at the thought and then noticed a movement out of the corner of my eye.

Moving toward us was a gentleman easily in his mid-seventies yet still strong and healthy looking. In my line of business, that wasn't something I saw very often. If I saw people in their seventies they were usually sick with multiple chronic medical problems. This man was nothing close to that. He had short, straight, dark hair with a touch of gray in it, not as much as most men his age. He wore jeans and a simple, cleaned and pressed button-up shirt with a sweater vest over it. He walked toward me with a presence that immediately put me at ease. He looked familiar, maybe I'd seen him somewhere before. He stood in front of me with an expression on his face that I couldn't comprehend. I heard Aaron speak up, "Max, this is . . ." Max held up a hand as if gesturing to wait.

"I know who she is. Hello, Megan." He held his hand out to me. I then noticed the red glow around him. I don't know why I didn't see it until then. I extended my hand to him.

"Hello, Mr. Reibolt."

He chuckled, "Mr. Reibolt is my father and he's dead, so I'd prefer Max."

"Okay then, Max, nice to meet you."

He continued to hold my gaze and kept my hand in his. "Well now Megan, we've been waiting for you a long time. It's nice to see you again."

Yes, I caught that, *again.* "I'm sorry, have we met?"

"Yes dear, but it was a long time ago, you were too young to remember. How are your parents?" He allowed me to draw my hand back, and I slid both my hands in my pockets, feeling a little uncomfortable.

"You know my family?"

"It's been many years, but yes." He offered no other explanation.

I thought about this for a moment and decided there must be some professional correlation between lawyers and doctors and left it at that for now. I had bigger questions on my mind at that moment. "They're fine, thanks. Dad's retired and they've been traveling."

"Great, good people."

I couldn't deny this. I just never had anything in common with them. So different . . . so completely different from me.

"So," I began, "Aaron suggested that I speak with you about who . . . what I am."

He smiled, "Ah, yes, I'm sure you have a lot of questions." He motioned for me to sit on a large leather couch.

As I moved to sit I noticed that he barely took his eyes off of me.

He sat down in the largest of two leather chairs to my right. I sat on the couch and Aaron removed a stack of papers from a chair so that he could sit across from me. Max took a drink from his coffee cup and then began, "Okay, so . . . yes . . . lots of questions. Where would you like to start?"

Suddenly I had forgotten all my questions. Where do I start? I suddenly thought of a question that I had not considered before. "Can you see my aura also?"

He smirked and drew his eyebrows down, "Yes."

I realized this conversation might be hard unless I started asking some open-ended questions. "Why am I the only woman who is like this?"

"An Aurator," he stated simply.

"Pardon me?" I asked.

"You are an Aurator. Why are you the only woman Aurator?"

I sighed. I guess I was still having trouble accepting it. "Yes, why am I the only woman Aurator?" The words struggled to make their way through my clenched teeth.

He stood and walked over to a collection of large antique-looking books. He ran his fingers across the spines until he came to the one he was looking for. As he pulled it off the shelf a small cloud of dust dispersed around it. He brushed the book off and came to sit back down with us.

"Maybe the better question to ask is *how* did we come to be?"

Well, I thought to myself, I suppose it would be if that were the question I wanted answered. A little annoyed, I nodded, humoring the old man. "Well then . . . ."

He chuckled, removed a pair of reading glasses from his vest pocket, and opened the book. He took much longer to find the information he wanted to share than I would have expected from someone who clearly had his own agenda. He began, "What do you know about Greek mythology?"

"Not much, but I'm listening." That is what I chose to say rather than, *Are you kidding me?*

He looked at me over his glasses and grinned. "Megan, I need you to have an open mind. This is going to be harder for you than for all the others."

"Why?"

"We'll get to that." He waved his hand around as if dismissing a two-year-old and settled on a page in his book.

"Have you ever heard of Asclepius the god of cleanliness, medicine, and healing?" He looked up from his book.

I shook my head no.

"Asclepius was a god from Greek mythology." He looked up to gauge my response. I tried to not respond at all. He smiled and continued. "Asclepius was the son of Apollo and Coronis. Coronis had been unfaithful to Apollo. As punishment she was killed, but the unborn child, Asclepius, was cut out of her womb by Apollo. Apollo named him after *asklepios*, the Greek word for 'to cut open' which was later changed to Asclepius. Since Coronis may or may not have been unfaithful, Asclepius may not have been Apollo's son. Apollo then took the baby to the centaur Chiron, who raised Asclepius and instructed him in medicine.

"So, Apollo was known in part for his medical abilities, and now so was his son. Asclepius married and had six daughters and three sons." He paused for a second as if trying to find his next words. "Many of his daughters were healers." He hesitated. "One of the daughters was like us, the first that we know of. She passed her genes down, and after generations in the ancestral line came Hippocrates. He was the most famous of our kind. Do you know who that is?"

"Of course I do, father of medicine, Hippocratic oath." I was actually starting to get interested. Being in the profession, I had always been fascinated by the history of medicine, but I had never gone this far back. "Is everyone . . . like us . . . in medicine?"

"Yes." Max stated simply.

I turned toward Aaron who replied, "Yes, I'm an anesthesiologist."

I smirked, "So is this where the God complex with you doctors comes from?" I'd always wanted to say that to a doctor, and now that the moment seemed appropriate I was giddy with my joke.

Max laughed a boisterous laugh, "Well it's better than *moron,* which is what you nurses *usually* call us behind our backs."

I nodded, "Touché." We all had a good laugh, then I continued, "Why are we all in medicine?"

"That's unclear. Asclepius was the supposed god of medicine and healing, and Hippocrates was the father of medicine. There is something in us that pulls us, as if a genetic drive toward medicine."

I thought about this. Why medicine? Why me, a woman? My head was spinning with information and more questions. I looked over and Max and Aaron were speaking together over the book. "Wait a minute," I interrupted. "Are you telling me that we are descendants from mythological beings? You guys realize how crazy that sounds, don't you? Mythology is just that . . . myth."

Max looked up from his book and quizzically grinned, "Is it?"

This response confused me. What seemed rational just seconds ago now felt like a difficult concept. "Isn't it?" I asked.

Raising his eyebrows and looking amused, "Some could say the Bible is fiction. Is it? Maybe, maybe not. The Bible is a compilation of stories of ordinary and extraordinary events recorded by man. Right?"

Although I grew up in the Catholic church, I had always grappled with the validity of some of the stories in the Bible. I waited for him to finish.

He sat back in his chair with a confident look on his face, seemingly happy that I was playing along with this theory. "Who's to say that mythology is not the same? These are stories that were verbally passed down because there was no adequate ability to record the events. Couldn't they also be a mix of ordinary and extraordinary events told throughout the generations until someone finally *wrote* them down into what we now call mythology?"

I couldn't argue with that.

He continued, "Then, could we not hypothesize that since these stories *may* be true and these people or gods *may* have lived, that they too would have had children who had children, who passed their genes down through the generations to us?"

Max then looked up and started speaking again. "Dear, to get back to the matter at hand, I believe you're wondering why you are the first woman with this gift since the daughter of Asclepius." He leaned forward excitedly.

"I hadn't thought of it that way, but yes, why?" My eyes were big and somehow full of hope that Max would have the answer.

"I don't know," he said furrowing his brow. "But I believe we are about to find out."

Then he looked up, murmured something to himself and shuffled off to one of the many bookshelves again. My jaw dropped. I looked at Aaron, who had the same confused look on his face, as if he too thought that Max would have the answer. I looked back at Max who now, talking to himself, reached up and pulled an old, intricately carved wooden box off the shelf. He placed the box on his desk and opened it. I moved forward in my seat and noticed out of the corner of my eye that Aaron did as well.

Max reached in the box and pulled out a small key. He then walked over to where I was standing and asked, "Can you stand up please?" I stood up and held my open hand out, thinking he was giving me the key. He smiled, put both hands on my shoulders and moved me gently out of the way, steering me over to the chair he had been sitting in.

"Have a seat, Megan. Aaron can you give me a hand with the rug?" Aaron stood and walked over to Max, who motioned for Aaron to lift the corner of the rug. They folded it over itself to expose the wide wood planks of the floor. Max motioned to stop. Then, after Max and Aaron exchanged a glance, Aaron walked over to lock the door to the room.

I joined them by the rug and Max knelt down next to a plank marked with an intricate carving of a staff with a single snake wrapped around it. He placed his hand over the symbol, and without even a touch the board moved downward. The board then slid underneath the board next to it, exposing an iron box, which he lifted out. He placed his hand onto the floor again, and the missing plank slid back into place on its own. I shook my head in disbelief as I looked toward Max, who had an amused smirk on his face, and then I followed both men to Max's desk.

He sat down and placed the box in front of him on the desk. He moved his hand over the box, admiring it for a moment and wiping the dust away. He then took a deep breath and leaned back in the chair.

"Aren't you going to open it?" I blurted out, excited to see what was inside it.

Aaron's mouth was open, "Is that what I think it is? Max?"

Max had a look of conflict on his face, somewhere between awe and fear. "Yes Aaron, it is."

"I thought that was just legend. It really . . ." Aaron was breathing fast and started pacing, running his fingers through his hair.

"Megan," Max began, "I spoke of Hippocrates because he was one of us. Also he was one of the first to chronicle his experiences."

"Wait," I started, "first, how did you open that floor?"

"We all have certain, well, talents? Mine is moving things without touching them. Large, small, it doesn't matter. I suppose I could move you if I wanted to. A telekinesis, of sorts." He answered my question but was a little preoccupied with the box. Aaron had stopped pacing and stood next to Max. It seemed that this was as far as I was going to get on this subject at the moment so I looked back at the box. "So, this box belonged to Hippocrates?"

Max moved the key to the top of the box, "Yes Megan." He looked at me with a desperate look on his face. "I've had this box for the past forty years but never imagined I'd need to use what was inside. You see, while he chronicled his experiences as an Aurator, he also wrote down what his talent showed him."

Aaron broke in before I could, "So he wrote down what he saw for our future?"

Yes, Max nodded silently.

So that was it, I thought—Hippocrates had the talent to tell the future? I wanted to be clear. "The future?"

"The future to him, which is now," said Max.

I was confused, "Now what?"

"He wrote about this moment . . . about you." Both men looked at me curiously. "Since I became my true self and met my mentor I have been told the story of Asclepius, Hippocrates, and his foretelling of the future. I never believed that his words would be realized during my lifetime."

He looked back down at the box and turned the key. I heard the box unlock and watched as it was opened. Inside was an old leather bound book, wrapped in plastic. Now I'm no archaeologist, but I was pretty sure that no paper would last over two thousand years. "That can't possibly be his, it would be dust. And, plastic isn't that old, either"

Max looked up and smiled. "You're right, this information has been passed down through generations of Aurators to the chosen keepers of the information. That's me. Our main job through the years has been to rewrite the contents of the book by hand into a new book and close it back up for safekeeping until the prophecy became reality."

I couldn't help thinking that a flash drive or CD would be easier nowadays.

Pulling the book from the plastic, he laid it on the desk. "I have not read the contents for many years, since the time I transcribed it nearly 50 years ago. The prophecy of a woman's arrival, what it would mean for us, and what you would bring."

"Me? I'm in that book?" Even as I said it, I knew how ridiculous it sounded.

"Yes," he answered simply.

He looked up at Aaron who was standing next to him. They both looked like kids on Christmas morning in front of the largest present in the room. Max opened the book and turned toward the back pages.

9. Hippocrates

Before reading, Max looked toward me. "Megan, these words have been rewritten many times and translated as closely as possible into English." I opened my mouth to ask a question, but Max stopped me before I could even ask what was on the tip of my tongue. "Just listen. He was trained in medicine, which was based in the Latin language because it was uncommon at the time. He believed that his words would elude most ordinary men of his time if it was in a less familiar language."

Max started reading out loud, "Let it be known, you who read this, that those before you have given you the truth to move forth throughout history. If she who is to be all-powerful and lead us has been birthed, then take these truths to heart." Max brought his hand up to his forehead and wiped the sweat that had accumulated. He then looked a little flustered as he searched for and found a handkerchief to wipe his hand before continuing on. "A woman, descended from Asclepius shall be born. She will possess more unique powers of purpose than all men before her. She will be skilled in many ways unknown to us, with much wisdom and medicinal knowledge. Most importantly, she will carry with her as the descendant the greatest gift of rebirth and will lead us to triumph over all. These will be confusing and disastrous times, and our people will need strength and guidance. Mankind will need help to return to the right path. Many will have gone off course, separating mankind and struggling for power, away from the Serpent Bearer. She will bring our kind together as one. There will be a great battle to regain proper balance. Without this woman, we will perish and the world will fall further into darkness." Max sat back and took a breath.

I waited for more, for the great answer that was supposedly in the book. But he was finished and closed the book.

"That's it?" I asked. "What the hell does all that mean?"

"Yes," Max began, "there are a few more entries after this but nobody has been able to make sense of those yet. He died soon after this. You see, Hippocrates could see the futures of certain people, more specifically, he saw his own bloodline's future. As the story goes he had a dream, a vision, of what was to become of him, his own death and he wrote down all of his experiences. He ended with this vision of what was to be. The coming together of all powers."

Aaron spoke next, "So, what does all of it mean? I have heard the stories of the woman to come, but it does seem a little unclear as to the specifics. Why?"

Max thought about this for a moment. "It is unfortunate that we don't know exactly what to expect from you, Megan. I suppose only time will tell. What I do know is that you will be a leader for us. You are meant to be great."

I couldn't take it all in. So much information. I suddenly flashed on something he had said earlier. "Max?" He was flipping through pages of the book and stopped to look at me.

"Yes."

"What did you mean when you said all of this will be harder for me to accept than others?" I had been perplexed by this and was glad I remembered to ask. So frequently I leave a situation or conversation frustrated that there was something I forgot to ask.

He raised both eyebrows and looked over his glasses that were low on the bridge of his nose, "You have not completed a purpose yet, there is no proof to give you reason to accept what we are telling you. Usually an Aurator has completed a purpose, then connects with one of us and is able to find out about our kind and accept the explanation because . . . well, it's hard to deny at that point."

Aaron cleared his throat and we both looked toward him. "I'm sorry, I just wanted to mention that Megan and I were discussing why she had a red aura if she had not completed a purpose. That's what prompted me to call you the other day."

"Ah, yes." Max replied, then handed the book to Aaron and got up. He walked over to the window behind his desk and looked outside. I looked at Aaron, who shrugged his shoulders in confusion at me. We waited for Max to reply. He suddenly sighed and hung his head. Without turning, he began to speak.

"You won't yet understand Megan. Who you are to us . . . to the future of all of us." He turned from the window and looked at me. "We, as a people, have been trying to keep up with the changing face of ills in this world. Over the past century we have become so outnumbered as our world is changing. I'm sure you've noticed how things have changed even since you were a child. Children can't play out in their front yards or walk down the street without fear of abduction or harm. If you take a leisurely evening stroll anywhere in a city, there's a fear of being attacked or mugged. And women . . . well, except for you . . . are at risk everywhere of physical or sexual attack. Our world has become an unsafe and sad place." He put his head down, slowly shaking it from side to side. "Our identity isn't even safe anymore," as he motioned toward his three computers on a table next to his desk.

I reflected on what he was saying. I was full of angst daily when it came to my girls. Always worrying about where they were and what they were doing. Was it safe for them to go to that friend's house? Did I know the parents well enough? If they were on field trips without my husband or me, was someone else watching them well enough? I experienced the fears Max was speaking of on a daily basis. From what I've heard from other mothers and fathers with older kids, that fear and worry never goes away. On several occasions I had tried to talk with my parents about this, thinking that they would understand exactly what I was feeling, but they both just shook their heads and said, "Things were different when you were a kid, hon. We just didn't have to worry the way you do today." I sighed at this . . . Max was right . . . sad.

I then noticed that Max had come over and knelt in front of me. "You, my dear, represent the birth of hope for us. A chance we can actually have a bigger impact in our world."

"I don't understand. I don't want to be a killer. How can I be one of you?"

"In time, in time." He then got up from the floor and went back to his chair, suddenly looking very tired. "You have a red aura because you are already stronger than any of us. You are already emanating the power of purpose. Your skill, whatever that will be, will come after completing your first purpose. You've had this aura your whole life."

"Well, what if I don't want to complete a purpose?" I asked.

"You don't have a choice." He said this so matter-of-factly and without looking at me that I paused to question myself.

"If that is true then why didn't I kill the boy in high school?" His eyebrows furrowed and he leaned forward. He spoke so slowly and with such intensity that I felt my breath catch.

"What . . . boy . . . from . . . high . . . school?"

Taking a moment to compose myself I took a deep breath. I retold the story of high school including the dark aura around John, the subsequent dream, the pain, shuddering at the memory of the pain, and the deaths of my fellow classmates.

Max appeared rattled and a little out of sorts. He began mumbling to himself, "That's impossible . . . he can't be . . . you would need incredible . . . that's impossible."

Aaron was the first to speak coherently. "Max, is this some sort of innate self-control?"

Max snapped out of his daze and looked at Aaron. "I don't think so, but I don't know." Then turning to me, "Megan, whatever happened to the boy?"

"I don't know exactly. He went to a juvenile detention facility but whether he got out or died, I have no idea."

Max pondered this for a moment, looking back and forth through the room as if searching for something. "We have to find out if he's still alive." Then he glanced at me with a curious look on his face. "There will be much to learn from you. I can see already that you are not cut from the same cloth as the rest of us. I will also call the Seniors to consult with them. They have all the original documents, aside from Hippocrates's journal, and these may hold answers." Nodding his head, apparently to himself, he stood and walked over to his desk, sat down, and began scribbling notes onto a yellow legal pad.

Aaron stood and approached Max, "What now? Do we search for the boy? If he is a designated purpose he could be creating chaos and will need to be removed."

Max stopped writing and fiddled with his pen for what seemed like several minutes. "You're right, Aaron, he will need to be dealt with if he's still alive."

"Wait a minute," I interrupted, "are you both talking about killing my old schoolmate?"

In unison, they quickly stated, "Yes." Then they went back to talking to one another.

Aaron first, "We will need to consult the Seniors. They may have some record or experience that will tell us what to do."

"Of course," Max replied. "I will contact them I do have a lot of questions for them. And, if you don't mind, try to research whether this boy . . ." turning toward me he continued, "what's his name?"

Slightly confused by the direction of the conversation, I replied, "John Steele."

Max clarified, "S . . . T . . . E . . . E . . . L . . . E?"

"Yes."

He then looked back at Aaron, "John Steele. See what you can find out about him and we'll go from there."

I was thoroughly and completely overwhelmed at this point. How had we gone from finding out more about me and this dysfunctional life I'm supposedly destined for to *Hey let's kill one of her old schoolmates.*

"Excuse me gentlemen," I interrupted their mutterings to each other. "You'll have to excuse me but I think I've heard about all I can handle today." Then turning toward Aaron, I said, "My girls will be out of school soon and I need to get them."

Max was the first to speak, "You have children?"

"Yes."

"Boys or girls?" He leaned forward with interest.

"Three girls."

"No boys?"

I tried not to sound annoyed restating my answer, "No, I'm pretty sure they're girls."

Max chuckled and nodded, "Yes, that makes sense. I admit that we did not focus as much as we could have on your questions today, Megan. This is all so new to us and we're all learning. Please be patient with us as we try to figure things out. Okay?"

I sighed and nodded back, "That's fine. I'm sorry, I know that I may seem a little irritable. I don't mean to be rude. I have never felt like I fit anywhere, rather out of sorts. Now I'm finding out that I do fit somewhere but to fit in there I have to accept that I'm a freak. Some sort of genetic mutant. It's a little more than I bargained for."

Something I said caused a look of sadness on Max's face. He rose from his desk and came over to me. Standing in front of me, he took me by both shoulders, urging me to stand. Then looking into my eyes his voice was smooth and I could almost feel his concern, "Megan, I'm sorry for your torment regarding feelings of not fitting in. Your life must have been confusing for you. You do fit. You fit with us. I'm sorry, but in time this will be easier for you, and eventually I believe you'll feel a sense of ease when your two halves become one."

His softness and sincerity caught me off guard and my eyes welled up. "I just want to feel whole. I don't want to have to wonder anymore where I belong."

He placed one hand alongside my cheek. "Then trust us, dear child. We will help you. But you will have to drop these walls you've erected to protect yourself and for once . . . trust completely."

I looked into this man's eyes. They were clear, intense, yet showed nothing in them that gave me reason to doubt. "I will try."

Max game me one of his cards. Same as Aaron:

Max
415-555-3422

We said our good-byes and left. Aaron and I didn't speak for the longest time on the ride back, and I appreciated the quiet. Then, breaking the silence Aaron spoke, "If there's anything I can do for you to make this easier, let me know."

"Thanks." That was all I could muster. I was completely spent.

I picked up my girls, thankful again for some normalcy. I listened to the goings-on at school. Who's playing with whom, who's mad at whom. How each one of them hated homework. I chuckled.

We got home and I sat to help each girl complete homework. As I sat at the table my mind toggled back and forth between the earlier conversation and new math. Ugh. I suddenly flashed to my most recent dream and the girl who had come to the emergency room. So much for remembering to ask everything, I thought. I filed the question away and pulled Max's card from my pocket, placing it next to Aaron's in my wallet.

My husband got home. It was Friday night. At our house Friday night was Couch Bed Night. We all dragged our top mattresses into the living room and watched movies until everyone fell asleep. We used to just sleep on the pull-out bed in our couch when we only had our first daughter. But after she learned how much fun it was to jump on the bed it broke. Hence, the mattresses. We just never changed the name. It was a simple tradition but something the family looked forward to all week.

10. Urge

I was off for the weekend and thankful for the break. We went to the park, did some shopping, and played in our yard. Enjoying the time together. Sunday night came and the reality of going back to work and school landed squarely down on top of us.

My husband got the girls dressed and tucked into bed while I made lunches. Halfway through, I sighed, realizing that we were out of bread and feeling like a bad mom for not having done all the shopping this week. I looked up at the clock. Nine o'clock, I could still run out for bread. My husband offered to go but he was already snuggled up with my two youngest reading one of their mystery books. I laughed as I walked out to the car. *You want a mystery, try spending five minutes in my head,* I thought.

Starting the car, I was off to the store and thankful for a few minutes alone. Since meeting Max two days ago, I still felt as if I was trying to process the information. If I was supposed to be the strongest Aurator ever, what did that mean for me and my family? Was I going to miss my oldest daughter's high school graduation because, "Oh I'm sorry honey, Mommy can't be there because I have to kill someone?" I muttered in my frustration. I shook my head and started to think that if I had been able to resist in high school then maybe Max and Aaron were wrong about me. I don't even remember having an urge to hurt anyone. The memory of the girl from my dream in the emergency room and the anger that accompanied being near her perplexed me. I don't usually get so angry. That was one experience I couldn't explain.

Finding parking at the store was tough. It seemed late to be so busy. I locked my car and started into the store. Placing my keys in my purse, I stepped on the rubber pad to open the automatic door.

Then it happened so fast that I had no time to process anything. I felt a cold slap to the left side of my face, my vision went blurry and everything was red. My entire body felt as if I had received an electrical shock, coursing from my core out through my fingers and toes. My breathing sped and my skin felt like it was on fire. Out of dizziness I grabbed at the metal bar separating the entrance from the exit. I heard a cracking noise as I dropped to my knees. Faces flashed in front of me. The faces from the dream . . . the women . . . the victims. I heard voices in the distance, saying something I couldn't quite understand, getting closer. Finally able to take a deep breath, I closed my eyes again, and intense anger inside of me seemed to emanate from every inch of my body. I noticed that I could feel every muscle in my body as if each one was its own entity that I was able to control individually. My head snapped to the side as I felt someone grab my shoulder. Straining to regain control, I was slowly able to focus on a gentle face of concern in front of me. "Ma'am, ma'am, are you okay?"

My whole body was numb except for something cold in my left hand. Looking over, it became clear to me that the cracking sound I had heard was me pulling the metal handrail out of the ground. I looked up toward what was now a crowd standing around me. I could hear them chattering excitedly as if in the distance, "Oh no, the handrail broke . . . she fell . . . is she bleeding? . . . did someone call an ambulance?"

I struggled to stand, still a little unsteady. "I'm okay," I finally got out. Everyone was looking toward me but I was looking elsewhere, searching . . . what was I looking for? I felt a pull and I turned slowly toward the parking lot. I scanned the cars that were around, difficult given that it was late at night.

Then I saw it . . . the dark aura, walking slowly away from me, gliding under one of the tall lamps. I felt a stab of pain and anger within my gut. It was a feeling that I had never had before. It took every bit of my strength to not go after it. There it was, my purpose, and I realized that at the core of who I was I would be unable to fight this pull.

I struggled to keep composure. There were several workers around me trying to make sure I was safe . . . probably wondering if I would sue for the faulty handrail. Little did they know I was the faulty one. I stood, unsteady on my feet but assuring everyone I was not hurt and I just needed a minute.

I looked around but the dark aura was gone. I walked back to my car and pulled out my cell phone. Dialing the number I still wasn't sure what I was going to say. I tried desperately to slow my breathing, closing my eyes and concentrating on my racing heart rate. I heard a voice, "Hello?"

"Max?" I tried to make my voice sound steady.

"Megan? What's wrong?"

I wasn't sounding very controlled. I took a deep breath and started. I described the events that took place, trying not to leave anything out. After I finished there was silence. I waited.

"You didn't do . . . anything?" he sounded stunned.

"What do you mean?"

"You didn't go after him . . . complete . . . your purpose?"

"No."

"I don't know what to say. How did you not go after . . . him? Or was it a her?"

"A him, I think, I don't know. I definitely felt the pull. I finally understand what you and Aaron have been talking about. But I just couldn't, it didn't feel right."

"Hmmm, well, as I said, I can see we will have much to learn from you. How are you feeling now?"

"Better, thanks. I think I just needed to speak with someone who . . . well . . . would understand."

There was a brief pause. "I'm glad I was here, but I don't really understand. You seem to possess a skill for patience that doesn't exist with the rest of our kind."

I thought of other questions I still had for him. "Hey Max, can I come by tomorrow?"

"Sure, sure, anytime. I have a class from two to four in the afternoon, but otherwise I'm free."

"Ten in the morning?"

"Sure. See you then."

"Hey Max?"

"Yes?"

"Thanks."

"You're welcome."

As I hung up the phone I began thinking about what had happened. I wondered who this dark aura was. I knew he was connected to the women from my dream but could he really be the person I was supposed to . . . *kill*? Was he a . . . ? CRAP! I just remembered . . . bread. The original reason I came to the store in the first place. I got back out of my car and looked around. He was still nowhere in sight. Had it really happened? I walked toward the entrance wondering, but then I saw where I had ripped the metal hand railing out. Reality.

I stepped over the remnants of my destruction, chunks of cement strewn around the front that some poor teenager who was just looking for a part-time job was cleaning up. As I went inside, one of the workers hurried over, looking concerned, and asked if I was okay.

I nodded yes, thanked her, and moved toward the bread aisle. After purchasing the item I walked back to the car. Dream state is probably the closest I could come to describing how I felt. This could not be real, could it? Everything in my head was telling me no. But my body . . . my body still ached to go after him, to find him. I wasn't sure what I would do when I found him . . . if I found him.

I went home and finished the sandwiches. Everyone was asleep. My nerves were shot. I walked into my bathroom, opened the medicine cabinet, and looked for a moment. Then I found it, a bottle of Xanax. I received the bottle during one of my visits to the doctor after a particularly difficult night in the emergency room. I got this prescription and a referral to psychiatry to talk about my *feelings*. The medicine I accepted. Psychiatrists? Not on your life.

I took one pill and went to bed. My husband was already asleep. I got in quietly, trying not to wake him, but he felt me in the bed and without waking turned over to curl behind me. His arm wrapped around me and I felt safe.

The next day after dropping the girls off at school I went to meet Max. I got to his door and was about to knock when I heard him say, "Come in, Megan." I walked in.

"Hello Max."

He got up from his antique wooden desk and walked over to me. Extending a hand, with a very warm smile that made his eyes close slightly, he said, "Hello, Megan. It's very good to see you again." Motioning for me to sit on the couch he offered me a cup of coffee. I graciously accepted. I didn't know many nurses who would turn down coffee.

He sat down across from me in his chair and began, "So, you've found your purpose. Any idea who it is?"

I found that question rather odd, "No, do you?"

This question made him chuckle as he shook his head. "Did you see his face?"

"No, he was walking away from me when I was finally able to look up. I'm not even sure he is a he. But based on the shape walking away, I think it was a man."

"Tell me again what happened."

I retold the story of going to the store, the cold, falling down after ripping the metal guard out of the ground, and the almost painful urge I had to go after him. He sat drinking his coffee and nodded as if he understood. Maybe this had happened to him. I suddenly felt as if, even though the behavior was odd, what I was feeling was normal. He then cut me off.

"Excuse me, Megan. You *pulled* the guardrail out of the ground?" He leaned forward, anxiously awaiting the answer.

"Yes, it was weird. I barely knew I was doing it. One moment I was grabbing it for support, the next I heard a cracking sound and it was in my hand, cement base and all. Everyone around me thought it was loose and I had fallen because it came out."

He sat back to think for a moment. "You know, we're not supposed to have greater strength except when we are actually completing a purpose or in danger. I wonder . . . ." He trailed off and looked up at his bookshelf. I expected him to pull out another old book holding more secrets and fables, but instead he stood and walked to the bookshelf, climbed up on his ladder to the top shelf and pulled down a metal ball the size of a tennis ball. Climbing back down, he walked back to the couch and handed it to me. It was cold, heavy, clearly solid metal of some kind with one flat part . . . maybe a paperweight. I looked at him.

"Now what?"

He smiled and pointed to the ball, "Give it a squeeze."

I shook my head, "This is crazy."

"Humor an old man, just a little squeeze."

I sighed. It took some effort to lift the ball. I squeezed my hand around the ball, but nothing happened. Looking back up at Max, I raised my eyebrows in an "I told you so" manner and tried to hand it back. He shook his head and gently pushed my hand and the ball back toward me.

"Try again, Megan." He knelt down in front of me and stared with an intensity I was not used to. "Think of the aura . . . your purpose you saw last night." I did and felt the anger brewing inside of me. My breathing quickened. Max saw this and continued, "Good, now I want you to picture the faces that appeared in your vision." I closed my eyes and after a moment the faces from my dream flashed back and forth in my mind. I felt a cold sweat forming on the top of my lip and noticed that my muscles felt as if they were warming, each moving separately but together. I shifted in my seat and heard Max in an excited tone, "NOW!"

I squeezed but could no longer feel the ball in my hand. When I looked down, I saw my hand clamped around a mangled piece of metal. I tried to open my hand but my pointer finger was stuck under some metal that had folded over. With my other hand I attempted to unfold the metal. It felt hard and unmovable again, so I took a deep breath and concentrated, this time with my eyes open, and tried again. I felt my hand warm first, then my forearm as I bent the metal off my finger. Spreading my palm to view the disfigured paperweight, I looked up at Max.

He met my gaze with a bewildered look of awe. Then suddenly he looked behind me, which made me turn to see that Aaron had just walked in. His face held the same look as Max's. "What the hell?" he said.

Max stood and extended his hand to Aaron. Always with perfect etiquette. "Hello Aaron, thanks for coming. You almost missed it."

"What was that? How did you . . . ?" Aaron walked toward me and reached for the metal to examine it.

"I don't know. Max asked me to and . . . well . . . you can see what happened."

We both looked toward Max who had walked back to the bookshelf and was shuffling through some old papers he had pulled out. He put a finger up toward us and started, "Asclepius was known to have the power over objects." Grabbing several papers haphazardly in his hands, he walked back to sit with us. He flipped through several of his papers then started again. "Since Asclepius was of the belief that he had this strength over objects and the ability to see auras like us, he came to the realization that the ones like us had certain talents. Each different. His daughter also had talents."

I raised my hand as if in class. Laughing at this, I put my hand back down and asked my question. "Didn't you say Asclepius was a god? A mythological being?"

Smiling at what I could only construe was the humor in my inane question he responded, "No, he was rumored to have been *made* a god by Zeus and placed among the constellations after Zeus killed him for raising the dead. We, however, know that he did not raise the dead, he saved those who were supposed to die by killing the ones who were to do the murdering . . . his purposes." He then turned a page of the many papers toward me to show me a picture of a statue. "This is Asclepius. Do you see the staff he is holding?"

Looking at the picture, I noticed what looked like a Greek-like statue of a man in a robe, curly hair and bare chest. In his hand he held a very rude stick which was taller than him. It looked as if the bark had been carved off by hand, leaving many channel-like impressions along the shaft. Around the staff was wound a large snake. "What about it?"

He pulled the paper back toward himself and smiled. "This is our symbol. This is the mark of our kind."

I looked up at Aaron and noticed a small pin on the lapel of his button up shirt; it was the same symbol. I then remembered when Max had taken Hippocrates's journal out of the floor and the board had this symbol on it. As I looked back at Max, he started speaking again.

"This is the symbol for those of us, all medical people by environment, and all Aurators by nature. The good of medicine."

I thought back to my nursing school days. When I graduated I was given a necklace by my father that said RN on it on top of the caduceus, a staff with two snakes entwined around it with wings on top of the staff. "I always thought that the caduceus was the sign for medicine."

"This is a common misconception," Aaron said. "The caduceus was the sign for the Greek god Hermes, who was the inventor of magical incantations, conductor of the dead, and protector of merchants and thieves. This symbol is usually mistaken for the symbol of medicine, but in reality it represents all that we fight against. The staff of Asclepius is the only true sign of medicine . . . well, of good medicine."

I thought about this for a moment. The caduceus was all I had ever seen in my career. It was everywhere. I couldn't wrap my head around the thought that it might be a negative symbol, but then I considered a possible explanation. "Max?"

"Yes."

"Does this mean that among the medical community there is good and bad . . . I mean . . . well . . . us and them?"

"Good question, but no. Those we fight against are not all in the medical profession. Some maybe, but a lot, at least of those that I've come into contact with, come from all different backgrounds."

I looked toward Aaron, who agreed, "All different, none medical to my knowledge."

"So," I began, "Asclepius was one of us?"

"Yes," answered Max, "but more specifically Megan, one of you. He was your ancestor. You are his bloodline, which is what makes you so powerful. We mentioned before that one of his daughters also had this power, but since then all have been men."

"Why her?"

"Good question. We may never know."

Although I enjoyed the history lesson, I remembered why I came in the first place. "What do I do about my purpose?"

Both men looked at me, Aaron now sitting on the couch across from me. "Complete it," they said in unison.

I laughed out loud. "Are you crazy? I can't kill someone. Besides, how do I even know where to look for this person?"

Max leaned forward and looked at me as a grandfather would look at his young granddaughter, "You have to complete it. If you don't, innocent people will die. If you don't, you will never be whole. This is your destiny . . . this is who you are."

"How?" I asked.

"How what?" Max asked as he leaned back.

"If I find him, how do I kill him?" I couldn't believe the words were even coming out of my mouth.

"That, Megan, is up to you. You need to follow your instincts."

"What if my instincts are telling me that killing is wrong?"

"You just need to turn it over. Close your eyes and ask for guidance. Ask to be shown the direction."

"Who am I asking?"

"Who do you think?" His eyes narrowed as if trying to place the answer into my mind.

"I don't know. God? That makes no sense, God would never guide someone to kill."

"Kill someone who is good? No. Fix a genetic mutation that he . . . or she . . . never created or intended and that is wreaking havoc in the world? Maybe. Just try it and let us know if we can help."

I stood up, realizing that I still had things to do before I got my girls from school. "I have some things to think about. I'll call you guys later. Thanks."

11. Purpose

The day progressed as normal. I picked the girls up from school after shopping and cleaning house. I was going to work that night so I had made dinner and decided to take a nap after my daughter Trina came up asking if I was okay. I had responded with the "fine honey" that I normally did when I was upset but didn't want my kids to worry. Along the way, I grabbed a quick kiss from my husband who was playing with Abi and dressed like a pirate.

I lay down and thought about everything Max and Aaron had said to me. I thought *I need help*, but then sighed and went to sleep. Except I didn't sleep well. I had dream after dream of killings. I was killing the same person over and over in different but all very gruesome ways. I awoke in a cold sweat, eyes wide and breathing fast. I looked around the room for someone but no one was there. I did however have a sense of resolve. I picked up the phone and called in sick to work. Then I dialed Aaron and told him where to meet me and what to bring.

He sounded stunned on the other line. "You want me to bring what?"

"Look," I started, "I did what you guys told me and this is what I came up with. I'm only doing what feels right. This is what I need to do. Can you meet me or not?"

He paused on the other line. "If this is what you were shown then it is my place to help."

"Thank you. I'll meet you at eleven-thirty tonight."

"Okay, bye."

"Bye." I got up, showered, dressed in my scrubs for work and packed my bag, but this time not with items for work . . . at least not my regular work. I gave each of my girls a kiss good-bye and then walked downstairs to kiss Luke, who was watching the news, and left.

I drove to the cafe, parked, and quickly changed into more appropriate clothes for where I was going. I was a little early so I finished my make-up and hair and waited. I wasn't sure if I could follow through with this. Could I do what was shown to me? Aaron pulled up right on time.

I stepped out of my car and walked to his door as he was getting out. "I wasn't going to do this . . . whoa, you look . . . wow."

It's true that I was dressed differently than I normally did. I'm a jeans and t-shirt kind of girl but when necessary I clean up nice. I was wearing a form fitting, almost down to my knees, sleeveless red dress that I wore when Luke and I went out last New Year's Eve. Luke liked the way the cut of the dress gave me a more voluptuous appearance. My make-up was definitely done up for nighttime and my hair was down instead of my usual pony tail. "Okay, okay, enough of the harassment. It's for a reason." I tried to reach for a bag that he was holding but he pulled it backwards.

"Hold up a minute. Just what are you going to be doing dressed like that?" He looked me up and down in a way that was teetering between annoying and flattering.

"Look," I began, do you think I would be dressed like this had it not been necessary? Just . . . well, can I have the stuff?"

I could tell he wanted to tease me a bit more but his face suddenly turned serious. "I didn't want to do this, but I called Max and he convinced me that we needed to help." He handed me a black leather bag. I took it and looked up at him. His eyes were filled with concern and a little fear. What I had asked him to do was unfair, I knew that. But the dream I had was clear, and I knew that the only way I would be able to complete my purpose was to carry it out in this way . . . with his help.

"Thank you. I know that I shouldn't have asked you to do this, but I don't know any other way. If I could do anything differently, I would."

"I know. I don't have to understand it to support the greater good that will come of this." Then placing his hand on my shoulder, he asked, "Are you okay?"

"Honestly? No." I answered so quickly that I had to backtrack. "I know what I have to do. The drive to complete this is getting stronger in me. I don't think I'll be able to control how I react much longer."

He nodded his head in agreement. I remembered the story of his first purpose and not being able to help himself. He asked, "When are you going to do this?"

"Tonight, right now."

His eyebrows furrowed in confusion, "How do you know you will see him tonight?"

"I dreamt it. I know where he'll be." I was looking through the bag to make sure everything I asked for was there when I realized things were a little too silent. I looked up to see a shocked look on his face. "What?"

"You . . . dreamt . . . it?" He seemed to have difficulty finding the right words.

"Yes, why? Didn't you?"

"No."

There had to be more than that. "No . . . but?"

"No buts, just no. It was random, at least it felt random. I know that there are larger hands at play here but I'm not aware of the game they're playing. I just move when I'm told to move."

I pondered this for a moment but then had what can only be described as an internal alarm clock go off in my head. "I'm sorry Aaron, we'll need to talk about this later. I have to go."

"Can I . . ." he started but I was already walking away.

"I'll call you tomorrow." I shouted back and got into my car.

I drove to the location in my dream. A bar. This was a bar I knew well, I had partied here during nursing school with a lot of friends from the Mission District. I was feeling pretty thankful that I didn't have the need to frequent bars, or even drink anymore for that matter, as I parked and looked around. No one here. I quickly changed and put together a bag of items that I would need.

It has always amazed me how it can be years since you've been in a particular place but the minute you walk in you are hit with a rush of smells and memories that transport you back in time. The table that my friends and I sat at was still there. The bar was the same. The bar was wooden, hand-carved mahogany with twenty or more leatherette stools. Behind the bar were all the usual bottles of alcohol and glasses hanging above the bartender's head. There were tables scattered throughout the rest of the room. A pool table sat in the corner with several wannabe pool champions hovering around it. The pictures on the walls were like any other bar, tacky, and clearly had not been updated since I was last here.

I walked up to one of the barstools and asked for a 7-Up. I sat down, placed my bag on my lap and waited. I could hear the chatter behind me. One man was breaking up with a woman who was in turn accusing him of cheating. Another gentleman was speaking with his male partner about their upcoming wedding plans and clearly having a difference of opinion regarding the theme for the event. I felt a little sad, wishing that these were my biggest concerns.

I sipped my drink and quickly reviewed in my head what I had seen in the dream. When he walks in I . . . OW! I was struck in the head by something cold. As I reached up to my head I looked toward the source of the pain. I stopped breathing. There he was, walking toward me, the dark aura emanating throughout the room, almost seeming to caress everyone he walked by. I took a breath, my chest burned, and I could feel my heart starting to speed up. I tried to look away but my body wanted to move toward him. It took all my strength to turn toward my drink and take some deep breaths. I could feel my body warming, the muscles tensing and relaxing. I looked to my right and there he was, sitting two stools down. I remembered the dream and knew that I had a part to play. I changed my posture to appear more nervous and insecure, glancing around as if searching for something.

After a few moments, I heard, "Can I help you? Are you waiting for someone?" I felt his words pierce my own heart. I reached for my chest and looked at him. His face had a familiarity to it that I couldn't quite put my finger on.

"Thank you," I said rather breathlessly. "I'm not actually waiting for anyone, just people watching."

His gaze moved up and down the length of my body. This sent a shiver down my spine, raising the hair on the back of my neck. I felt the anger welling up inside me. I wanted to kill him. This thought pulled me out of my moment of self-absorption and I turned back toward him. Our faces were just two feet apart.

"Can I buy you a drink?" he asked.

"I have one, thanks." I tried to play coy. Luke always said I was terrible at this but maybe that was because I never wanted to be coy with him.

"My name is Amber," I said, "and you?"

"Oh, well I'm J.J. Nice to meet you. Can I interest you in conversation?"

"Sure, what do you want to talk about?" What am I missing, I thought to myself. There was something about him. Was it the dream? Sitting there in front of me an average but not bad-looking guy, brown hair either intentionally cut into one of those windblown, bed-head haircuts, or else he just hadn't gotten a haircut in a long time. His eyes were a bright blue that would have been beautiful if their appearance were not overshadowed by an immense sadness that emanated from them. His face was one of someone who had, in my dad's words, been around the block once or twice. He looked as if he had lived more than one life. He smiled at me, and the softness I had felt in that moment was gone. He was evil. I felt the urge to spring forward and take care of him quickly. I looked back down at my drink. *Play the part, play the part.* This plan would only work if I continued to play my part. Although I felt the strength and a new sense of inner courage building in me, I needed to come off as insecure and weak.

I looked at my drink and concentrated on taking a more weak posture. He responded by moving closer, onto the stool next to me.

"Are you sure you're not meeting anyone?"

"No, why?" I turned to look at him just as he sat down next to me.

"Just wondering why a woman as beautiful as you is alone. Seems a shame." I could see how his words could be charming to someone who was lonely, or rather just wanted to be with someone.

"Thank you." I responded softly. "But I'm not beautiful. Nobody ever seems interested in me." I tipped my head ever so slightly forward as if to seem sad.

I felt a sharp pain but didn't move as he placed his hand on top of mine on the bar. "Maybe you've just been waiting for me."

I felt nauseated. My muscles wanted to flex and respond to his touch but I wouldn't let them. The internal fight was almost painful as I took a ragged breath in. Looking toward him I saw that his face was excited and he took my response to mean, well, something much different.

I took a deep breath in, "Yes, maybe I have been." I looked away quickly so as to seem shy.

"Well, do you want to get out of here, maybe go get something to eat?"

I looked up at him. It had worked, I couldn't believe it, just as I had seen it in my dream. Could I go through with it and finish the way my dream did? "Okay, I guess," still playing the part. He got up from the barstool and stood with his hand out. I didn't trust myself to touch him, so I reached for my bag instead, clutching it to my chest. I turned to walk out the front door but he motioned toward the back door.

"My car is in the back, do you mind if I drive us?"

Is this what he does with all his victims? And they fall for it? We walked out the back door into the alley between the two buildings, and he motioned for me to walk down the opposite way from the street. The alley was not quite big enough for a car to fit without going through like a pinball machine, and there was nowhere to run . . . not that I wanted to. He followed behind me until we were at least forty feet away from the door, then he placed his hand on my shoulder.

"Wait," he said in a throaty, urgent tone. "Stop for a moment."

That's when I felt it, an urge unlike any other. My shoulder where his hand rested felt as if on fire. I wanted to turn and dismember him, I wanted to hear him beg for his life. I turned and was startled when I saw him holding a knife.

"It's okay, I'm not going to hurt you."

Things happened so quickly. I remember standing in front of him staring at the knife, but then in a blur of movements I had disarmed him, the knife clattered to the ground, and I had taken control. Within a second, I saw myself standing over him holding him down by his throat. His eyes looked up at me in terror. What a turnabout this must be for him, I thought.

"Who are you?" he choked out.

What is it about his eyes? Why are they so familiar? "Who are you?" I did not release my grip but instead tightened my fingers around the curve of his throat so that I could feel his pulse for a split second and then it disappeared. "I could end you right now."

"I'm J.J. I already told you that. Why are you doing this to me?"

Fascinating really . . . the feeling I was having. So many nights my heart raced as I walked down a dimly lit street at night, worried someone could attack me. But now . . . I wasn't afraid of anything. My muscles ached to finish him. Then I saw it, the images so vivid in my mind . . . the women from my vision, the woman from the emergency room and then suddenly they shifted out of focus and visions of the kids from my school who were killed came forward. I tried to shake the images out of my head but was unsuccessful.

"What is your real name? J.J. is short for what?" I tightened my grip just slightly.

"John Jeffery," he spit out.

"What is your last name?" I asked the question, but just as the words left my mouth I knew the answer. I could see the young boy's face in the weathered one before me.

"Steele," he sputtered out. My grip had gotten a little tight and I loosened it ever so slightly. I gasped.

"Why do you care?" he asked.

"We went to high school together, and I remember what you did." His eyes were wide with awareness and fear.

"That was a long time ago," he struggled to say.

"Not so long that I could forget it," I barely got the words out of my throat.

"That's what this is about? You're *avenging* them?" He had a slight smirk on his face.

"No." Yes, them too, I thought. "I'm here because of the recent tragedies you have created." Now his breathing was fast and uneven. He knew exactly what I meant. He struggled but, even though I had to adjust my grip, I was stronger than him. It felt amazing. His body was like an eggshell, and with one twist of my hand I could end his life. I felt powerful. Enough talking. It was clear what he had done, and the urge to end this was overwhelming.

I reached into my bag with my free hand and pulled out one of the two syringes that Aaron had brought for me. It was a paralytic, which I quickly injected into his vein. I felt the fight leave him and released my grip.

I stood and removed two latex gloves from the bag. I put them on, grabbed a roll of tape, and taped his eyes open. I looked down at him. "You know, John, it didn't have to be this way. You had a choice to be something else . . . someone better . . . you had a choice." In those words I realized that I, however, didn't have a choice. I held the syringe in one hand, now gloved, and held my other hand up. I felt so strong . . . so different . . . changed in some way.

This is it . . . the resolve . . . this is who I am. I never asked for this. As I stood there viewing the surreal scene set in front of me, I struggled to fight the fear and the nausea . . . the excitement. I became acutely aware of every muscle in my body. One by one, flexing and extending as the blood pulsed hard to supply what my muscles needed to keep each one satisfied. My heart was pounding and racing . . . aching. A sudden chill vibrated through me as drops of sweat accumulated above my brow line. The back of my neck felt moist as a slow trickle slipped down my back. I took in a deep breath and, noticing my ragged breathing, I quickly steadied myself. I smelled the scene and the aroma of victory took me over, making me shudder as I felt the high. I could taste it on my tongue, which made my mouth water, and I had to swallow hard. I felt my saliva moving down my throat, feeling a bit cold in my overheated body, only to land in my now quivering stomach. I sighed, realizing that the nausea had finally passed.

I stood and looked at him . . . my victim, with contempt and just a hint of sadness. He never saw it coming. His limp body twisted into an unnatural position on the ground, still but not dead . . . not yet . . . and a smirk spread across my face.

But as the breeze of reality kissed my cheek, my face dropped just slightly with sadness. *The others . . . they were right . . . I have been created for this.* I closed my eyes for a moment as I felt a strange sensation. A feeling to do something, but what? Is this what they were talking about? I was drawn here and it felt right, but could I really finish it? As I took a deep breath, a sense of calm took over my body. It was at this moment that I understood who I was to be and how far I had come to get here. In front of me lay my past, present, and future.

He deserved this. His breathing was slow, shallow, clinging to life, lying motionless from the paralytic I had just injected. His eyes were wide with fear, taped open so that he could see me, see what was coming. I didn't want him to miss a thing. I wanted him to see me doing this. I wanted him to feel the fear and pain that he had put his victims through, the pain that he would have inflicted again if he were allowed to live. Not today.

This was premeditated, I had searched him out. The syringe, still in my hand, was cold even through my latex glove, but comforting. I could almost smell the metallic taste of its contents and sighed. I walked slowly over to my bag. I retrieved the other syringe, already loaded. I checked it for air, silly, it wouldn't matter. I knelt down next to him, looked into his eyes for a second, then spoke. "You will NEVER hurt anyone else again." I felt his chest, his heart, beating as if I were holding it in my hand. I unsheathed the needle, it caught the light across the alley and sparkled. Slowly, methodically, I felt between his ribs and plunged the needle into his heart. He looked scared as I stared into his eyes. Then I emptied the contents of the syringe into his heart. Slowly drawing the needle back out through his skin with a last tug, I felt for his heartbeat on his right wrist. Was this what nursing school really trained me for? I was thankful for my ER nursing experience now as I waited . . . it slowed . . . then stopped. No movement, no shudder from him, just silence.

I stood over him, watching him. I waited. Then it came. I felt oddly aroused. The need that I had denied for so long, the daily obsessive thoughts, clouding my own thoughts, rendering me completely helpless. *What am I doing . . . my husband . . . my children . . . what am I doing?* I dropped to my knees, beaten by the need, the obsession, all my strength to fight this off was gone. But, I needed . . . and wanted more. A new strength began to build in me. I could do this, I could be this, I needed to be this. I could feel my heart pick up, beat with the strength I had been craving. A warmth started in my gut, like fire I felt it start to burn each organ as it spread throughout my body. Images flashed in my head, images of would-be victims of this man, now safe. I started to shake, a tremor that shuddered through my body. I was breathing hard and fast. It surpassed any feeling of ecstasy I had ever experienced. I tried to calm my mind, my body, my heart, my breathing. Slowly, the sensation receded along the same path it had climbed through my body. It was over. I had been preparing for this moment my whole life.

12. Beginnings

I walked to my car, reviewing all of the night's events. Had I cleaned everything up? Were there any DNA left? I couldn't worry about that, nor did I feel I needed to. I needed to sit and think. As I walked up to my car, I saw two figures in the dark standing next to my car door. I could feel my muscles tightening, but they relaxed when I noticed the red auras.

"Max . . . Aaron," I said matter-of-factly . . . almost calmly.

"Megan," they both replied.

I squinted at both of them, "How did you know where to find me?"

Max glanced toward Aaron who suddenly looked uneasy. "I followed you. Wow, you still look great." His face then put on a boyish grin and I rolled my eyes and looked toward Max.

"Well, how are you?" Max asked clearing his throat.

"Other than feeling I'm still in the middle of a dream . . . or nightmare, I'm great. You?"

Close enough now to see their faces clearly, I noticed Max frowning. "You're not sick?"

I opened the trunk and placed the bag into it. "No. What do you mean sick?"

Max and Aaron looked at each other.

"You completed your purpose?" Aaron questioned.

"Yes, why?"

Max interrupted, "I'm curious, did you get his name?"

I took a long breath in and out and nodded, "Yes, it was John Steele from high school."

"Fascinating," Max stated in an awed response.

Aaron continued, "Megan, it is difficult after our first purpose . . . and the transformation . . . to be, well, okay."

Max moved toward Aaron and put his arm around him. "What do you say we treat Megan to a coffee and talk about this somewhere else."

Aaron nodded in agreement, and we each drove off in our respective cars. *Transformation,* Aaron had called it. *Is that what happened?* I took a moment to survey myself in the rearview mirror. I looked the same. My body felt the same, although I had to admit that something was different, I just couldn't put my finger on it.

We stopped at one of my favorite coffee shops and all went in to sit down.

This time I started the questioning, "Max, what does transformation mean for me? How am I different?"

"I can't believe she's okay," Aaron again remarked, looking at Max.

"Agreed, Aaron, agreed. But there is a lot that is going to be different when it comes to her." Turning toward me, "So first tell me, tell me everything."

I raised my eyebrows in surprise, but then retold the events. They both sat across from me and nodded in agreement to much of what I said. When I was done, it was Max who spoke first.

"So, this dream you had, it showed you where to find him and what to do?"

"Yes."

"And was the dream correct?"

I had to think about this for a moment because once I was in the heat of doing what I had to do I hadn't connected it to the dream anymore. But, yes, it was . . . exact . . . except for the knife. "Yes," I finally responded, "it was mostly right on."

"You can see certain futures. Fascinating. I wonder what it means," he responded.

"Max?" Aaron interrupted, "The transformation?"

"Right, right. So tell me Megan, did you feel any pain after you completed your purpose?"

I had to think about that. There was no pain, just a feeling of heat and, well, arousal. I looked at both men and didn't believe I could share this detail so I just answered, "No." They looked at me a little bewildered. Aaron's expression even held a hint of jealousy. I felt a heat and tensing all over my body but no pain. "Was I supposed to?"

"All of us do . . . well, all of us except you," Aaron chimed in curtly.

"What does the transformation mean?" I asked, getting back to my original question.

Max looked at me for a long minute and then smiled. "Your eyes are a little lighter, and your skin looks a little darker."

"What?"

"A transformation," he began, "is just that . . . we transform. Our DNA actually change ever so slightly. Usually so slightly that unless you're really looking for it you wouldn't know anything had happened."

"Why does this happen?"

Max smiled, "It's funny how we seem to be genetically equipped to handle the ever-changing technology in the world. How long do you think we'd last with the new police forensic science? Do you really think you didn't leave DNA at the scene?"

My eyes were wide. I had thought about it as I was walking away but did not consider being caught, maybe because I couldn't be. "I thought about it, yes, but something just let me abandon the worry."

"So, what is it? What let you forget about it?" But somehow I thought this question was rhetorical so I waited. Max continued, "Instinct . . . genetics . . . a higher power? Maybe all three? Maybe someday we'll know for sure, but right now we just have our faith that it is something bigger than us. We change each time, just after the last heartbeat. Is it our own DNA that changes or something in our purpose that triggers us? A lot of questions, but not a lot of answers."

I pondered this while Aaron asked Max what kind of coffee he wanted, then went to get us all coffee. I did feel different, but I couldn't exactly say how. I was very aware of my surroundings, my body, others. Wow . . . I looked around and the whole cafe was lit up. I had never seen so many auras so bright and big in my life. "Am I supposed to be seeing more of each aura now?"

Max's eyebrows crinkled in confusion, "What do you mean more?"

I looked around and found one person who had an almost white light around him. It was huge, but I could still see through it, expanding out almost six feet from his body. He was walking past Aaron, whose red aura was solid, strong looking, also expanding out six feet but as their auras passed each other the white aura buckled and bent around Aaron's. I tried to explain what I was seeing to Max.

He said, "I see the red and white of their auras but do not see their interactions. Hmmm."

"Hmmm what?"

"Your skills are getting stronger. We already know from your purpose that somehow you have the ability to see some futures, although we don't know how much yet. You can also sense auras stronger than anyone I've known of. They will be interested to hear this." He trailed off in thought and I barely caught the last words. Aaron walked back to the table with three coffees. I guess he remembered what I drank from meeting for breakfast. Taking a drink confirmed this, coffee, half and half, and sugar.

"Thanks, Aaron."

"You're welcome."

Then turning, I said "Max?"

"Yes?" Still not looking at me, he was lost in thought.

"Who are "they," and why will they be interested in this?"

Aaron looked up from his coffee at Max and asked, "Are they coming?"

"Yes."

Aaron sat back in his chair. Then looking at me. "Wow, they haven't come over here for at least one hundred years. You sure know how to draw a crowd."

I looked again at Max. "Max please, who?"

He sighed, "The Seniors from Greece."

"Which ones?" asked Aaron.

"Aleck, Nicholai . . . and Tomas."

Aaron's mouth fell open. He got up from the table and walked outside.

"What's going on?" I felt as if there was a secret being thrown back and forth in front of me.

"These men," started Max, "are the Senior Aurators in the world. As we said, no one's been to this country for over a hundred years. But of course no one has needed to come. Until you." Max turned his coffee cup around in front of him and looked a little uneasy.

I guess I could understand why they would come. According to Max and Aaron, I was the prophecy and descendant of Hippocrates, although I thought this was crazy. What I couldn't understand was why these two suddenly felt uncomfortable. I placed my hand on Max's arm, "Okay, I'll bite . . . what's the problem with this?"

He cleared his throat and sat up straighter. "What do you mean?"

"I can see you're uncomfortable. Why?"

Then a voice behind me started, "We don't want them here."

I turned to face Aaron, who had come back in and was standing behind me, fists clenched.

"Why not? If they are the leaders, isn't that good? Aren't all of you . . . us . . . good? Isn't this what you keep trying to tell me?"

Max removed his other hand from his coffee cup and placed it on my hand, which was still on his arm. His hand looked a little weathered, touched by time, but his hand was so soft and comforting, much like a grandfather's hand on a child would be. I took a breath and looked at his face. I could see doubt in his eyes . . . something troubling him.

"Megan, for some time now we have doubted the intentions of our newest Senior, Tomas." he said. "His actions and decisions have not always been the best, in our opinion, for us." He looked at Aaron, who nodded in agreement and then looked back to me. "Remember . . . while the sense of purpose you have is a genetic gift, with years of experience and exceptional control you can make different choices and turn the strength toward a different purpose. This is what Aaron and I think he has done."

"So why hasn't anyone tried to stop him?"

"It's much more complicated than that."

"Why?"

He pulled his hands away gently and sat back. Aaron sat down and both of them looked a little overwhelmed. "Right now," Max began, "it's just a theory, there is no proof. And to take on the Seniors would . . . well, challenge the hierarchy. There is a protocol, and to speak with them about this without proof could be a reason for them to ostracize us from the group. Since I have been given such a position to hold Hippocrates's journal, I would not want to do anything to jeopardize this."

I turned toward Aaron, "Why not you, then? What do you have to lose?"

"Those who have gone against the Seniors have never been heard from again," Max explained. "We think they are disposed of for fear of Aurators going to the Caduceus. However, most who challenge are not trying to go to the other side, just to effect change. The Seniors have used this as an excuse. Not all of them mind you, just Tomas . . . we think."

"How many are there?"

"How many what?"

"Seniors."

"Twelve." Max then leaned forward, "We're not going to resolve this issue tonight. Can I change the subject back to your painless transformation?"

"Sure, I guess. What causes the transformation?"

"We think it's something called your serpodus."

"My what?"

"Your power, the reason you're an Aurator. Broken down, serpodus simply means power of the serpent rod. Specifically the Rod of Asclepius. This is where the power emanates from and why it is our symbol." He paused as his eyes squinted at me slightly. "Hmmm, have you ever read the Bible?"

I thought back again to my days at church. Short of gathering ammunition for spit balls, I don't think I'd ever opened the book. "No."

"Revelations tells us of the end of evil. It is written by John, a disciple of Jesus. Whether you believe the Bible is the word of God or a great fictional novel, it's important to read and understand the contents of the Book of Revelations. A gift from God, an angel, comes down during an epic battle between good and evil and throws the evil serpent, which we know as the caduceus, into Hell. Some say this is Armageddon, the end of time. From our history we've learned that this interpretation is not true, it is just the end of the major evil in the world . . . as we know it . . . for one thousand years." He chuckled at what appeared to be a private joke that only he knew. "I've come to view it as God's reset button, a sort of . . . do-over."

This was fascinating to me, and not like our earlier conversations where it felt like some far-fetched, make-believe story that had nothing to do with me. I *felt* this story, as if something deep inside was pushing me toward something. "So, this . . . battle . . . this has something to do with me? This is why I'm here?"

Max wrinkled his forehead, "We think so, yes. Obviously Hippocrates's prophecy is interpreted. But yes we think you *are* part of it."

"Do you . . . we . . . know what is to happen? What *kind* of battle?"

Max turned toward Aaron and motioned for him to continue. Aaron looked at me, clearing his throat. "Nostradamus, know the name?"

"Sure. Loose predictions that are hard to prove or disprove, right? What about him?"

"He is one of your ancestors," Max broke in, unable to contain this bit of information. Aaron rolled his eyes and looked generally annoyed. I didn't have the patience to be codependent around Aaron's poor bruised ego and turned toward Max.

"What do you mean ancestor? Another relative? That can't be right. Why haven't my parents told me any of this?" My father was a name dropper—if he had known about Nostradamus being a relative, he definitely would have been boasting.

Max looked a little uncomfortable, shifted in his seat, and cleared his throat. "Well, let's just say they don't know about this."

"What do you mean they don't know? Don't you think they would know their own relatives?"

Max closed his eyes and sighed, "This is a conversation for another day. I'd like to get back to Nostradamus if that's okay—it's why we're here."

I was irritated by this. Here was a man claiming to know more about my family than I did, or than my parents did, and he wasn't willing to go any further. "Fine," I said with a seven-year-old attitude. I had to chuckle at myself, I was so familiar with the emotional problems of a seven-year-old girl. This self-realization, however, did not prevent me from folding my arms over my chest with a harrumph in defense of . . . well . . . something.

Max smiled, "It's okay, we'll talk about it later." Then he motioned for Aaron to continue.

Aaron took a sip of his coffee, then continued, "Nostradamus was an apothecary, then went to medical school."

"Another doctor?" I interrupted.

Aaron nodded his head, "Yes, but not the conventional way. He went to medical school but was kicked out when they found out he was an apothecary. This job was considered menial labor, lower class, blue collar. However, in those days you could apprentice with another doctor and then practice, which is what he did. He wrote books on medicine as well as predictions of the future."

Max raised his hand to interject, "He was a future teller also, like Hippocrates . . . and you. And by the way, Walt Whitman was also a nurse, as well as being a writer and one of us. We're not all doctors. There are Aurators in all areas of medicine."

I lowered my head and raised my hand toward my head as if tipping an imaginary hat. "Thanks for that, I was beginning to wonder."

Aaron cleared his throat, "Can I continue?" I raised my eyebrows and Max chuckled. "His predictions were never supposed to be publicized, they were written, just as Hippocrates's were, for the benefit of our kind. To help us positively affect history by eliminating those most evil. He was conned out of his writings and they were published. This warned the Caduceus side, and they were able to protect the people his prophecies told about longer than they should have been. Subsequently they were able to engineer much more evil than should have been allowed."

I had to ask, "Who were these people he wrote about?"

"Napoleon . . . Hitler . . . and it is suspected that the third person in his predictions was Osama Bin Laden, but there's still no proof that he's the one. It is very difficult to interpret the writings."

I had to agree that all three men created far more havoc on earth than most. "Was there an Aurator who had him as a purpose?"

"Yes," answered Aaron, "but it was suspected that some of the Caduceus had infiltrated his troops so that he was under constant protection and guard. He may not have been the next in line but he created enough havoc."

Max spoke, "It is important to realize that while we need to eliminate certain people because they are the incarnation of evil, not all evil can be eradicated. Good cannot survive without evil. We would cease to exist. This is why your serpodus is so important for us. We may have the chance, through you, to offset what has been done. To prepare for what others refer to as Armageddon. We believe the other side is organizing for the first time ever because according to Nostradamus's predictions. If Bin Laden was the incarnation of the third person, then he was to be the last of these leaders. The end result of all of this, my dear, is that with your direction we will be able to organize ourselves to fight that which intends to rid the world of all that is good."

I turned toward the window and noticed that the first light was creeping into the night sky. This was my favorite time of day. Every day a chance to start over . . . a new beginning.

I looked at my watch and announced, "I should go. They'll be expecting me home."

Max nodded in agreement, "What an amazing night! Thanks for letting us be a part of it."

Aaron and Max stood as I did, and Max reached out to give me a large hug. I sighed and felt the turmoil inside me, churning between a feeling of being overwhelmed and a sense of purpose and design.

Max cradled my chin in his hand. "This will be okay, this is your destiny. Next week when the Seniors get here, we will get more organized."

I didn't speak, I just nodded my head and left. I changed into my scrubs in the car. After all, I had been at work all night . . . not murdering someone. I walked into the house. I took a deep breath . . . home, then walked upstairs to change into pajamas and wash my face. I climbed into bed and snuggled up next to Luke. He made a slight moaning sound to acknowledge my presence, and I fell deeply asleep.

13. Truths

I was happy to undertake simple household and family tasks. I cleaned the house, cooked, played and did homework with my girls, and spent some much needed quality time with my husband. I was happy and lying with him after some much needed one-on-one time when he asked, "What's going on with you?"

I closed my eyes, grateful to be facing away from him in bed so that he couldn't see my face. "Nothing, why?" My voice did not sound convincing—how could it when what I said wasn't true.

"Well, I just noticed that you haven't been yourself lately. You've been a little distracted. Do you want to talk about anything?" He was twirling his fingers in the hair at the base of my neck and I shuddered as a chill raced through me. I turned over toward him. I loved how our naked bodies felt next to one another. I reached up to his face and placed my hand aside his cheek.

"I'm fine. Maybe it's just the beginning of a midlife crisis." I smiled, trying to appear nonchalant about the whole thing. His eyes squinted ever so slightly as he looked at me.

"Are you going to a tanning salon?"

My heart sped, how could I think that he of all people wouldn't notice the difference. "No, why?"

"Wow, you just seem so tan, and it makes your eyes look a little lighter and brighter." He was examining me very closely, and I was starting to become uncomfortable with having to avoid the subject.

"Your mind is playing tricks on you." I said as I reached around his neck and pressed my lips to his. "Round two?" I asked. He smiled and rolled over on top of me. I had to admit that while I felt terrible about not telling him everything that was going on, these distraction techniques always worked and . . . well . . . I never seemed to mind either.

At work I was noticing subtle changes. I always had what is called a nurse's "gut," meaning that I sensed when something wasn't right. Many nurses have this, some more in tune than others. Mine was always spot on. I had once walked down the hall, and as I passed a patient room I stopped, sensing that something was wrong. I had walked into the room and found a man who was in an unmonitored room . . . unconscious. I had called a code blue to let everyone know there was a patient who needed resuscitation and we saved him.

But what I was feeling now was . . . different. I walked up to my patient and could feel, somehow *feel*, that his heart was beating irregularly. I placed him on the monitor and his heart rate was, in fact, irregular. While it was not a life-threatening rhythm, I shouldn't have known this. I mean . . . a feeling is one thing, but this was different. I would have to remember to talk to Max about this.

That night while sleeping I had a dream . . . well maybe now I can call them visions. I was with Max and Aaron when Max got a call that his office had been ransacked and he needed to return to the university immediately. Upon arriving we stepped into his office, which had been completely turned over, books pulled from shelves, furniture cut open and stuffing strewn about. His desk had been smashed practically into splinters, and several holes had been made in the walls to expose studs. I focused on the floor where Max had kept Hippocrates's journal and noticed that the board was missing and the box was shattered . . . the journal was gone.

Then in the doorway a dark figure appeared, no face, just a feeling of impending doom. My eyes were drawn toward something brilliantly bright in the middle of the object, and as it came into focus I realized what it was . . . the sign of the Caduceus. I put my hand up and the object flew backwards and disappeared.

I woke suddenly, covered in sweat, heart pounding, and gasped to catch my breath. My husband woke and put his arm around me. My heart rate immediately slowed and I felt calm . . . how does he do that? I explained it was just a bad dream and got up to splash water on my face. I looked up in the mirror and wasn't sure who I was looking at. I was changing so fast I felt as if I was losing who I was, or who I was supposed to be. I hung my head and silently asked for guidance. From whom I do not know.

I met Max at his office the next day because he wanted to bring me up to speed on the organization and what I could expect from the visitors. I knocked and heard, "Come in."

"Hello, hello Megan. Good to see you." He stood and came over to give me a hug. He motioned for me to sit and I walked over to the couch.

As I sat down I started, "I know you want to bring me up to speed, but there's something I need to tell you first."

Seeing the urgency on my face he furrowed his eyebrows and nodded for me to continue.

"I . . . I had a vision." It was hard for me to say that, almost as if he would laugh at how ridiculous that idea actually was. Instead he leaned forward with eyes wide.

"Go ahead, what?" He said this with so much enthusiasm that for a moment I lost my train of thought and had to regroup. He waited patiently while I flipped through the memories in my head trying to put together what I was going to say.

"Okay, last night I had a vision that while you, Aaron, and I were out you received a call that your office had been broken into, everything was in shambles, and the floor, where the journal is, was open, the box had been removed, smashed, and the journal was gone."

Max's breathing sped and he seemed a bit nervous. He looked around as if to see if anyone else was around, but then turned back to me. "What else?"

"When I looked toward the door there was a dark figure there and in the middle was a shining object." I paused.

"What was the object, Megan?" I could tell he was a bit impatient that I wasn't telling the story fast enough.

"It was a Caduceus."

Max exhaled sharply, "No!"

His exclamation startled me. "Did I do something wrong?"

"No, no, but this means that they may know where the book is and, more importantly, they're strategizing . . . organizing. Megan, we have to get the journal out of here. Somewhere safe. But where? Did anything else happen in the vision or was that it?"

After his last response I hesitated to tell him but explained how I had put my hand up in an act of protection and the object flew back and disappeared. He nodded as if he understood something that clearly I did not, got up, and walked over to his desk, flipping through a Rolodex . . . wow, do people still have those? He pulled out a number and dialed the phone. "Hello?" he said into the phone. "Yes, hello, look, I'm sorry, but this is a business call. Megan had a vision."

He continued to tell the entire vision to the unknown person on the other end. When he finished he was silent for a long time. Then he put his head into his hand, "No, I don't think I can do that . . . what if they . . . I know but . . . I know, I know you're right. Very well then, I will . . . and . . . I know I don't have to tell you this, but I think this information should stay between you and me." Then looking up at me, "And, of course, Megan."

Hanging up the phone, he walked over to the journal's hiding place and again moved the floorboard without touching it. He pulled out the box that housed Hippocrates's journal and moved to hand it to me. "You have to take this."

I hid my hands behind my back, "What are you doing? I can't take this . . . what are you thinking? I can't . . . I won't."

Max hung his head, "Megan you are our only hope . . . possibly our last hope. This is your destiny, your vision proves that. You are to be the keeper and protector of the journal."

I reluctantly extended my arms and took the box. He sat down, looking so tired. Then, motioning for me to sit, he started to explain. "You had the dream of protection. I had a similar dream, but no one was trying to take it. You must take this, hide it, and protect it. No one will know you have it. It is perfect, that as powerful as you are, you become the next Guardian."

"Guardian?" I hadn't considered that yet another role in this new life would be to protect a prophecy.

"Yes, I have been the Guardian of the journal, this has been my title. But for some reason this is to be your task now. What I don't know is why you are to be a Guardian *and* the one we have been waiting for. Perhaps the Seniors will have insight into this."

I sat back down and placed the box next to me. "Question. If Tomas is . . . possibly . . . not to be trusted . . . why would we ask him?"

He put his hand up. "We're not. We are secretly meeting with Nicholai beforehand. He agrees that Tomas cannot be trusted, but he does not have enough proof and is not willing to risk the secrecy of the journal to find out."

I thought about this statement for a minute. "Is that who you called?"

"Yes. He agrees that you are to be the Guardian but is also perplexed by the . . . well . . . dual roles. Typically a Guardian is just that. But everything is new to us now, and we may not fully know the reasons for what we are doing . . . we may not need to know the reasons to move forward. He is very excited to see you."

He then stood, "Wait . . . there is something else I have for you." He opened the right top drawer of his desk and pulled out a small leather box. I set aside the box with the journal as Max handed the smaller box to me, and I looked at it for the longest time. On it were the initials GB. "For your special day."

I looked up at him, "Special? Wait, who is GB?"

He smiled a very warm smile and whispered, "Your grandfather."

I looked at the box closely. My maiden name is Alcosta. "This was my mother's grandfather?"

"No. Why don't you open the box?" I looked at his face, which appeared quite conflicted, and decided not to press further.

"Okay." As I opened the box I noticed the lush thick velvet inside. I remembered the same velvet in the box in which Luke had presented my engagement ring. As the box opened completely, I saw a small gold object and focused on it. I had come to know this symbol very well: it was Asclepius's staff. I pulled it out and noticed it was a pin for a shirt or tie. I looked up at Max. "Okay, what's going on? Some of my family know about this . . . they are . . . were a part of it . . . but my parents have no idea? This doesn't make any sense."

He sighed, "No, I don't suppose it *would* make any sense. To be honest with you, I wasn't sure how or when to talk about this, but I suppose now is as good a time as any other." He walked over to his desk. "Tea?" I motioned no. He poured himself some tea from a plug-in pot, then opened a drawer, pulled out a small flask of alcohol, and poured some into the tea. Looking toward me again he held up the flask, "You sure?"

"I'm sure, thanks," holding up my bottle of water.

He sat back down, took a few deep breaths and started talking. "Back some years I was a new Aurator. I had just completed one purpose, met my mentor, and had a vision similar to yours, which is how I became the Guardian of the journal. Just like you are now, I was a little overwhelmed with all that was happening in my life and wondering what to expect. My parents were not Aurators, so I had very little guidance from my family. My father's brother was one of us, and he saw me at Christmas after I completed my first purpose. We stared at each other's auras. I had never seen a red aura in my family. He worked with me alongside my mentor and taught me all about the Aurators, Asclepius, Hippocrates, and the Caduceus."

He stopped for a moment and took what I thought was a big drink of his tea, then after a few deep breaths he continued. "I had another vision sometime later with three victims, two adults and one child. I was disturbed by this because I had never had a vision of a child dying. But this vision was confusing because I could not see the child's face. It was, well, for lack of a better word, blurry. Most faces of victims I had seen were sharp and in focus. It was a week or so after the vision before I could sleep normally again." He paused with a pensive look on his face.

I didn't interrupt, even though I had a ton of questions. He took a deep breath. "One night I was out to dinner with my wife."

Wow, Max is married? I had never considered that and I looked down and noticed the simple gold band on his left ring finger.

"I saw something that amazed and confused me," he continued. "I saw the people from my dream. My mentor had told me that we usually did not run into the victims, just our purpose. So I sent my wife home in a cab, excusing myself to go back to do some work in the office, and I set off to follow them. As I got closer to them I saw that the woman was pregnant and around her belly was a red aura. I could only extrapolate from my teachings that this meant she was carrying an Aurator.

"I followed them for a while, at a distance. Even though I was, I didn't want to appear to be stalking them. Just then, a dark figure came out from behind a building and stabbed both adults. I felt as if a bombshell had gone off in front of me . . . this was not how it was supposed to be. People screamed and ran. Instinctively I lunged for the figure and completed my purpose, but apparently no one saw me because they had run away in fear. I then turned toward the victims . . . the man was dead. The woman was looking up at me, struggling to breathe . . . she was obviously bleeding into her airway because there was gurgling when she tried to breathe.

"I dropped down next to her as I started to feel the pain of transformation, but then she reached out and grabbed my arm. My pain stopped and I felt a sudden surge of adrenaline. 'My baby,' she tried to say, gasping, 'you must take my baby, please . . . for all of us.' Then her arm dropped and I could see her breathing becoming very irregular.

"For a moment I couldn't think straight, but then I remembered the aura I saw around her belly . . . I must get him out . . . a future Aurator . . . this woman must have known she was carrying one of us, but how?"

He stopped and tears welled in his eyes. His right hand raised up toward his chest and the words were broken as he tried to compose himself. "I know I need to tell you this, but the memory burns in my chest. The pain is almost too much to bear."

I held my hand out to him and laid it on his arm, "Then don't, if it's too much."

"I have to, you need to know. You need to know *everything*." A tear rolled down his cheek. "I had spent the entirety of my career up to that point saving people . . . and I had to make peace with the fact that I was an Aurator and my purpose was to choose to end others' lives. Now I was being asked to do the unthinkable."

I furrowed my brows. "What do you mean? What did you do?"

"I picked up the knife that had just ended both of their lives and performed a very crude cesarean section on the mother, who looked to be about eight or nine months along. The baby took a breath. I cut the umbilical cord, tied it in a knot and wrapped my jacket around her to keep her warm."

"Her?" I interrupted. "A girl Aurator? I thought they've all been boys . . . men, until me?"

He looked at me, waiting for me to catch up to where he was in the story. My mind searched for what I had missed.

"Wait . . . Max! Are you saying that baby was me?!" I stood up and started pacing across the room. Now it was my turn and my eyes welled up. "No!" I tried to scream but no noise escaped. My whole life as I had known it lay in shambles in front of me. I searched the floor as if looking for an answer to a question I had never asked. "So my parents are not my . . . parents?"

Max stood, looking considerably older and tired suddenly. "No, they are your parents . . . just not your birth parents. A parent does not need to give birth in order to love and be a parent to a child."

I felt dizzy suddenly and sank to the floor as the flood of tears fell from my eyes and rolled down my cheeks. Max tried to console me, lowering himself to the floor with me and wrapping his arms around me, but I shrugged him off.

"How . . . why?" My words were barely audible.

Max sat back from me on the floor and hung his head. "I'm sorry, I thought what I was doing was right."

I looked up at him. I could hear the sincerity and agony in his words. "Please tell me what happened."

Sighing, he looked up at me, taking my face in his hands. "Trust me, if it had not been *necessary* then I would not have done any of this." Then he helped me up from the floor so that we both could sit on the couch. He reached over and took a large drink of his tea. I immediately understood why he had made the tea the way he did. Again he lifted his cup up toward me to ask if I would like some, but I shook my head no. He then set his cup down. "You don't drink?"

"No."

"Problem or choice?"

"Choice." Yes, it had been a choice to abstain from alcohol once I finished nursing school because I knew of my parents' past problems and I was attempting to avoid any genetic potential to become an alcoholic myself. I guess I didn't have that worry anymore.

He smiled and then continued, "When I saw you in that moment you were born, I knew who you were. Remember when we first met and I told you that you had your red aura your whole life?"

I tried to remember back to everything that had been said that first day. Mainly, I could remember leaving his office with many questions. I shrugged my shoulders, and he chuckled.

"I saw that red aura around you from that very moment. I knew who you were . . . well, who you were going to be. I was shocked to realize that you, just like Asclepius, had been born by means of a crude cesarean section, although it wasn't called that in his time."

I remembered the story very clearly and thought back to how terrible that sounded. "If I remember correctly, Asclepius was cut out of his mother's womb, right?"

"Yes, otherwise our kind would not have existed. Without you being born in the same fashion, our kind would not be saved."

My breath caught at this thought. "So, then what?"

"I took you home to my wife and told her what had happened. We wanted to keep you, but I was concerned, since I was known in the Aurator world, that if someone saw you who was not . . . well, of good intentions . . . your life would be in danger." Pausing, "We had just gained another child as well from a friend who had just passed, and, well, that was a terrible time. We had lost a lot."

I had never considered the fact that he was a father. "Do you have children?"

"Yes, two . . . both boys."

"Was one the other child you were speaking of?"

"No, we needed to find a good home for that one as well. Such a sad time."

"Are your boys . . . like us"

"No, they are both in their forties and are civilians."

I looked down at my hands which were still clasped around the box holding my great-grandfather's pin, and Max started again.

"I knew that for you to be safe I needed to find a family to raise you. I struggled with it and called a Senior whom I trusted, but his only advice was to trust the direction." He rolled his eyes, remembering something that I wasn't privy to.

"What?"

"Well," he chuckled, "I too had a lot of difficulty accepting my role and sometimes . . . at least in the early years . . . had trouble grasping the idea of being guided."

I sighed and nodded my head. This I understood.

"We had been caring for you two or three days, when I had a dream in which I was speaking to a man inside a bar I recognized, a bar that was around the corner from where I worked at the time. Not sure what the dream meant, I tried to formulate a plan to somehow protect you. I called an old friend of mine from high school who had taken a . . . well . . . different path than my own and asked if he knew of anyone who could forge documents. He told me of someone he had worked with and I called him."

I shook my head. This was sounding more Hollywood by the minute. Max suddenly said, "You know . . . where do you think Hollywood gets all their stories? Real life!"

I squinted at him, as if accusing him of mind reading. He retorted, "It was obvious why you were shaking your head."

"Okay, go on."

"On the phone, this man asked me to meet him at the same bar that I had just dreamt about. Okay, I thought, I'm supposed to go there . . . for him? Something still didn't feel right about it."

He stood. I thought he was going to get another drink of tea, but instead he went to the small refrigerator behind his desk and got a bottle of water. He offered me one and I accepted.

After handing me the water he continued to stand. "I got to the bar with all the information I wanted on the documents and half the money he requested. When I walked into the bar, it smelled like old beer and whiskey and the smoke was heavy in the air. Those were the days before 'No Smoking' sections. It took a minute for my eyes to focus through the smoke. I could hear 'I'm a Believer' by the Monkeys playing on the jukebox." He shook his head, "I never understood the fascination with that musical group."

I motioned with my hand to move ahead with the story.

"Okay, okay, anyway, I saw someone who fit the description of the gentleman I was supposed to meet and I walked over to him. We introduced ourselves and I gave him the envelope with the information and money. He told me to meet him back in the same spot at the same time in two days and he would have the completed documents. I nodded and off he went.

"I was disgusted with myself, wondering, how could I have done this? I sat to have a drink and, just as I ordered, there was a voice next to me. 'Tough day?' I looked at him, and there was a gentleman with the whitest aura I had ever seen . . . good to the core as I had come to know it."

He took a drink of water and looked at me, "You okay?"

I nodded yes but did not believe it myself. As he looked at me, I could tell he didn't believe me either.

"I struck up a conversation with him. He was a newly hired attorney with the District Attorney's office in San Francisco. I don't know why . . . well, now I do . . . but he started pouring his heart out to me. He and his wife had one son and had been trying for another child for many years. He admitted that the situation had driven them both apart and to the bottle for comfort. His wife was terribly depressed and he feared for her sanity . . . and his.

"After listening to him for quite a while, I realized that our position in the bar was exactly as I had dreamt it and that he was who I was supposed to meet. Without thinking, I started to tell him about being a doctor and knowing of a baby whose mother had died. He was tentative at first, but I gave him my information and told him to look me up to verify that I was who I said I was. However, I warned him, this baby could not be adopted in the most legal of ways. It was a leap of faith for me. This could have ended my career. I told him to meet me again in two days, same place and same time if he were interested. We said our good-byes and I left. My heart was racing. I had never done anything even close to illegal before, and even though I knew why I was doing this . . . it was scary for me."

I couldn't believe this was all about me, it sounded too surreal. I had to keep reminding myself to take deep breaths.

Max continued, "Two days passed and I met the man who provided me with the documents for you and paid him the rest of the money. Then the same attorney came back. He asked how much the baby would cost. I told him there would be no charge. You see, I had done my own checking and discovered some information about him as well. I had only one condition, which was that he and his wife had to stop drinking. He was stunned by this but assured me he was willing to do whatever it took to have a good life and give his wife a baby.

"Are you sure you want to hear all of this?" he suddenly asked me.

He must have read the overwhelmed expression on my face. "I knew that my parents stopped drinking, I just didn't know this was why," I said. "I'm sorry, it's a lot to take in. Please finish."

"We agreed to meet the next week," he continued. "I figured they needed a few days to sober up. I went home and told my wife that I had found a new home for . . . you . . . and she cried. She had named you and wanted to keep you."

"The next week you and I met with your soon-to-be mom and dad at their house . . . the same house you grew up in. Your mother's aura was equally as bright as your father's, and I knew they were the right people. Your mother was so happy and she wanted you immediately. As I handed you over to her, I felt my heart break. Even though I knew it was the right thing for you, I have to admit I wish we could have kept you."

I was acutely aware that my breathing was fast and I felt oddly nauseated. "My parents have been sober since."

"I know. I've watched them throughout the years."

"You've watched me all these years?"

"Yes, here and there. I felt . . . responsible . . . to make sure you were okay." He put his head down, "I've always felt horrible for not getting to your mother and father in time."

I could see his face and knew that his pain right now probably rivaled my own. I sighed and leaned toward him. "Max, I do understand how that must have been hard for you. You've kept this a secret all these years." I reached out and put my hand on his arm for the first time in an attempt to comfort him. "While this is unbelievably difficult for me to wrap my mind around right now, I can say that I appreciate what you did for me. I *know* that I would not be here if it weren't for you. Thank you."

He looked up at me, taking my face between both of his hands. "I hope you *really* understand who you are. And who you are *going* to be. We will perish without you. I'm sorry for any pain this has caused you, but it was necessary for the future of our world. The consequences of what I did to you I will have to live with, but you being here is bigger than both . . . all of us."

My head shook slowly side to side in disagreement, the idea that I was to save everyone was not only unthinkable, it didn't *feel* true.

I decided not to make Max feel any worse than he already did. "I will do whatever is asked of me."

He smiled, "Well, we have gone over quite a lot today. What do you say we save the briefing on the Seniors for another day?"

I had to admit that I was fairly full emotionally and didn't think I could listen to anything more today. I agreed, and we hugged good-bye.

14. Reality

I drove home in a daze, not realizing where I was going. Could all this be true? I was at a stoplight when I looked down and saw the journal next to me. What was Max thinking, giving this to me? I slipped it into my purse. *Guardian. Ha!* I felt like I could barely manage my own life, let alone guard the book that holds our prophecy.

My head was spinning. Adopted? I had to pull over. I looked at my watch and saw that I still had two hours before I needed to pick up the girls from school.

I pulled my phone from my purse and dialed the familiar number as my heart began to race. An answering machine picked up, "Sorry we're not here right now, leave a message and we'll call back." *Crap.* I hung up and dialed a second number. "Hello?" said a sleepy voice on the phone.

"Dad?"

"Hi honey. What's up? You okay?"

"Uh . . . yeah. Where are you guys?"

"Paris, honey, remember?"

It took me a minute to process what he had said . . . they weren't here. "Yeah, sorry dad, I remember now. When do you guys get back?"

"Two weeks . . . honey, is everything okay? You don't sound right."

I could hear my mom in the background asking what was wrong, but my dad responded I was okay. I couldn't figure out how to bring this up over the phone. "Sure, Dad, everything's great. I'll see you guys when you get home. Bring the girls t-shirts, okay?"

I never needed to remind them to bring the girls anything. They were always so generous, of course, since the girls were their only grandchildren. My brother still hadn't found anyone foolish enough to marry and have kids with him. Brother? Wow, I really wasn't related to him. All those years

I couldn't figure out how the two of us could have shared the same genes, and now I knew we didn't.

"Honey? Honey? Did I lose you?" I didn't realize he was still speaking to me.

"Sorry, Dad. I'm here. I love you. Have a great rest of the trip, and I'll call you when you get home."

"Okay sweetheart . . . we love you."

I found myself choking back tears at this statement. "I love you both, too." As I hung up I burst into tears. This morning when I woke up, my biggest problem was that I was some sort of prophesied *coming* to rid the world of evils. Yeah, that's a pretty big problem. But now, adopted?

My breathing was rapid and short. I felt a little dizzy and realized I was hyperventilating. I started holding my breath, trying to slow it down. I looked around, no paper bag. Concentrate. Concentrate. As my breathing slowed, I started to think about my girls. Suddenly the reality hit me that the three of them were the only other people with whom I was genetically related to, at least among the people I knew.

I wanted to see my girls. I drove to their schools and picked them all up early. I made an excuse of doing something special with them. We bought ice cream and drove to a park where I watched the two youngest play on swings and slides while I sat with my oldest and heard all about teenage drama. I felt so grateful. I couldn't imagine my life without them.

What now? I thought. I heard a voice in my head saying, *It's okay, you have a bigger purpose.* My middle daughter came over to me. She stood right in front of me as if she were looking for something. "What honey?"

"I don't know, Mom, you just seem sad. You okay?" She leaned in and gave me the biggest bear hug anyone could ask for. I felt an immediate sense of calm.

"I am now, baby. I can always use a hug from you." She stood up straight and smiled.

"Better, Mom?"

"Better, baby." She ran off to push her sister on the swing. I must be the luckiest woman in the world. I looked up at the sky and thought, *I hope you have a plan in mind, because I'm not sure what I'm doing, or what you want from me.* I realized that I had not spoken to God or whatever was up there since I was a little girl. But suddenly I was very confident that I was not in charge and that there was *something* greater than myself.

We left the park and drove home. The girls did their homework and I made dinner.

Even though I couldn't hear the front door open, I could tell when my husband got home because I saw the girls' auras sparkle and shimmer with a million tiny lights. They always did this when he walked into the room. I knew he liked to surprise me, but I was rarely surprised. The girls jumped up and ran toward the door. I went back to cooking. Then I heard it . . .

Happy Birthday to you . . .
Happy Birthday to you . . .
Happy Birthday, dear Mommy . . .

Oh no . . . I forgot my own birthday!

Happy Birthday to you!

There was my husband standing at the doorway to the kitchen with flowers and a present. My girls stood around him with their own wrapped presents. I paused for a moment and blinked. My husband's aura looked muddied, darker for some reason. Was it the lighting? I shook it off as a temporary break with reality as a result of my day.

"Oh my God, I completely forgot! Thank you, guys." I went over and hugged each of them.

Trina asked, "Mom, isn't that why you picked us up early from school?"

I giggled, "No, Mom actually forgot her own birthday. I just wanted to spend some time with you guys." She hugged me super hard, and I felt very grateful for my family. Flashing back on this afternoon, this must have been what Max meant by a "present." Of course he of all people would remember my birthday.

After dinner we opened presents and ate some apple pie. Luke always remembered that I preferred pie to cake. We put the girls to bed and I got ready for bed myself, suddenly grateful that I had taken this day off months ago for my birthday. As I walked out of the bathroom, Luke was there in bed. "Okay, what's wrong?" he said.

"Ugh, I hate that! How do you always know?"

He grabbed me and pulled me to the bed. "Because I've made it my personal goal in life to know everything there is to know about you. You are my favorite hobby."

I smiled and fell into his arms. Then, I couldn't help it, the tears just started coming and I couldn't stop the torrential downpour. My body felt hot and I was shaking.

"Oh my God! What's wrong?" My husband was almost panicked. He was grabbing at me, trying to bring my face up to his, but I just kept fighting to stay buried in his chest. I always felt so safe there. I soon lost the battle, though, and I was looking square into his beautiful eyes. I stopped sobbing after a few moments but couldn't talk. He waited patiently.

I took a deep breath and found that I was breathing in the same ragged way that my girls used to after they'd had a good cry. "I have to tell you something," I said. He sat very still, not interrupting, waiting.

"I recently met this older doctor through a friend. He used to know my parents when they were all younger."

I could see from his eyes that he was trying to see what I was going to say before I said it.

I started crying again and he held me close. "Take your time," he said.

After a few moments I sat back up and looked at him. "His name is Max." I decided to leave the Aurator stuff out for now. "We've been talking quite a bit lately. He's a wonderful man."

I could see that Luke's breathing was faster, though he was trying to stay focused for me. I continued, "He told me . . . he remembers my parents."

I started crying again, I couldn't say the words out loud.

"He told you what, honey?" His voice was so calm, like silk, but I could hear the undercurrent of concern.

"I'm adopted," I blurted out. It was the only way. Here I was, a grown woman, and I couldn't believe how hard I was crying, the pain I was feeling. My life had been a lie.

Luke's breathing stopped. "What?! Honey, are you sure? You just met this guy . . . how would he know?"

I couldn't believe I was saying this. "He arranged the adoption. He met the parents . . . my parents." I didn't know what else to say. I hated lying to him.

He held me tight. "I'm sorry, sweetheart. You shouldn't have found out this way. Have you spoken to your parents yet?"

"Which ones?" I said rather curtly.

He took a deep breath and held my face in his hands. "The ones who raised you."

"I tried to call. They were in Paris. I forgot."

He nodded, "Oh, that's right. What are you going to do?"

"I don't know . . . I don't know anything right now." I suddenly felt very tired. I just wanted to go to sleep and not feel anything.

"Remember, Meg," Luke started, "I'm also adopted."

I know the look on my face was one of confusion. Even though I knew this, I found myself slightly irritated. We were talking about me. "Yes, I remember. Why?"

"Did I ever tell you about the letter from my birth mother?"

"No." I remember the story of his adoption. His mother was thirty-five and he was a newborn. His mother, beautiful to a fault. I loved the pictures of her. She was diagnosed with breast cancer. Somehow it went away without any treatment, but then she died anyway. As a nurse, I always thought that sounded a little sketchy. In all the stories, though, I can honestly say I had never heard of a letter.

"My mom wrote a letter to me telling me about our family and how I was to always remember where I came from. I never got over losing her, but to move on I had to forget about my birth family. You see, no one in my immediate family wanted me, and I was adopted out to strangers."

My heart broke for him. I could see the pain that he had concealed all these years. I ran my fingers lightly over his cheek. "Well, it's a good thing a couple of throwaways like us found each other."

He looked up at me with the same love in his eyes as the day I married him. "You will never be a throwaway. I have to admit though . . . for a second I thought you were going to tell me that you'd met someone else."

I gasped. "Are you kidding me? You ARE my someone else."

"And you mine."

He reached down and kissed me, not a hard passionate kiss, but sensitive and soft. I fell into his arms and he stroked my hair. "You should sleep . . . it's been a tough day."

I looked at him and blinked. Why was his aura different? I sat back for a moment and looked him up and down. The gold shimmer was gone and I was looking at a muddy shadow of what used to be.

He looked at me inquisitively, "What?"

What could I say? Anything would have sounded downright crazy, "Nothing . . . I'm sorry, I'm fine."

His eyebrows furrowed as he looked at me. Was there something he was going to tell me? "Go to sleep," he said.

I tried to say no, but I didn't get that far. I drifted off in his arms.

15. The Meeting

One week and many cries later, I received a call from Max. The Seniors were coming in that night and we would be meeting at his house.

"How are you, Megan? Since our talk?"

"I'm okay. It's been a lot to think about this week."

"Yes," I could hear sadness in his voice. "I'm sorry about that. There really was no easy way to tell you."

"Agreed, it's okay. Can we make the meeting time late tonight so I can make it look like I'm going to work?"

"Sure, eleven-thirty?"

"Great."

"Oh, and by the way, how was your birthday?"

I chuckled. Of course he remembered. "It was great. Thanks."

"Good." There was a pause. "Nicholai is asking if we can meet with him beforehand, you know, because of Tomas. Can you meet this afternoon with Aaron, Nicholai, and me?"

"Okay. Can we meet around noon so I have time to drop off the girls and get a few errands done?"

"I'm sure that's fine. They all got in last night and are each going their separate ways today. I'm sure he can get away."

"Where?"

"We'll meet at my house." He gave me the address, and I finished getting the girls ready for school. Dropping them off was always so bittersweet. I just wanted to spend every minute with them. I had not told them about my newly discovered lineage. No sense upsetting them before I had a chance to speak with my parents.

After running my errands, I drove to the address Max had given me. I wasn't sure what to expect. I got the message from both Aaron and Max that Nicholai was the one who could be trusted. What was this Nicholai going to be like . . . what would he think of me?

I pulled up to Max's house and stopped in front. It took me a second to get my bearings and realize that I was in the Diamond Heights area. I looked up and down the street, admiring the very large, expensive houses. I had been so preoccupied with my own thoughts that I hadn't been paying attention to where I was going, and certainly not to where I ended up.

I parked on the street and looked at the entrance in front of me. There was an arched iron gate bridging two brick walls that encircled the enormous property. Looking through the gate, I saw a long cobblestone driveway with a fountain in the middle. At the end of the driveway was a grand house with peaked roofs and brick facing laid in curved designs, almost mirroring the landscaping behind it.

As I walked nearer the gate, I saw ivy encircling the windows, climbing the exterior walls and arching over the eight-foot double doors, taking over the building. Upon reaching the gate, I saw a small speaker box with a call button. Pressing the button, I waited.

"Hello?" said a friendly, but unfamiliar female voice.

"Um, hello. This is Megan . . ." then I heard a buzzer and the gates separated and swung inward.

I walked up the driveway, and just as I was about to knock, the doors parted and opened. A tall, strikingly beautiful woman with salt and pepper hair stepped through the open doors. She was dressed impeccably in pressed slacks and a white button-up shirt with a silk scarf loosely tied around her neck. She flashed a smile that immediately made me realize that I had been holding my breath. I exhaled . . . I felt welcome.

She looked as if she were about to reach out and hug me but restrained herself and extended her hand to shake mine. "You must be Megan. My name is Vivian, Max's wife. It's a pleasure to see you again." So, he told her about meeting me again. She knew about Aurators? For a split second I contemplated telling Luke. Only for a second.

"Yes, hello. It's very nice to meet you," I said. Wow, what a brilliantly white aura. Her warmth and the feeling I got just standing next to her were almost intoxicating.

She motioned for me to follow her into the house. As we walked in, my eyes were immediately drawn toward the vaulted two-story ceiling, where a painted mural was lit by several lights. I looked down the walls to the windows that curved around a winding staircase made of marble. Again I had to remind myself to breathe.

The wooden floor looked newly refinished, with an inlay of different colored woods designed in the shape of a star directly below the painting.

She motioned for me to follow, and we walked into a room directly off the entry. As I walked through the doors, my senses were hit with the scent of old books and a musty hint of mothballs. I chuckled at this. The walls were floor-to-ceiling shelves filled with books. Too many and too far away to see titles. The rest of the room mirrored Max's office at the university. A large wooden desk with papers piled high and stacks of magazines and other periodicals on the floor. There were four leather chairs, no couch.

Standing in the middle of the room were Max and Aaron, both of whom came over to greet me. Max first with a big hug that felt more like making amends than saying hello. Aaron and I shook hands and then quickly parted . . . pleasant enough.

Out of the corner of my eye I saw someone else moving toward me. I turned and met eyes with another man, taller than average height and dark curly hair, deep thoughtful brown eyes and an olive complexion. His aura was a brilliant red and much larger than either Max's or Aaron's. I wondered how mine compared. He was a very attractive man, maybe in his sixties.

"Megan," Max interjected with a bright smile on his face, "may I introduce you to Nicholai."

He stopped just before me and took a deep breath and exhaled. Then with the most beautiful accent that would melt any woman's heart, Nicholai said, "I've waited forty-two years to meet you. You look just like your mother . . . beautiful."

My heart began to race. "My mother?" I looked at Max who nodded at me. Looking back toward Nicholai, "You knew my mother?"

He reached his hand up toward my face but then lowered it, changing his mind. "She was my sister-in-law."

I looked back and forth between the men, searching for some missing piece and breathing faster. "Your sister-in-law? She was married to your brother?" Everyone was silent, as if waiting for me to catch up. "You're my uncle?"

He smiled, "Yes."

The room was spinning, coming and going, and as I reached out in front of me, I felt several hands catch me. As they lowered me to the floor, I focused in on the face in front of me. "Give me a minute," I barely got out.

Max and Aaron helped me by raising my feet for a moment. Vivian appeared next to my head with a cold compress. I sat up slowly. "Uncle?"

My voice sounded more irritated and demanding than I had intended it to be . . . but . . . so be it.

"Yes . . . Cos . . . I mean Megan."

"What did you say?" I caught that he almost called me by another name.

"Cosette. That was the name your mother and father had picked out for you. It means *people's victory*. Which is what . . . who you are."

"They knew I was a girl and who I was?"

"Yes. Your grandfather and I saw the red aura around her abdomen, and when they found out through ultrasound and told us they were having a girl, we were astonished. Your father was not an Aurator, but apparently he carried the right gene for you and was chosen for a much higher purpose."

I had another question but he said something that just didn't seem right. "Ultrasound? I thought those weren't mainstream until the seventies?"

He chuckled, "True, but there were used in the very early 1960s, and your dad pulled all the strings he could to get several until someone on the east coast was actually good enough that they were able to tell them the sex of the baby. But no, it was not widely used then. At first he was really disappointed. Dad and I thought he was hoping for a little Aurator of his own. Little did he know." He smiled widely as both eyebrows climbed upward on his forehead.

I rolled my eyes and remembered my earlier question now, even more poignant. "He knew about you?" This surprised me. Apparently I'm the only one who keeps secrets from my family.

"Yes, our father spoke with us about who he was, why he would disappear sometimes, and who we might become. He spoke to us about privilege and our duty to do what is right. As young men, we paid very little attention to this. But then in my late twenties I completed my first purpose, and your father was devastated. He thought he was not to be chosen. But soon he met a woman whose beauty I have yet to see matched. That is, until you. They fell in love, married, and she got pregnant. As I said, your grandfather and I saw the red aura around her abdomen. When we heard from your parents that they were having a girl, we sat down to discuss who we thought this child was to be." He walked around mimicking a proud father with his chest out, pretending to boast. "Your father felt on top of the world. He was a brilliant surgeon who was offered an incredible job opportunity in San Francisco and jumped at the chance." His head lowered as he remembered this. "We took them to the airport and said good-bye. I didn't realize that would be the last time I would see them alive."

He looked up at me. "Until now. I see them . . . in you. If it weren't for Max's quick thinking, we would have lost you too. All these years, I've wanted to come see you, but I knew that it might put you in jeopardy if anyone followed me. I needed to be patient. You see, your mom and dad knew exactly who you were going to be and thought that they could better protect you outside of Greece."

I was concentrating on taking slow deep breaths, trying to comprehend everything that was being said.

"Let's everyone sit . . . on furniture . . . and continue our conversation." Max said. It was at that moment I realized I was still sitting on the floor. I stood cautiously with Nicholai's help, moved to a chair, and again Vivian was right there, this time with a cool drink.

When I was settled, I looked back at Nicholai. "Do you have children? Is my grandfather still alive? Do I have other family?"

He smiled at me and chuckled slightly. "Yes . . . no . . . yes."

I motioned for more details. He continued, "Your grandfather had hoped to be able to meet you, but he died of a heart attack two years ago."

Strange, I would have thought that with such extra . . . powers . . . we would be less prone to regular, run-of-the-mill ailments. But apparently, no.

He continued, "You have a lot of family in Greece, on the island of Kos. That is where you are from . . . well, your family."

"And you?"

He shifted in his seat somewhat, "I live in Kos. I'm gay and have a partner. I knew it was important for me to have children so we got a surrogate and I was able to father two boys."

"And are either of them . . . ?"

Smiling, with a somewhat playful look in his eyes, "What? Gay?"

I frowned at him, "No. Like you . . . an Aurator?"

Smiling wider, "Yes, one. Why?"

I stood and started pacing across the floor. "I don't know. Maybe because two weeks ago I had a family that . . . while I never saw how I fit in, they were still my family. Now they're not my family . . . at least not biologically. But I have another family who I *am* linked to biologically, but I've never met them. This is nuts. This stuff doesn't really happen outside of movies!"

I sat back down, breathing fast and my eyes welled up. I'm tired of crying, I'm tired of feeling out of control. I asked, "Is this why you wanted to meet with me before the others?"

He reached over and placed his hand on my arm. "Yes. The others, while they knew you were coming, did not know that I already knew of you. This withholding of information on my part could have compromised my position as a Senior. Especially the part where we are related. I have had to hide the knowledge of you all these years." He hung his head and stared at the floor. "How I wished that I could have kept you when we lost my brother." Then looking at me, "I couldn't compromise your safety."

I could feel myself surrendering in exhaustion. "What now?"

"Now we meet with the others tonight," Nicholai said.

"Okay." I looked up at Aaron, "Did you know about this too?"

He shook his head, "Not until today. You're not the only one confused here."

"The others . . . if they don't know we are related, where do they think I came from?"

He wrinkled his forehead, "Yes, that is going to be difficult to explain, but you need to make them believe that you don't know anything about your birth parents or that you are adopted."

That shouldn't be hard, I thought, since I don't know anything about them. "Why?" I asked.

Max and Nicholai looked at each other. Then Max spoke, "We believe that information is coming from someone inside the Aurators and being given to the Caduceus side. If they find out who your family is . . . they will try to kill them all."

"Caduceus *side*?" This is the first time I'd heard the Caduceus used that way.

"Can I answer this?" Aaron finally spoke. Everyone nodded. "It's my job, Megan, to know how the other side is organizing. For some time now, someone from our side has been organizing those who we fight against . . . the Caduceus. But they are organizing at an alarming rate. Just last week I learned that they had a meeting to discuss information regarding you. Right now they don't know who you are, only that you exist. Since we were the only ones who knew about you, someone in our camp leaked information."

I started thinking back to the different dreams I had over the years, flashes of faces, fighting between groups of people I didn't know. Was that a premonition of this? I looked up and the men were talking among themselves. I could hear them in the background like white noise. What was happening to me? Was I going to faint? I felt hot and overwhelmed. I saw lines of red, white, and black connecting in my mind. I suddenly couldn't feel my body. I closed my eyes.

Get a grip, I thought to myself. My breathing was fast and hard. I saw hordes of men, some of them talking, some of them fighting. I saw older Aurators swirling around in front of me. Talking to me and telling me the past. I saw myself as if looking in a mirror with my family around me as we passed through darkness. Then suddenly a bright red light, almost blinding, directly in front of me. I brought my arms up in defense, somehow knowing that if I walked toward and trusted the light I would be fine. Electricity coursed through my body and my eyes shot open.

Suddenly I realized I was two feet off the ground. I looked around and saw the three men standing around me. Max and Aaron with shocked looks on their faces and Nicholai with a knowing smile. Looking at my body, I felt each muscle flexing and extending, just as I had during my first purpose. My breathing slowed and I consciously brought my body toward the ground. As my feet touched, I looked at each man standing in front of me. Somehow I knew what was and what would be.

"We will need to be prepared for these men tonight," I started. "I agree that Tomas is the weak link and will undermine us at the first opportunity."

Aaron's jaw dropped open and he looked at Nicholai. "What just happened?"

Nicholai's smile had not yet left his face. "She has transitioned and become one with her past, present, and future . . . who she is meant to be."

I felt an inexplicable anger toward the Caduceus and a sense of purpose to rid the world of them.

Nicholai walked over to me, "This final transformation was not to happen until you were ready. You are ready to lead us. And we will follow. You will know what to do now."

"How do you know this?" Even though I also knew this was my heart of hearts, I was curious about his knowledge.

"Nostradamus," he stated very simply.

"What about him?" I became aware that as soon as I asked the question I knew the answer. "He prophesied us all coming together under these circumstances to combat the Caduceus."

All three men looked at me, as if my eyes were open doors. "Yes, I know everything now."

"Yes, you do," Nicholai added. "Your ancestors are now a part of you."

"Wow!" said Max. "I didn't see this one coming. But I guess if you live long enough among those with special gifts you will eventually see something that takes your breath away."

Realizing that I needed to get ready for tonight and set the scene at home so that no one suspected anything, I announced my departure. After saying good-byes, Nicholai walked over and hugged me. As he pulled back he simply stated, "Tonight."

I nodded yes, and with that I left.

16. Powers

Driving home, I was acutely aware just how different I felt. I wasn't afraid of anything. That was a very odd feeling for me, since I had been afraid of everything my whole life. I was more profoundly aware of everything around me. I saw minute movements that caught my attention. Control over myself was the only way I could describe it.

The night went by smoothly. I kissed everyone goodnight and left for "work." I stopped at a coffee shop, changed out of my scrubs, got a coffee, and went to Max's for the meeting.

His house was so beautiful and majestic, all lit up in the dark, that it almost took my breath away as I drove through the gate. I noticed a rental car in the driveway. As I turned off my car engine, I stopped to take a breath. I was ready.

I knocked on the door, and Vivian opened it, greeting me once more. I felt much different entering the house this time. Strong . . . powerful.

I turned the corner into Max's study. Standing next to Nicholai were two other men. Max stepped forward and began in a formal tone, with flourishes of his hand, "Gentlemen, please welcome Megan. Megan, these are our Seniors, Aleck, Tomas, and Nicholai."

Aleck stepped forward first. He was a beautiful man, and I don't say that about too many men. Dark curly hair, warm olive skin, and clearly in good shape. His aura was brilliant. It sparkled red. He was wearing a short-sleeved shirt, which I thought was odd given the cool temperatures of springtime, and each muscle was clearly defined along his arms. He smiled at me as he approached.

"Hello, Megan," he said with an excited tone in his voice. "I'm *very* pleased to finally meet you." Looking closer at his face, I was surprised because he had to be in his late sixties or even seventies, but his body shape and stance were closer to someone my age. My body relaxed and I smiled; until this moment I had not realized how tense I was.

I looked over at Tomas who was approaching, and my body tensed again. I pondered this. Was it because of everything the others had told me or was I sensing something? I tried to tune in to this. He stood in front of me while Aleck moved to the side. He was smiling, but his face was not as easily warm as the others. I had a brief flash of nausea, then I felt heat and a shiver of electricity shoot through my body. Feeling each of my muscles tense ever so slightly, I wondered why I was having this reaction. His aura was not brilliant red like the others. It was more of a dull, muted, brick red, as if all happiness had been drained from it.

He sensed my reaction and paused. His head tilted downward slightly as his gaze on me intensified. We both stood staring at each other for what felt like hours but was only seconds. In that moment, I saw flashes of pictures in my head. They seemed disjointed and didn't make any sense. An open grassy field . . . flowers . . . glass shattering and strewn about. He smiled and then took the last few steps toward me. Extending his hand he voiced a greeting.

I barely heard what he said, still pondering the images flashing too fast for me to put them together. I snapped out of my self-imposed trance. I noticed his bright red, wavy hair curling softly around his ears. He had hypnotic green eyes that seemed to be trying to read my face. He was an attractive man, but there was something wrong that I couldn't put my finger on.

I reached out and took his hand. Not realizing my own strength my muscles tensed in response to his touch.

"Ow," he said softly and pulled his hand back.

"I'm sorry," I replied.

Neither of us took our eyes off each other. I was then interrupted by a sense of ease when a hand reached over and touched my shoulder. It was Nicholai. I turned and we shook hands and introduced ourselves as if we had never met.

Then Max interrupted, saying, "Okay, everyone. I'm sure we all have questions and there are many things we need to talk about. But first things first." He motioned for everyone to sit.

Vivian entered the room and set tea down on a table. She looked at me for an instant and I could see the concern written into the creases on her forehead. I nodded ever so slightly at her and she nodded toward me. I felt a kinship with Vivian now that I had learned that she first cared for me.

"Now . . ." began Max, "since we've all met Megan, we can start to discuss the next step."

I heard voices but they trailed off. I saw images flashing in my mind. Again, there was the open grassy field . . . flowers . . . and glass all around me. I saw dark figures in front of me but couldn't make out how many. I saw a beautiful island with seven white pillars surrounding its cobalt blue shores. Seven pillars stood erect on the island. There was blood and screaming. The pictures stopped, and I held my hand up to interrupt the men in the room.

"Excuse me," I started, "the Caduceus side will be organizing." All heads turned toward me with surprise in their eyes. "I see two places to start with." I paused to review the pictures before continuing.

"What do you mean, two?" started Aleck, but Max placed his hand on Aleck's arm and motioned to wait.

"There will be two conflicts . . . fights." I continued to search for more clues in the pictures. "Soon."

"When and where?" asked Aaron.

I looked up at him. "Very soon, and from what I'm able to see, one will be here."

Nicholai began to look uncomfortable, "Do you see faces?" He glanced over to Tomas.

I thought about this and said, "No." I decided to keep one of the visions to myself since I suspected it was here in San Francisco and I had an idea of where it was. I did, however, have a question about the second. "Is there a place that has seven pillars that any of you know about? I also see these on land with very blue water next to it. Is this Greece?"

All eyes were wide and bearing down on me. "What?" I asked.

Nicholai began first. "Megan, have you ever been to Greece? Or studied Greece?"

He looked as if he knew this answer already but was setting up his next statement. I said, "No, why?"

"There are seven pillars at Asklepion. Ruins of the original temple that was built to honor Asclepius." He leaned forward. "Your ancestor."

I remembered the story and had been doing some online research about Asclepius, but I didn't remember any building associated with him and had not researched going to the island. I looked inward for some doubt, some shred of my former lower self-esteem that might make me question my story. However, I couldn't find it anywhere.

Discounting my own belief systems—gone. I stood a little taller in that moment. "There *will* be a fight soon, at this place you mentioned. The date is not in my vision, but the location is crystal clear. I do see a few faces but I do not recognize them. And . . . well, there will be deaths."

There was silence in the room. Everyone looked at each other. Aaron spoke first, "Who dies?"

"I don't know, it's a blur. I just see bodies," I answered.

"Well," started Nicholai, "this is what we've read about, so now is the time. Aaron, can you please connect what Megan is saying with Nostradamus."

"*Nostradamus again?*" I thought.

Aaron stood up and started pacing, he looked at Max and exchanged a look before beginning, "Nostradamus's predictions for *us*, not the general public, were a continuation of Hippocrates's. He said that you, Megan, were coming, and that this would signal the great 'coming together.' He urged that we, as Aurators, start organizing because the Caduceus side would be doing so also. There would be many small battles as the two sides were growing. These battles are to take place on several continents worldwide. There are predicted to be deaths . . . many. Both sides will lose individuals. However, at some point in the near future, which hasn't been determined yet, everything will come to a crucial point and all will converge around the earth for the final battles."

"Wow," I said, "I have to admit I don't see all that. We don't know when?"

Aaron scratched his head, "I don't know exactly. There are a lot of references to the number eighteen in the writings. But remember that things were written in code so that the other side wouldn't know what, who, or when it was coming. Remember, we already lost so much with Hitler and Napoleon. As much as I can tell, we are not supposed to know *when* until after you have arrived."

Everyone nodded in agreement.

Aleck raised a hand to interject, "Okay, so what I'm hearing is that right now we will have two battles on a small scale, one here and one in Greece. Is that correct?"

"Yes." I answered with such confidence that it surprised even myself.

"Okay then," he continued, "we should return to Greece and be watchful for this event. Is there anything else you can tell us?"

I thought back on the flashes of images in my head. "People are in long sleeves right now in the visions." "It's cool there right now?"

"Yes," stated Aleck as he looked to the two other Seniors.

"Then it will be soon." Something in my vision caught my attention and I looked off as if looking into the distance. "Soon, two to three months."

The room got quiet. It was very clear everyone was pondering this last statement. However, the silence was broken by the phone in Max's study ringing. He stood and strode over to the desk. Lifting the receiver from the base, he answered, "Hello?" But it sounded distant. I was still lost in thought regarding the visions of the fight here at home and what I thought looked like the location.

"What?!" I heard Max shout, and it pulled me from my thoughts. He was looking directly at me while the person on the other end of the line was obviously saying something rather involved. "When? . . . I'll be right there. Yes, thank you for calling . . . *I'm glad I gave the journal to Megan.*" He turned slightly away from us, leaned against the desk and hung up the phone. Why did he say that out loud? I looked around but nobody seemed to flinch at the idea that I had the journal. Thank God.

Everyone looked back and forth at each other. It was Aaron who spoke first. "What happened?"

Max turned slowly, suddenly looking very tired, shaking his head back and forth. "That was the campus police. My office was broken into tonight. It's . . . in shambles. They said that even some of the floorboards had been ripped up." His eyes passed over me quickly as if trying to direct my eyes somewhere else. I followed the intended direction and looked directly at Tomas. He was the only one not making eye contact with anyone else in the room. I also noticed the very slightest hint of a smirk on his face. His aura was shifting, almost clouding more, becoming more muddied.

"Oh my God, Max!" said Aleck whose utterance returned my thoughts to the conversation. "Did you have anything . . . *important* . . . in there?" We all knew what he meant.

I flashed on the vision of his office and remembered the break-in. God, it had actually happened. How could I know these things? If my ancestors were future tellers, was I truly destined to be one as well? I wasn't sure I really wanted to know everything that was going to happen, but in this case the knowledge had proved to be advantageous by allowing us to keep the journal safe.

Max looked back at Aleck, "No. There was nothing in my office. I . . ."

Aleck interrupted, "The journal?" He sounded stressed.

"I had just moved it." I thought I saw a slight smile starting on Max's face. He looked smug, and Aaron looked toward me.

Out of the corner of my eye I saw Tomas shift ever so slightly, looking more uncomfortable. Everyone else in the room sighed. "Thank goodness," I heard someone mutter.

Walking slowly over to the group, Max announced, "If you'll excuse me, I have to go. I need to see to my office."

"I'll come with you," Nicholai started first and then everyone followed suit.

The door to the study opened and Vivian entered. Every man stood out of respect for her, not only because she was a woman but because something about her seemed almost regal. As she hurried over to Max, the worried look on her face was obvious. His face softened as he looked at her. Slowly raising his arms to meet hers, they clasped hands as she asked, "Is everything okay? I heard the phone ring and then heard you. What's wrong?"

He raised a hand to her cheek, caressing it softly. "Don't worry, someone broke into my office, but everything's okay. We are all going over there right now to check it out."

She nodded in agreement. "Okay, be careful."

Max kissed her lovingly on her forehead and we moved to leave. I drove with Max and Aaron while the three Seniors piled into their rental car.

Aaron began speaking as soon as we drove away. It was as if he had a terrible secret and couldn't wait to talk about it. "Okay," he began, "did anyone else notice how uncomfortable Tomas seemed?" We both quickly agreed. This fact had been painfully obvious.

"I have another question," Aaron began but I cut him off and answered with irritation in my voice.

"Look Aaron, I'm apparently now the Guardian of the journal. I didn't ask for this, but the job is mine. Max gave me the journal last week."

Both men were quiet and looked at each other. In my mind I reviewed what I had said . . . I didn't think I had said anything that would have offended anyone or that was a secret. "What?"

Aaron chuckled, "I never asked my question, Megan."

"Funny Aaron, I clearly heard you speaking. Don't try to make me sound crazy. Max, back me up here, he's messing with me."

I saw Max's eyebrows furrow in the rearview mirror, perplexed by something I said.

"What Max?"

"Megan . . . you really thought you heard Aaron speaking?"

"Of course I did, and you did too. This is ridiculous."

Max glanced at Aaron. "Did Megan answer the question you were about to ask?"

I looked at Aaron, and answered him again, "What do you mean, *Yes, but she beat me to it.* This is nuts. You both are nuts."

Aaron's head whipped around, "Would you please let me talk?"

I sat back and gasped, "You really didn't just say something?"

Looking forward, he folded his arms over his chest with a huff. Max chortled, "Well, this does put an interesting spin on things. Can you hear what I'm thinking?"

I listened but didn't hear anything. I shook my head. Then suddenly I heard, *"Now I'm thinking about you."* I gasped.

"Ahhh," said Max.

Aaron threw his arms up. "Why am I the last one to know what's going on?"

Reaching over to Aaron, Max placed a hand on his arm. "Megan can hear things that pertain to her. Only to her."

I suddenly realized what he was saying and flashed back to an earlier conversation at Max's home. "Max?"

"Yes?"

"When you received the phone call about your office, did you say that you were glad you gave me the journal . . . out loud?"

"You heard that?"

"That would be a 'no' to the *out loud* part, Megan," Aaron interjected.

"Yes, I did hear that. I thought it was odd that you were announcing it."

"Well . . . ?"

"I get it. You didn't."

The car got very quiet and it was clear that everyone was trying to wrap their minds around what had just transpired. *"Why does she get all the cool tricks?"* I heard from Aaron.

"Grow up, jerk," I mumbled

"Crap," he retorted back.

Max snickered.

17. Questions

Walking down the hallway we could see the light emanating from Max's office. Scraps of paper were strewn throughout the hallway just outside his door.

"Oh Max," I whispered.

Max reached over and squeezed my hand.

We walked in and surveyed the damage. The furniture had been sliced and the inner stuffing pulled out as if someone had been looking for something inside. Boxes were opened and dumped out. Books were pulled out of shelves and thrown into piles across the room from their original homes. His desk was upside down and all the drawers smashed into pieces. The floorboards were pulled up haphazardly throughout the room leaving large holes in the floor.

I heard the sound of men's shoes coming down the hall.

"They're heeere," Aaron sung out.

Max leaned toward me. *"Best if we don't tell anyone about your talent."* I was looking right at him but didn't see his lips move. I rolled my eyes but nodded in agreement. I was able to hear a slight echo this time to his voice.

I heard someone gasp behind me. I think it was Aleck.

We were all in the office. Tomas walked toward the window and looked out. I wished I could hear what *he* was thinking. Then he turned to Max.

"Max, I'm so sorry. This is terrible."

"Thanks Tomas," he said quietly as he picked a couple of his books up off the floor, looking at them for a moment before dropping them back down. "So much of this is not salvageable."

Once we had gotten the okay from the campus and city police, each of us set out across the room to help Max clean up the mess. We were quiet for the most part since the police were still finishing up their work.

Max climbed up his ladder to the top shelf as if looking for something. "Awww. My yearbook from college is destroyed."

This struck me as funny. Here was a man who had accomplished so much in his life. Probably earned more degrees and awards than anyone else I would meet in my lifetime, and he was worried about a college yearbook. He turned on the ladder and sucked in a breath. I jumped because I thought he was falling. He motioned for me to not worry, pulled out his cell phone, and snapped a picture.

"Hello?" I heard behind me. I turned to see Detective Charlene McGuire. I recognized her immediately. My stomach felt as if it dropped six inches.

"Um, hey there. How are you?"

She surveyed the room before looking back at me. "You're from the emergency room, right? Mandy?"

"Megan," I corrected her.

"Megan, right." She continued to look at me. "You know, about that patient that night?" She raised her eyes in a knowing fashion hoping to prompt what may have been a buried memory of mine.

I could see that answering too quickly might give me away. I tried to listen closely, maybe I could hear her thoughts. Nothing. "Um . . . sure . . . that's right, that girl. Yeah, I remember, why?" Of course I asked the question, but I'm not sure I wanted to hear the answer.

"We found the guy connected to her attack, and well . . . quite a few others."

"Oh really?" She was still looking at my face . . . examining.

I could also see heads turn cautiously around to look. I'm guessing because they heard the hesitation in my voice. "*Megan . . . is she talking about your purpose?*" It was Max. I could see him looking at me. I nodded ever so slightly but not subtle enough for Detective McGuire.

"What?" she said.

"What?" I asked. I learned early on in my life to always answer a question with a question.

She looked a little confused, "Well, we don't have to worry about him anymore . . . we found him dead."

I tried to look surprised but was not sure how well I pulled it off. "That's terrible. Well, good for the other possible victims but terrible that someone had to die." Seemed a reasonable response.

Her eyes narrowed a little as she examined my face. "Yes, I suppose. He was taken out . . . very . . . medical like . . . injected with something. Well,

I probably shouldn't talk too much about it but the investigation is already done. We are looking for the killer's killer now. Ironic, huh?"

"Ironic." Sort of, but not as ironic as the fact that she was talking to the killer's killer.

"Okay," she suddenly blurted out as if announcing to the whole room. A few of the men jumped. "Time to go. Done here. Good to see you . . . Megan." She extended her hand in a gesture to shake. I hated this act of etiquette. I reached out and took her hand. She held it firmly while making eye contact. I was surprised by how calm I was and how steady my hand was. I really didn't have anything to be afraid of, I thought.

She smiled at me, released my hand, and motioned good-bye to everyone in the room. After clearly hearing her footsteps all the way down the hall everyone turned toward me.

"How did you complete your purpose?" Tomas asked.

I looked at Max who nodded to go ahead. "Well, since I wasn't sure what to do I came up with a plan to inject a paralytic, then inject potassium to stop the heart. Crude, but effective."

Jaws dropped open. Funny, I hadn't expected that reaction. I looked at Max, hoping I'd see some clarity in his face but I didn't.

Max, picking up on my clues, cleared his throat to get everyone's attention. "Gentlemen, we are in uncharted territory here. Can any of you tell me what skills or abilities she is *supposed* to have?"

Everyone looked a little confused yet, glancing at each other while shaking their heads, no.

"Exactly," began Max again. "Megan, did you have any kind of *instinct* or *urge* to do something else while you were completing your purpose?"

I had to think back. I shook my head no but then remembered something, "Wait, I do remember when I was with him I had an urge to reach out to him. Is that what you mean?"

"Anything else?" Tomas asked.

"No."

Everyone looked back at Nicholai. Since he was the oldest of the Aurators, he was the one everyone turned to for answers.

Scratching his head and looking toward the floor, he was silent for what seemed like several minutes. "I don't know what to think, honestly. Megan, we just know to go inside and trust our instincts. I would probably suggest, however, that the next time your instinct takes over you should go with it. The *medication* route is probably not your best offense. You just haven't found your way yet. Aaron, was there anything written about this by Nostradamus? Or from Hippocrates, Max?"

"I'd have to go back and check, Nicholai. I'm not sure," Aaron hesitantly responded. I could tell Aaron was disappointed he did not have the answer.

Max was still thinking. "A woman, descended from Asclepius shall be born. She will possess more unique powers of purpose than all men before her. She will be skilled in many ways unknown to us and with much wisdom and medicinal practice. I believe that's what he wrote. What it means . . . well some is obvious and some is still a mystery. I'll have to check. Can I get back to you?"

Everyone agreed that we would check the written documents we had and would speak again.

After a couple hours of cleaning up the office, Aleck stood and motioned to the others. "Well gentlemen, I suppose we should be getting back to our hotel."

Max walked over to Aleck, "You're leaving so soon?"

Smiling a very warm smile that instantly made me feel peaceful, Aleck reached out and the two men hugged. "Yes my old friend. We came specifically to meet Megan," as he turned to look toward me with a wink. "But sadly, we are leaving early in the morning." They broke and Aleck walked toward me.

Letting out a long sigh, "Megan, I cannot tell you how much meeting you has meant to me. I do not know what our paths are to be. However, I do hope that they come together again. We will keep a watch at the Asklepion Temple and let you know if anything happens." He hugged me and then turned to say good-bye to Aaron.

Tomas walked toward me, and I could feel my posture stiffen. The tension in the room escalated as everyone's eyes turned toward us. I tried to extend my hand to meet Tomas's outstretched arm but found my arm struggling with the move. Forcing every fiber of my muscles forward, I met his hand. As our hands wrapped around each other I could feel a sense of unease stirring deep inside of me, as if something had awakened and now was trying to climb out in attack. His hand was colder than mine and just a tad clammy. Nervous? Interesting. My confidence grew and with it I felt the size of my aura expanding. This did not elude Tomas, who looked around me, almost in admiration, at my aura while still holding my hand. My eyes stared at his, trying to get some shred of truth from somewhere. Could he really be bad? How could he be an Aurator and still be this nefarious?

"Tomas," I said with as little emotion as possible.

A smirk grew on his lips, "Megan?"

"Will we be seeing you again?" It was a question that I had not realized I wanted to ask before the words left my lips. I felt an intellectual pause as I searched my memory for the thought that preceded that question.

"Most definitely. After all . . . you *are* who we have all been waiting for . . . right?" Without breaking eye contact, his head cocked back in an arrogant fashion.

"Maybe not everyone. Agreed?"

His self-confidence seemed to disappear in an instant. "Well, I suppose the . . . other side . . . is not as pleased as . . . we are."

I nodded in agreement and dropped my hand. Tomas stepped back several steps before finally breaking eye contact.

Everyone exchanged pleasantries and good-byes. Nicholai gave me a very tight hug that almost took my breath away. Then I heard his thoughts, *"Please take care of her."*

I knew enough now to listen for the echo. I knew it was a thought and just hugged him back.

As they headed toward the door, Aleck turned around, "Oh yes, and Megan, if *you* see anything . . . you'll let us know?"

"At once." Of course I would make sure *not* to let Tomas know.

I looked at Nicholai who had a confused look on his face and heard, *"Interesting."* Then they turned and walked out the door.

Max, Aaron, and I looked at each other for a while before Aaron finally started. "So, Megan has the journal, has special powers that no one else knows about, and there's going to be a fight soon? Is that the summation of what just happened?"

Max was smiling at me. "Pretty close," he said. "Okay . . . you left out the location of the fight here . . . why?"

I had almost forgotten about that. I had seen the beautiful building surrounded by flowers and knew immediately where it was, but I saw something else that I knew shouldn't be shared.

"Yes, I did leave it out. Not to keep the location a secret, but rather because of who I saw there."

"And?" Nothing ever eluded Max.

"And . . . . Tomas is there . . . at least someone who I think is him. But how can he be here and there?"

"Good question." Max stepped over several piles of books and began to sift through papers. "Megan, have you had a chance to look through the journal for any clues about you?"

"No, not yet. Why?"

Still looking through papers, he motioned as if to swat a fly. "Just, well, just look."

"I will." Then remembering something from earlier, I said, "Wait a minute. What did you take a picture of?"

"Picture?" he questioned, but then a sudden change on his face displayed that he remembered from earlier, "Oh, right, right, I forgot."

Aaron walked over, "You saw something?"

Max pulled the phone out, "Here, look."

As the picture loaded onto the screen we could tell immediately what it was. The contents of Max's office that had appeared to be strewn around were actually meticulously arranged in the corner of the office into the shape of a caduceus. Aaron shook his head.

I frowned saying, "Is this surprising? I mean, who else could it be?"

Max nodded, "Agreed, it's just that leaving such a blatant sign leads me to believe that they are ready to make a move. Why else leave such an obvious calling card for us? They want us to know that the inevitable is upon us."

"The inevitable?"

"The switch . . . days end," Aaron stepped in.

"I'm sorry, are you guys talking about the end of the earth?"

"No, not exactly Megan" Aaron began. "In the predictions, our kind and the Caduceus will come together in a great battle that has been building for centuries. And this will coincide with a switch within the earth's magnetic core."

It took me a moment to catch up with this last thought. I found myself back in college physics discussing the theory of the earth's polarity and how it has switched randomly throughout history. "I'm sorry, somehow we are connected to the earth's polarity?"

"Everything is connected between earth and space. Yes, we are connected to the magnetic core."

"So what does that have to do with the timing of us fighting and, as you put it, *the end of days*?"

Aaron's eyes moved back and forth as if he were reading from the pages of an invisible book, "You see, the earth is due to change its magnetic poles. Switch, north and south. Currently the magnetic current in the earth's core runs from north to south and is . . . well has been changing for some years now, at least since Hippocrates's days to run the other way. This will cause the magnetic core to temporarily destabilize, and in Nostradamus's predictions when this happens all of our kind will come together to fight." His forehead creased and he looked at Max.

"That's as much as we know," Max began. "Unfortunately we don't have details. We know from modern science that the destabilization of the earth's magnetic core really won't cause a major catastrophe. The switching of poles, the Aurators coming together, a fight, and . . . you . . . are connected but that was all Nostradamus wrote. There really isn't an end of days. Rather a beginning. At least that's the hope. A chance to do something different with the world we've been given."

"So there's no Armageddon?" I asked. "What about all those movies and predictions about the end of the world. All of it is . . . made up?"

Aaron stepped toward me, "Sort of a lie, yes. But most people don't have the information we do so they can come to no other conclusion to the predictions than Armageddon. You know . . . the world blows up . . . California and half of the western United States fall into the ocean . . . blah blah blah. Come on Megan, I know you're smarter than that. It would take a cataclysmic event of gigantic proportions . . . several of them . . . to occur simultaneously around the world. Honestly, the idea of the end of the earth has always bothered me. Okay, separate from what I already know being an Aurator. Armageddon, unless God him or herself came down to earth and caused it . . . is a scientific impossibility." He paused. "Now if a meteor, say six miles wide, hit the Earth . . ."

"Okay, okay, that's enough." Max interrupted.

"Wasn't there something about the Mayan calendar?" I asked. It ends and the world is supposed to end?" I remembered this from one of those history shows that Luke and I loved so much.

Max chuckled, "What makes you think that's why they ended the calendar? What about the possibility that . . . well . . . they just got tired of chiseling those calendars out?" He mimicked chiseling in the air in front of him. "It would be a rather ridiculous assumption to think that the Mayans would just keep making calendars . . . we don't even do that. Have you ever gone to the book store and tried to find a calendar for five years from now? Impossible. Throughout history all the *end of days* predictions come and go with nothing to show for them."

My head was spinning, and I was feeling the fatigue of the night. Aaron walked over and put his hand on my shoulder. "I'm sorry but we have more questions than answers. I think that's why you're here . . . to fill in the blanks."

The dawn was starting to light up the fog, and I suggested that it was time to go home. The others agreed and we drove back to Max's in silence. Getting into our respective cars after nodding to each other, we left.

18. Assets

I drove through the streets toward home. I felt hungover. My head hurt, I had trouble remembering last night, and my body ached. Plus, my ears felt like they were plugged because I kept hearing echoing sounds . . . crap, I hoped I wasn't getting sick. I didn't have time for *normal* stuff anymore.

Then it hit me like a huge life-altering epiphany. I wasn't normal. I never had been. At least I never felt normal. I let out a sigh of relief that was immediately replaced with a feeling of angst. On the one hand, yes, I was different . . . very . . . and would never be normal, but . . . growing up . . . I never was . . . *normal.* Ironic. That which I wanted so badly in my youth was now painfully unattainable forever.

Odd. A couple of weeks ago this would have caused me severe distress. However, today, at this moment I felt the angst pass and a sense of relief settle into every pore. My body felt relaxed and warm. I . . . finally . . . fit. There was no other way to explain it. I definitely belonged, but something about it wasn't right. Max and the others had told me over and over again that I was the one to lead us to defeat the others.

Something wasn't right about this.

I pulled up to my home and breathed a long sigh. I loved my family. What would all of this do to them? Should I tell my husband? Max's wife Vivian knew and she accepted it. Could I expect as much from him? Then I chuckled when I realized that in all the excitement I had forgotten to change back into my nursing uniform. Luckily the bag was just in the back seat. A quick change and I was walking into the house.

The house was still. I took in a deep breath. I loved the smell of my home. I went upstairs, careful not to wake anyone and showered. I knew I should be tired but I wasn't, and all I wanted was to spend some time with everyone. After showering and dressing, I found my way downstairs to cook breakfast and make some coffee.

I could hear the movement beginning upstairs with my husband first, then my girls. Alex waking up the younger two, who seemed to be fighting it the whole way. I smiled at this. I had never put the responsibility on her to take care of her sisters but it was a job she willingly accepted. She has always been such a wonderful, sweet character. Kind to others. Always the first to stand up for what was right and fair in the world. Fighter for the underdog, my husband would always say . . . that is, as long as the TV wasn't on.

Trina was the first to complain about getting up. She loved to sleep. When she was a baby, the doctor had told me to wake her up every two hours to feed her, whether she liked it or not. She didn't. My only child who slept through the night from day one. My intuitive one. Trina cared about others like Alex, but it was because of her uncanny ability to understand how people felt. She has always had a brand of empathy far beyond her years. Also, she was our only child who at the age of two could scale the tallest dresser in 2.3 seconds.

Then there was my Abigail, my baby. We weren't sure if we were going to have another child. I was fine with two but my husband pushed and pushed to have one more. *We're such great parents . . . we should try to get as much good in the world as we can.* An inflated opinion of our parenting skills, but I could see that it meant more to him to have another child than it did to me *not* to. So . . . Abigail. I wouldn't have changed it in the slightest. What a bright spot on the planet. So full of love and happiness. Everyone always said she was the happiest baby they had ever seen.

I took a deep breath in and a long drink of my coffee. This has got to be the closest to heaven anyone ever gets.

My husband came down the stairs first. Looking somewhat stunned to see me dressed and coherent, he smiled. I couldn't help noticing that his aura seemed even darker this morning. Why? What was happening? Walking over, he wrapped his arms tightly around me and I noticed that I did not have the familiar sense of ease I usually did. I closed my eyes and breathed in and out, wondering, *Is it me?* Throughout our marriage any time we had an argument, which was very infrequent, all he needed to do was wrap his arms around me and all the cares in the world were gone, nothing could hurt me, and it was going to be okay. He didn't possess this skill with just me. He was also the go-to guy when the girls were sick. When they had fever, pain, or just plain didn't feel well, he would go to them and wrap his arms around them . . . instant "daddy medicine." I used to love to look in on our girls when they were sick, and Luke would be there sitting or lying on the floor next to the bed, sound asleep but with one hand on them in some attempt to be there for them. I was the nurse, yet he was the one who comforted them the best when they were sick. But for some reason his "skill" was not there right now.

He pulled back from his hug and looked at me with those gorgeous eyes that made me fall in love with him from day one. "Good morning, love," he whispered.

My brows furrowed, "Good morning." I felt confused and a little off balance. But he held me securely in his arms and started kissing my neck.

"Mmmm, Bengay. Sexy," he murmured. I laughed out loud this time. I was a little sore from all my . . . exercise lately, along with some serious lack of sleep, and had put some Bengay on after my shower.

I'm sure this new . . . aura . . . is about me . . . right? I must be just seeing things differently. I thought.

We both turned our heads toward the thunderous pounding of six feet barreling down the staircase.

"Morning," they bellowed in unison.

"Morning, girls," we echoed back.

We sat for quite a while eating breakfast, and I spent more than a few minutes examining each of my girls' features. Trina's bright red hair. This made me chuckle. Alex looked so grown up. And Abigail . . . my baby. My eyes welled up and I turned to avoid anyone seeing. They are getting so big and the time was flying by so fast. My husband got up and kissed me on my cheek, then walked over to put on his shoes.

Time. How much would I have? I wondered if I were doomed to hide from my own family . . . afraid that every time I left the house I wouldn't return. It was at this moment I realized I needed to appreciate every moment with them.

Everyone moved slowly toward the door as they finished getting ready for the day. I grabbed my purse and keys and announced that I would take the girls to school.

In the car, the girls babbled bits of gossip that they had been privy to and I hadn't. I relished every minute. Trina kept looking at me from the back seat through the rearview mirror.

"You okay, honey?" I asked her.

"Sure, mommy, are you?"

The other girls stopped talking and also looked up. I was suddenly aware that there was an unspoken question that I needed to answer.

"Girls, mommy has been working a lot and in . . . different areas than I'm used to. So it's just an . . . adjustment for me." There, I thought, the truth, sort of. Alex and Abigail smiled at me and shook their heads in agreement. Trina definitely seemed a tough sale on this. I should have known better, she was always so intuitive. But she smiled as she squinted at me inquisitively.

I exhaled.

After dropping them each off I went back home. Luke was already gone for the day. I was actually working at my real job tonight and should probably get some sleep. I walked upstairs and sat on the edge of my bed while taking my shoes off. I suddenly felt my breathing getting heavy.

I struggled to take a breath. Then I couldn't breathe. I wasn't near water, yet I could feel my chest being compressed as if I was going under. I gasped again. I felt like I was going to pass out.

Then I saw it . . . as clear as if it were happening right in front of me . . . a victim. A woman . . . no, a young girl. I sucked in a deep breath. She was being dragged backwards from me. I didn't recognize the face but I knew the panicked look. She was in trouble. I reached out to her. She was so real that I thought I could feel her, save her if I could just reach her.

She disappeared in a foggy black cloud and was replaced by several other faces circling around me. The same pain . . . anguish. They were screaming at me . . . *help me . . . it hurts . . . stop . . . please.* I screamed and threw my hands over my ears. My ears pounded and sharp pains shot through my head. Dropping to my knees, I clutched my chest. Breathe, breathe, breathe!

Then it stopped.

What the hell was that, I thought. The pain ended, the faces, the anguish, all gone. But then I felt a growing warmth inside again, just like before. I saw my daughter Alex's high school suddenly. My muscles stiffened, as my hands formed tight fists. I let out a noise that was something just short of a growl.

I put my shoes on and quickly ran to the car. The tires squealed as I tore out of the driveway. *What's wrong?* I heard, but I didn't stop to think about it. I just shook my head and continued on. I drove through every stop sign and stoplight. Again I announced my arrival as the tires squealed into the parking lot at the school. A few boys who were in the parking lot turned to look toward me, obviously cutting class.

Getting out of my car, I could feel a pull. I knew where to go. Walking slowly so as not to miss any subtle cues, I walked around the outside of the school then out toward the fields. There was a small football stadium, and at one end was a wooden baseball backstop. I walked slowly toward it. Yes, I was going the right way. I was distracted for just a second when I felt my phone vibrate in my pocket but I ignored it.

I crept around the backstop, and there he was.

I hadn't seen his face in my visions, but all the faces showed up and floated around the back of his head as if drawing a bulls-eye. In front of me was a man of medium build kneeling down behind the backstop, watching. But what was he looking at? My eyes followed where he was looking, and just past the bleachers was a girl in a cheerleader uniform, getting ready for practice. She was standing by herself and I traced back to the man. He was breathing hard and brought his arm up to wipe the sweat on his brow with his sleeve. *Oh my God,* I thought, *this is why I'm here.* My muscles tightened, my breath quickened. I was here for him. I closed my eyes. Everything inside of me was guiding me here. *Listen to what you feel, Megan,* I heard and my eyes shot open as I briefly looked left and then right. No one else was here.

"Hey!" I hollered out.

I looked toward the young cheerleader. She had heard me and was looking in our direction, but unable to see us, she appeared generally uncomfortable and grabbed her bag to walk briskly toward the school.

The man was standing in front of me with anger dripping off his face. I smiled and said, "Good, we're alone." This newfound smugness on my face must not have been quite what he was expecting and his eyebrows furrowed.

I paced and stalked like a cat around the space where he was standing, then asked, "What's your name?"

"What does it matter to you?" He looked me up and down. "You know, you're a little old for me but you're kind of cute."

I stopped and my head cocked slightly. "Your name?"

"Craig . . . yours?" He was now looking me up and down.

I could feel the anger boiling inside of me. My muscles tightened and I started to walk toward him. He moved to grab me, but with a strength I was now becoming familiar with, I pushed him to the ground. He struggled to stand but I was holding him down. His eyes went wide. "Who are you?!"

"That's a good question." After considering whether I should tell him my name, I concluded it wouldn't matter since he would be dead soon. "Megan."

"What is this to you?" He was having trouble breathing. I could feel him struggling against my hand on his chest, but my strength was greater.

I looked him up and down. Enjoying this, and smiling again, I said, "I'm someone who is going to make sure you never hurt anyone again." And with that, I could see his color changing. He was grasping at his chest. I put more pressure and he gasped. I could feel and hear bones cracking and he struggled to scream. I knew that if I could put enough pressure at just the right area of his chest and compress his heart with enough force then it would not be able to beat . . . to pump the blood around his body . . . to live. He would slowly die . . . from lack of blood . . . from the inside. A whimper escaped his lips as I watched him for a moment and he took his last breath. Dead.

I looked at my hand. There was nothing different about it. Warmth filled every corner of my being and I realized that I was about to transition, as they called it. Time to go. I noticed students beginning to mill around in the distance and walked around a different way to avoid contact with anyone and any unwanted eyes from pot-smoking, class-cutting boys in the parking lot.

I got into my car and drove away. I could feel my arms and legs shaking and knew that I had to get far away from the school before anything worse happened or, God forbid, the pain. Turning onto several streets until even I didn't know where I was, I finally pulled over and cut the engine. I felt the ache slowly creeping over my body like the fog coming in off the bay. I grabbed the steering wheel and braced myself for the worst. A sudden rush of ecstasy rushed through every cell in my body as my breathing raced ahead of me. Then it passed. I felt nothing else. My breathing slowed, the feeling inside me stopped, and my body felt normal. Well, better than normal actually . . . strong. I started the car and drove home.

Walking into the house, I felt a little stunned. I put my keys on the front table, dropped my purse onto the floor, and walked to the kitchen for a glass of water. Wow, no pain, no intense transition. Then remembering that I was supposed to change, I ran to the bathroom and turned the light on. Looking in the mirror I was searching for something that would show me what had changed. Studying my reflection I saw that I was exactly the same, no difference.

My phone suddenly vibrated and I reached for it. I opened the front and saw for a split second that I had one missed call, then I noticed that it was Alex calling me. "Hi honey, everything okay?"

"Mom? Mom? Can you come get me?" Her voice sounded shaky and scared. I didn't understand. I had taken care of the man . . . Craig . . . who could have hurt her.

"Yes baby, calm down, what's wrong?"

Now she was crying on the phone, "Mom, there was . . ." her voice trailed off.

I was scared and raced through my memories. I was sure I had gotten rid of him. He was dead.

"There was what?" My voice tone was rising with each word. "There was what?!" I repeated even louder.

"Someone was found dead at our school. There's police everywhere. Please come to get me."

I took a deep breath and my heart ached. My actions to protect her and her friends had caused her pain and fear.

My eyes closed for a moment. "I'm on my way. Where will you be?"

"The teachers won't let us leave without an adult, so you have to park and walk up."

My stomach dropped. Go right back? Did someone want me to come back? Had someone seen me and were they using my daughter as bait? "I'm coming baby, I'll be right there." I heard her start to cry as I disconnected the call. Grabbing my keys and purse again, I ran to the car. Driving toward the school my mind went over and over what had transpired. What did I do wrong? Did I not complete the purpose? I must have, I felt his pulse, *I'm sure of it.* I felt different. I raised my hand up and looked at it with wonder.

I looked up just in time to slam on my brakes. Traffic. At least a mile of cars lining the street to pick up students at the school. I was too anxious and would not be able to wait. I pulled over and parked. Getting out of my car, I was almost hit by another frantic mother trying to get to the school. She glanced at me apologetically, but I just nodded my head in an understanding way. We were all panicked.

Walking too fast toward the school, I must have stumbled half a dozen times, almost falling on my face. At least I was in good company because it seemed most of the other parents who had chosen to walk were doing the same. As I approached the school I saw yellow caution tape strung across the front of the entire school. For a moment it was almost as if I were back in high school after the shooting. I tried to shake that off. Not a place I wanted to go right now.

A hand rose above a sea of parents, and I could hear my name being called. Well, the voice was yelling "Mom," but I could hear it plain as day, this was my child. It always amazed me how several children could be yelling mom, and each mom could pick out her own child's voice in the crowd. My pace picked up. Dodging through the cramped group of parents, I reached for and connected with my daughter's hand. Pulling her through the crowd toward me, I wrapped my arms around her. There was chaos all around. Teachers and police officers were trying to keep everything orderly but had clearly lost the battle.

Holding on to her, I moved backwards through the crowd. I could feel her sobs on my chest. When we finally made it out I held her away from me to get a closer look. "Are you okay, did you get hurt?"

"No . . . oo . . . oo" she got out. She was having trouble breathing with those quick breaths children get when they have been crying hard for a while.

I wrapped my arms around her again and tried to calm her. Everyone seemed to disappear around us, and the noises become muffled. Her crying was on the brink of hysteria, and I tried to slow my breathing down so as not to contribute to the stress. We stood there for what felt like several minutes. Slowly her breathing began to pace with mine until we were both at a reasonable rate. I felt her take a deep breath in and sigh. Her body relaxed against my hold, and I had to increase my clutch on her to absorb the extra weight.

After a minute or two she pulled slowly away. "Mom, why would someone be killed at our school?" Her breathing started to quicken. I heard murmuring all around us, *There was a man found dead on campus. No kid was hurt. What could have happened?*

"Shhhh, what matters is that none of the students were hurt and that you're okay. The police will figure the rest out."

She nodded in agreement and we started walking toward the car. We had not gone more than twenty feet when I heard someone from behind us say, "Excuse me, excuse me, Miss?" My heart stopped as I turned.

A male police officer was walking toward us. I gulped hard. "Yes?" I didn't sound very confident.

He approached us slowly, "Can I talk to you for a moment?"

"Um, yeah, I think so." Oh crap, I thought, this is it, someone saw me. So much for leading the Aurators to rid the world of all that is horrid and terrible. I'm going to get caught for an impulsive sense of purpose. Even though I was strong and steady in my conviction, my former self inside was shaking.

"I'm a friend of your brother. He just wanted me to make sure that your daughter was okay."

Great. My self-imposed moment of drama has been completely obliterated by my moronic brother just giving a shit about his niece. I smiled rather nervously at the officer, "We're good, thanks. I'm just going to take her home."

"Okay, I'll let him know. Take care."

"You too." I breathed in a deep sigh, realizing the complete insanity within my own mind at that moment, and turned to take my daughter home.

19. Liabilities

I tried to explain the day's events to my husband, but he seemed too preoccupied to listen and, quite frankly, I couldn't stand to look at him with that dark aura, so we had very little interaction. After tucking all the girls into bed, I finally had a moment to myself. Standing in the kitchen, I could hear the newscaster on the television in the living room.

"It was a terrifying day for some high school students today at Seven Hills High School, where a man was found dead behind the school. The victim has been identified as Steven Timmons, a registered sex offender living in the city. Timmons had been convicted twice of lewd conduct with underage girls in the past. He had recently been on warning with the Probation Department for not complying with the terms of his probation. The school groundskeeper found Timmons dead, and initial reports from hospital spokespeople are that he died of a massive heart attack related to injuries sustained . . ." The news trailed off, and I didn't hear the rest of the story. *Good*, I thought.

I looked out the kitchen window for a moment and a picture of an ocean scene flashed in front of my eyes. I blinked but it was gone. Then it was there and I blinked again. I shook it off. I'm losing it.

Reviewing the events of the day, I decided to call Max to talk everything over with him. As I opened my phone, I saw that I had missed a call and a voicemail. I remembered that when I was crossing the field toward my intended purpose I had felt my phone vibrate. I clicked on the missed call to see who it was. Not recognizing the number, I decided to listen to the voicemail.

"Megan! Megan! This is Nicholai . . . oh . . . well . . . you need to call me as soon as possible. It's very important."

He had a rather feverish tone to his voice so I called back using the number he had left me. It rang only once.

"Megan?"

"Yes, hi Nicholai. I'm sorry I didn't call sooner, I . . ." but he interrupted.

"I know, I know everything. I saw you walking toward him, your purpose." He was talking so fast I could barely keep up.

I was completely confused. "Wait, Nicholai. Wait, you what? I'm sorry but I can't keep up . . . it's been a long day."

"I'm sorry Megan, let me start over. I was walking near the beach when all of sudden my vision shifted and I saw a field in front of me. I could hear your thoughts struggling to figure out what to do with this man you were approaching. I tried to talk to you but I didn't know if you could hear me. So I tried to call you. I didn't mean to interrupt, but I was trying to help."

My thoughts raced back for a moment to my experience at the school. *Listen to what you feel Megan.* These words had caught me off guard in the moment.

"Megan?"

"Yeah, I'm sorry. Did you . . ."

"Yes, I said, *Listen to what you feel Megan.*"

Shaking my head in disbelief, I asked, "How is that possible?"

"I've only heard of this happening once before, centuries ago. But they too were relatives and descendants of Asclepius. Just like us. I first noticed it when we were in Max's office. Occasionally I would hear another voice that was not my own, and I figured out it was you. After I got home I tried to see if I could hear you from Greece. I concentrated and when I finally heard something, it was you thinking about your purpose. This time, however, I also saw you. Well, saw what you saw. I watched the whole thing."

I could hear his racing breath over the phone. "This is . . . I don't understand . . . we can hear each other?" I barely got the words out.

"Yes, and apparently we, or at least I, can see through you."

"Wait a minute . . . did you say you were near water today?"

"Yes, twice. Once earlier and just now before you called. Why?"

I looked at the clock that read ten o'clock at night. "What time is it there?"

"About eight in the morning, why?"

"Well, after I put the girls to bed I was looking out a window when I had a sudden flash of ocean. I wasn't thinking of the ocean, nor was it any body of water that I know."

"Maybe it was the ocean I was looking at."

"This is nuts," I said.

Chuckling on the other end, "I agree, but, my dear, these are the cards our maker has dealt us. What we choose to do with them is up to us."

Thoughts began swirling in my mind. Our maker? Who's doing this to me? Who do I get to blame for this unrequested chaos infiltrating my life?

"Easy there, Megan, this is a gift, not a curse," Nicholai said softly.

"That was a private thought."

"Not anymore."

I rolled my eyes. It was hard to get mad at him. Everything he said rolled off his tongue with such a sweet Greek accent that it could make even the most harsh words sound lyrical. "Okay, so what now?"

There was silence, and I could hear his thoughts bouncing back and forth between possibilities. "Well, we can practice this new serpodus . . . or skill, if you prefer, to see if we can master it a little more."

"Not tonight, I think I'm done."

"I understand. Are you still going to call Max?"

I had forgotten about that. "No, now after everything I have to go to work."

"Okay, Megan, have a good night. And take care."

"Thanks Nicholai . . . for everything."

"Thank you as well. It's nice to have a long lost piece of my family back."

After we hung up I thought about that last statement. Family. What did mine look like? My mom and dad? They raised me, but there was no biological link there. Funny. I think part of me always knew. I had heard adopted children say that they sort of always knew, but here I was having my own realization of this idea.

In my head I knew that I shouldn't feel this way. That the family that had raised me and loved me was my family. No less than if they had given birth to me. But somehow this wasn't right. I walked over to the couch, sat down, and closed my eyes. I felt so strong right now in so many ways except for this side of me . . . the illusion of stability within my life. What was I supposed to feel? As I sat there, I could feel the two sides of myself struggling for control. The older, insecure, and scared side that wanted to run away and hide somewhere, that longed to rock back and forth on the couch, trying to shake some reality loose from my mind.

And this other, very foreign side of me that was strong. I didn't understand her. I wanted to, but she negated everything I had ever known my entire life. I could almost feel the ripping inside myself as I caught my breath. My heart ached. I longed to cry, to release all the fear and pain, but nothing happened. Why couldn't I cry? It would be so easy to release this into the universe, which is the way crying had always felt for me. The pressure would build and then eventually explode in a torrent of tears, spilling outward as water, dripping over my cheeks and eventually off my chin. I imagined the newly deposited saline spots, no matter where they landed, drying and evaporating into the space around me and leaving on the next breeze or waft of air passing by, taking with it my fears and pain.

This was not to be today.

Instead I sat, increasingly more aware of the line drawn between my two halves. My eyes shot open. I needed to see my parents.

20. Progenitor

All the way to my parent's house, I heard Nicholai's words resonating in my head. Past and present.

Nicholai, get out of my head. I'm just going to talk to them.

"Megan, please, there's no reason to hurt them. Please just think through what you're doing and the motivation behind it," he pleaded.

Why do you care anyway? All I could hear was chuckling. It was irritating. How I wished that this new serpodus worked like a radio and I could just change stations—or better, turn it off.

"Hey! I didn't ask for this either, but here we are."

Ugh. I gripped the steering wheel. *You didn't answer my question.*

"Okay, okay," Nicholai said through my thoughts. Look. From a practical standpoint, most, if not all of the Caduceus don't know you exist. If you maintain your everyday family life then you don't appear different than anyone else. However, on a more . . . emotional level . . . Megan . . . they raised and loved you. If they love you half as much as I love my children or, for that matter, half as much as you love your children, imagine what this would do to them. Knowing that you know."

I took a deep breath. I love my girls and felt a sharp pang in my gut as I imagined myself in my parent's shoes.

"That's it, Megan. You have to try and understand . . . empathize with your parents before you attempt to speak with them."

I rolled my eyes as I pulled up to the house. *Come on Nicholai. I need some time to think about things before I go in. Can we say good-bye?*

"All right then. Good luck and let me know how it went. Take care and . . . I love you."

I was caught for a moment. *I love you?* These words always were so difficult for me to say, except to my husband and girls. Yet here was this man who represented a quintessential stranger to me. Well he is a stranger who is a relative. I shook it off.

Then I heard, "It's okay, Megan, just let me know how it goes and try not to overthink everything too much. Sometimes things just *are* and don't have specific reasons or explanations."

Okay, thanks, I'll talk to you later.

My mind filled with questions. How would I approach the subject? What would I say? Would they be angry, hurt, relieved? How would I feel after? What was my motive for this?

This last question I decided to ponder before going in. Nicholai had asked me this. As I thought about it I had to admit that my motivation seemed unclear. On the one hand I wanted answers about my past. I wanted to know the truth. On the other hand I knew the truth was painful for them and I didn't want to cause them any more pain. Would I have done the same thing if I had come upon one of my children in the same way? Would I have wanted them to know that I had broken the law to obtain them?

I looked toward the house and suddenly saw, felt, and smelled a rush of memories sweeping through my mind. The Christmases dragging trees through the house and leaving needles everywhere that my mother would curse for the next two months. The wrestling events between my brother, father, and me that they would sometimes even let me win. Watching my mother and father dress up to go out on very infrequent date nights and thinking how beautiful my mom was. Wishing I would look like her when I grew up.

Looking down at my hands that were clasped a little tightly in my lap, I noticed they were slightly sweaty. After taking a deep breath I realized that it was now or never.

As I walked toward the front door I was hit with a rush of emotions. They crashed into me as if trying to push me back through time. I stopped just short of the front steps and, turning toward the grass to my right, I could see my brother and me running in the sprinklers while my mom and dad sat in their lawn chairs drinking lemonade. I could almost hear the chatter, "*Mom, he's hogging the water . . . No I'm not, she's lying,*" and then mom piping in, "*All right you two, just get along . . . Dear, would you like some more lemonade?*"

Simple chatter. Nothing really. Yet now every word was fraught with lies. "*He's hogging the water—because he's your real son . . . no I'm not, she's lying . . . because you bought her on sale . . . all right you two, just get along—or we'll have to give Megan back . . . Dear, would you like some more lemonade—you liar?"* I tried to shake it off. Why did I always have to be so judgmental?

The house was typical for San Francisco. Tall, narrow, and about six inches from the neighbors on either side. As a child I always thought that was so when the earthquakes came, the house couldn't fall over because the ones next to it would hold it up. The drapes in the front bay window were open so that you could see the table set squarely in front with my grandmother's heirloom vase. My parents recently updated the house with new windows and painted the exterior gray. It was about time. I don't think the house had been painted since I was ten.

I counted the twelve steps up the narrow walkway. I raised my hand and knocked. My mother's voice rang out in song from inside, "Come in."

I entered and my mom glided across the floor to meet me. She was always so graceful and I admired that about her. I chuckled to myself. Being graceful myself, I actually thought I got that from her.

Her arms wrapped around me in a loving embrace, clearly glad to see me. "Hi honey, I'm so glad you're here. But why do you insist on knocking? This is your house too."

I rolled my eyes. Always the same question, and I grudgingly gave the same answer. "Mom, I'm respecting yours and Dad's privacy, the same reason you knock when you come to my house."

Her hand went up toward her mouth as if trying to keep in a secret, then looking back and forth she leaned toward me, "You're about thirty minutes too late to catch us *doing* anything." Then she giggled.

"UGH! MOM! No offense, but please, not in front of the children." She seemed caught off guard for a moment.

"Oh, are the girls with you?"

My lips pursed, I was not amused. "No mom," I started through clenched teeth, "Me!"

My mom laughed, "Honey, you really do need to lighten up."

In most situations I would not be referred to as a prude, but I would be hard-pressed to find anyone who wasn't grossed out in some way to think about their parents having any relationship beyond a hug and kiss hello and good-bye.

"Come here, honey." My mom motioned for me to sit on the couch. As I sat, she handed me a photo album with a picture of the Eiffel Tower on it. *Figures*, I thought to myself. They've been home less than seventy-two hours and my mom has a completed photo album already. "You look, I'll make tea," she said.

Then she was off to the kitchen. Looking through the book, I began to drift into thought. What was I going to say? I examined how I felt. Somehow this wasn't feeling right. My body wasn't relaxed and I was rather anxious. Shouldn't I feel anxious before I have the "hey you bought me off a guy in a bar" conversation?

"It's not supposed to feel right."

Ugh, Nicholai, get out of here!

"Sorry, sorry. I was just worried."

I slammed my hand onto one of the pages of the photo album just as my mom walked into the room. She stopped a few paces from me with her eyes curiously wide and eyebrows raised. "Everything okay?"

I took a deep breath as I looked down at the picture. "Yes, I was just looking at the Champs Élysées and wishing I could go there right now." Then as if pretending to wipe something off the page, I listened for Nicholai but he was gone. Thank God.

"Oh honey, you'll go there once your kids are older. It's a lot of work to take little children there." She set the cups of tea down and started turning pages in the album while it still sat in my lap. I looked at her face. There were more wrinkles now but they seemed to complement her gray hair. She really was a beautiful woman. Her skin was pale but she had a lovely complexion and was still fit because she walked every day. I always admired my mom for staying home with us while we were growing up. Now being a mom myself, I definitely understood how hard she worked. Our house was always clean and well stocked with food and necessary items. She had been involved in both of our schools as well as dropping us off and picking us up every day. At least until we got our licenses. Even then she was waiting for us when we got home with snacks and would sit at the table anxiously awaiting the teenage tales of the day. I looked toward the dining room table and reflected that some of my best memories were with my mom at that table, dishing about the drama at school. She always appeared to be so interested. Most of the stories I brought home were for her benefit. Since I was not part of the drama myself, I had to rely on hearsay from others, usually something I overheard at the lockers so I would have some juicy tidbit to share with her. She really was a great mom.

My kids adore her. Even at her age, she's the first to get on the floor and wrestle with them. Boy, do they love to wrestle with her. It was cute when they were one and two years old, but as they got older and stronger, I started having muscle cramps and backaches after our nighttime matches. But Nana didn't seem to care. She probably spent the next three days after a wrestling match lathered up with some liniment and dosed up on anti-inflammatories, but it never stopped her from participating again during the next visit.

Then suddenly I heard a loud, "Hello? Megan?"

"Hey, dad. I'm in the living room."

My dad walked through the door that led from the kitchen to the dining room. As he turned toward me his face lit up with a huge smile. I felt an ache in the pit of my stomach thinking over and over how I was going to bring up the subject of adoption and effectively wipe the smile off his face.

Placing the photo album on the coffee table, I stood and met his open arms with my own. My dad's hugs were always so comforting to me. While I hadn't often opened up to him regarding my pain and troubles growing up, when I did he was always there with a hug. Always nonjudgmental and a great listener. Maybe it's a lawyer thing. Or just a dad thing.

My dad and I sat down together, while my mom popped into the kitchen to check on the tea. My dad took the photo album from the table. "Okay," he started, looking around to make sure my mom wasn't listening. "You know your mother. We have a few good photos and the rest are sunsets . . . hundreds and hundreds of sunsets." Shaking his head with a smirk on his face he flipped through the many sunsets and pointed out the few photos of monuments they took.

I looked at my father instead of the photos. He was an attractive man with strong features. Even at his age he was not that gray. If it weren't for the wrinkles on his face that trailed down his neck, it would be difficult to gauge his real age. He still worked out several times a week and consulted for local law firms. He had always said that if he stopped moving he would die.

My parents' marriage was one I had admired and hoped to emulate when I found someone of my own. They were and are best friends. After he showed me the photos and told the corresponding stories, he closed the book.

"Okay now. What was the midnight phone call for when we were in Paris? It wasn't just because it was your birthday, was it, because we didn't forget."

"No no, Dad, that's fine. I'm sorry about that late night call . . . I . . ."

"Tea," sang my mother as she walked into the room.

After pouring tea for each of us, she sat down across from dad and me. My dad turned back toward me.

"Well?" he asked.

"Well what?" asked my mother.

"I was asking Megan why the late call when we were in Paris. She sounded upset on the phone, and I was about to find out why."

"Oh, that's right," mom said. "Did you get our birthday card? Sorry to interrupt, go ahead dear."

I winced. I hated when my mother called me dear. I always tried to remember my own feelings so that I would never call my children that . . . or patients for that matter. I looked back and forth from my mom to my dad.

"Oh guys, you know me. I got a wild harebrained idea to have a big family reunion this summer and wasn't thinking about where you were or what time it was."

They both looked at each other and then looked at me. I don't think they believed me, but I could tell from their faces they wouldn't press me on it. I quickly moved on.

"Anyway, then I thought that it was too short notice for everyone and dropped the idea altogether." I tried to change the subject, "The girls missed you guys."

My mom was great about accepting whatever I said at face value and moving on. Dad, however, was not an easy sell. While I was talking with mom about the girls coming over to spend the night, I could see my dad staring in my direction. As I child I knew that it was best not to make direct eye contact with dad. Especially if I was trying to get away with or avoid something. He had a special gift of looking at someone and getting them to talk. It was probably a very useful skill in his profession, but it was terrible if you were his child.

I saw him turn away, get up, and move toward the kitchen. Mom and I finished plans to have the girls stay overnight soon, and then she handed me a large bag with French writing on it. Presents for the girls.

I gave my mom a huge hug, told her I loved her and went to say my good-bye to my dad. I walked into the kitchen and saw him standing against the sink as if looking for something in the drain would help him make sense of his daughter.

"Dad?"

He wouldn't turn toward me, "Yes honey?"

"Um, I'm leaving . . . I love you."

I saw him take a breath and turn slowly toward me. His face was crowded with worry lines and his eyes dark with sadness. "Any . . ." his voice cracked, "any time you want to talk . . . you know . . . about anything . . . I . . . just let me know."

My face softened. "I know, Dad." My heart ached. My omissions were hurting him. But my real questions might hurt him even more. I stretched up onto my tiptoes and kissed my dad on his cheek, then whispered, "I love you."

He smiled at me then gave me a big hug. "Back at you."

I smiled. I tried to read his face but all I saw was a tangle of emotions running through the lines. My smile disappeared as he raised his hand to my face. "*She knows . . . no she can't . . .*"

My stomach dropped. How could he have guessed that? I heard him but his lips didn't move. *I do know,* I wanted to shout. But even more, I wondered how I could have heard him. I thought that was only for Aurators. My head lowered. Maybe now was the time to ask him. Then I heard him thinking, "*Maybe I wasn't enough. Maybe I wasn't a good dad.*"

Tears filled my eyes. "Dad?"

"Yes, my darling daughter."

"You're the best. The best dad I could have ever hoped for. Thank you . . . for everything."

He hesitated for a moment as if waiting for something, "Of course . . . what else could I do . . . I . . . well . . ."

I hugged him. "I love you, Dad." And he hugged me back with such an intensity that I knew no other words needed to be spoken.

I said my good-bye and left. I sat in my car for a moment, absorbing what had happened. What did I accomplish? Did I hurt him even more?

"You did great Megan, I'm very proud of you."

I smiled at the now familiar voice inside my head. *Thanks Nicholai.*

"That's Uncle Nicholai to you."

Ha ha.

"You okay?" he continued.

Yeah, thanks.

"Okay, I'll talk to you tomorrow. Give me a call."

Sounds good.

21. Complications

I was happy to go to work that night. I went along during my shift, checking on patients who had been there for hours and admitting many new ones. With the chaos of my newly acquired dysfunctional life, the comfort of the sick and dying at work was . . . well . . . I guess it shouldn't be comforting, but it was.

"Megan?" My boss was standing behind me as I was charting a medication I had just given.

"Oh hey, Deloris. What's up?"

"Can I talk with you for a moment?"

"Sure." I followed her out into the hallway.

"Hey," she started, "you okay lately?"

"Um, yeah. Why?" I know that my face showed my confusion. Had I made a mistake at work? Did I miss a shift?

"Well, you've missed a few days recently and . . . well . . . you never have before. Anything going on?"

I wanted to laugh hysterically at this question. Anything going on? Where do I start? I wanted to shout out, *Look sweetie, just be glad you're not in my head . . . it's getting kind of crazy and crowded in here.*

Instead I just replied, "Nope. All is good."

"Well, I was just worried. You've worked here for several years with only a few sick calls and they were always related to your kids, so I guess I was just wondering if they were okay."

Good opening, so I said, "Well, things are good. Abigail's asthma has been acting up lately and you know how it's always worse at night." This was partially true. I just left out that it was only affecting her during P.E. at school.

Deloris's face immediately relaxed. "Oh, I'm sorry to hear that. Well, if there's anything I can do let me know. You're one of my best nurses. I was afraid you were thinking about leaving."

I laughed, "I can't imagine leaving here."

She gave my arm a reassuring squeeze and turned to walk away. "Well, I can't imagine this place without you either. Have a good shift."

Shaking my head, I started walking down the hall toward my patients. I knew calling in sick was rather out of character for me. Luke usually stayed home with the girls since he had that natural ability to soothe them. I never minded. Anything so that my girls were better while I was at work. Being a self-diagnosed workaholic, I don't tend to miss work very often, until recently that is.

I felt a sudden shock walking down the hall, and my stomach dropped. The feeling was almost painful, and I was hit by a wave of nausea. Moving felt slow and sluggish, and voices around me echoed in the halls in low tones. The hairs on the nape of my neck stood on end, sending a chill down my back. My vision blurred for a split second and then cleared only in the center, creating a tunnel effect. Shades of gray encircled a doorway at the end of the hall. I knew that I was walking toward the door but I could not feel the floor beneath my feet. For a split second I wondered if others around me were aware of my sudden behavior change, but patients and coworkers walked in and out of the grayness, coming in and out of focus, seemingly oblivious to me.

As I moved into the doorway I saw a single bed with a male patient who at first appeared to be peacefully sleeping. My breathing sped up. Something was wrong. I cautiously moved toward the bedside. Looking back and forth, I saw a young man, maybe in his twenties, healthy looking in every way. There was a white aura surrounding him but something was different. It was changing, shifting shape and then abruptly it began to fade away. I snapped out of my haze and realized that he was dying. I felt for a pulse and found it was very weak. I reached up to push the code button that would alert everyone to the situation but then hesitated. Instead I put my hands to his chest and started compressions. Pushing down and releasing his chest, I could almost feel a quivering below the skin. I tried to picture this sensation in my head . . . his heart? The object stopped quivering and began to move on its own, weakly at first but then stronger and stronger until I felt a regular pulse in his wrist.

His pulse continued after I moved my hand from his chest, and when a few moments had passed I pushed the code button. People rushed into the room, and I quickly explained that I found him unresponsive. We moved him into the appropriate room and another nurse took over. They saved him that night. The young man had an underlying heart condition that had never been identified, and while he had come to the hospital for what appeared to be simple flu symptoms, there clearly was much more going on.

A few people told me "good job" on the way out the door that night, but I must admit I was a little too preoccupied with what had happened to absorb the accolades.

I got to my car and lay my head back. "What am I doing?" I thought out loud as I pulled my phone out and dialed.

"Hello?"

"Max?"

"Hi Megan. Are you okay?"

"I don't know."

"Nicholai called me and filled me in," he said.

I had to admit I was a little relieved that I didn't need to explain much. "I know I'm supposed to know what to do . . . and on some level I do . . . but . . . sometimes it's just a bit much. Maybe it's just happening too fast. I don't feel ready."

"You will Megan. Trust."

I hung my head. Just then I heard a beep on my phone. It was Luke clicking in. "Max, I'm sorry but that's Luke on the other line. Can I talk to you later?"

"Sure. I'll talk with you later."

I clicked the call waiting over. "Hi honey, what's up?"

"Hey there, how was work?"

Hmmm, truth or not? Not yet at least. "It was okay, I'm actually in my car, just leaving now."

"Okay, just wanted to know if you remembered that you're going on the field trip with Abigail's class today." His tone was curt and he sounded a little off.

"Shit, I forgot. I'm on my way," I replied

"Okay, I'll have her ready for you."

"Thanks." I was just about to hang up when I decided to ask, "Hey honey?"

"Yup?" He still sounded curt.

I hesitated but then took a breath to speak. "Are you okay lately?"

He spoke almost before I could finish my question. "What? What are you trying to say?" His tone was gruff and accusatory.

His response caught me completely off guard, it was so unlike him. I didn't know how to respond. "I . . . I just have noticed that you've been, well, a little short lately and wanted to know if maybe I had done something wrong?"

A half huff and chuckle broke through the line as he spoke, "Really? Why do you think everything is about you?"

I suddenly pictured him in my mind as tears welled up in my eyes. His aura had changed from golden to dark lately. Just now I was making the connection to what that might mean. Before I could say anything else he spoke again.

"Listen, I gotta go. Don't forget about the field trip. Bye." And he hung up.

It was another five minutes before I realized that the phone was still against my ear. What could I do? Did his dark aura mean the same as other's auras? I put the phone down and shook my head. No, I said to myself. It's not possible. He is one of the most gentle men I've ever met. I have to keep believing that.

Spending the day with my daughter should have been something that would allow me to let go of everything and enjoy, but my head was filled with so many thoughts: Luke, the upcoming fight, and questions about my role in it all. I decided to let go and ask for guidance, just as Max and Nicholai had suggested. *Please show me how I can be of service*, I thought. But I wasn't sure who I was speaking to. I listened for a moment then laughed in relief when no one answered.

The San Francisco Zoo. I forgot that was the destination for the field trip. Thank goodness. It was a nice day in the city, a little overcast as we pulled into the parking lot. We stepped out and I smelled the exhaust from the school bus that we had been riding in. I smiled, remembering my days in the school band and going on trips to compete. I think I still have my flute somewhere. Then I felt a little sad that I could barely remember anyone from high school. "Absent" was the word that came to mind. Even though I had been present in body, my mind was never present at school. There was always somewhere else I would have rather been.

As the exhaust dispersed, the salty air from the beach across the street caressed my face and lit up my senses. I took a deep breath and grabbed Abigail's hand. We divided into groups, so I was chaperoning Abigail and three other girls. Winding through the different exhibits, we made our way to the monkey cages. This was always my favorite exhibit.

As we stood there talking about the different monkeys, a sudden brush of cold hit me from behind and took my breath away. I turned just in time to catch a glimpse of darkness creeping around a corner. Another mother's group was next to us, and I asked her to watch my girls for a moment while I went to the restroom. As I walked toward where the darkness had disappeared, I felt my muscles tense.

"Careful, Megan. Something's not right here," I heard a voice whisper.

I know Nicholai, let me concentrate.

My breathing was fast. I stopped at the corner and looked around before moving further. Then the presence I felt was gone. Just like that.

Nicholai, what happened?

"I don't know. Did you see who it was?"

No.

Just then I heard a scream. I whipped around and realized the scream came from where I had left Abigail and the other girls. I broke into a run.

As I reached the monkey cages I saw the other mother shuffling the girls away from the cages.

"What happened?" I almost yelled, but no one answered. I moved through the group to where Abigail was, grabbed her hand and gathered up the other girls. Then I noticed others looking into the cage. Moving toward the cage while still holding on to Abigail, I saw a bloody figure lying twisted at the bottom. I turned toward another onlooker.

"What happened?"

"I don't know," a nearly frantic mother said. "One minute we were looking into the monkey cage and everything was fine, and the next moment there was a man lying at the bottom. The monkeys were all still in the top of the exhibit. I didn't see him there at first, not until someone looked down. Oh God, it's terrible!"

I looked back toward the body at the bottom of the cage and gasped as I saw it. A red aura faded in front of my eyes. I moved toward the fencing. "No!" I screamed in my head as the aura completely faded. Then my eyes swept to the left where red letters on the cement wall read, "YOU ARE NEXT."

Nicholai?

"I saw it."

Who could have done this? There was a pause before his answer.

"Call me when you can."

I steered Abigail and the other girls back with the group moving away from the cages. Abigail tried to ask me what had happened. I said that it was a grown-up problem and there was nothing to worry about.

Our group was in the front of the zoo waiting for the buses to return. Some of the children had seen the man and were crying. Others were confused and scared. The police were coming and going, and then a television crew arrived. The camera panned over the front and then attempted to move through the gates before the police stopped them.

Just then I heard a familiar voice, "Well, hello there. We need to stop meeting like this."

I looked up to see Detective Charlene McGuire again. Ugh.

"Megan, right? You always seem to be where the excitement is, huh?" She looked at the kids around me, raised one eyebrow and walked away after tipping an imaginary hat my way.

"Have a nice day," I tried to say as pleasantly as possible. Unsuccessful. I was thankful when the buses arrived and we all piled on. It seemed like a much longer trip back to school than it had been going to the zoo. When we finally arrived, the teachers tried to return some normalcy by announcing that students should go back to their classes for the rest of the day.

I was thankful. I knew that Abigail hadn't seen anything and seemed happy as she skipped off for lunch. I pulled my phone out and dialed.

"Megan?"

"Hi, Max. I . . ."

"Can you come to my office now?"

I was caught off guard by this. "Yes, I, um, I'm on my way."

Driving to Max's work, I battled to make sense of what had happened. I felt a sharp stab in my chest and then anger as I realized that my daughter had been with me when this happened. What if something had happened to her? I hit the steering wheel out of anger and helplessness and sped up.

22. Choices

Walking down the hall toward Max's office, I heard the drone of a television newscast. I knocked softly and peeked my head through the door, but Aaron was standing in the room instead of Max.

Relieved, I walked into the office, just thankful to be with someone I could talk to.

"What's wrong with you?" That was not the greeting I was expecting from him.

"What?"

"Haven't you seen this?"

Confused, I turned to where he was pointing. The news was reporting the death at the zoo. I saw our group as the camera panned across us.

I shook my head at him in an effort to express that I didn't understand. He walked over to the television.

Pointing at the picture, Aaron said, "Right here . . . you . . . you're all red. Your aura? It's now broadcast for everyone to see. You've put us all in danger! You've put yourself in danger!"

I squinted my eyes to see what he saw, but all I could see was me. "I'm sorry, Aaron, but I don't . . ."

I turned and he was standing just a few inches from me. I stepped back but he reached out and grabbed my arms. His eyes softened from their original intensity as he spoke. "Megan, you can't see your aura, but all of the rest of us . . . and them . . . *they* can. We need to avoid the media. Didn't anyone tell you that?"

I couldn't remember anything specific about the media. There had been so much information I'd had to absorb. "No, I don't . . . I don't remember anything. I'm sorry."

He took in a long deep breath. "If anything had happened . . . to you . . . I . . . we . . . ." As he trailed off he looked into my eyes. His eyes became wild and intense, his pupils dilated. He raised his hand to touch my cheek.

What is he doing?

He moved closer to me and everything inside of me begged to move away. *Run, run!* But I was frozen. My breathing was picking up and my heart was thudding in my chest. I noticed that his breathing was becoming as quick as my own as he began leaning toward me. *Move, Megan, move!* It was hopeless, and as much as I did not want advances toward me at that moment I could not move.

Then as if waking out of a deep sleep, his intense eyes broke contact with my own and he lowered his gaze. "Megan . . . I . . ."

My chest was tight as I struggled to breathe. "I . . . Aaron . . . I can't."

His hand fell from my face, "I need to go." There was sadness and confusion on his face.

"Wait," I urged.

"No, I'm sorry, I don't know . . . I'm sorry." Turning, he walked toward the door just as Max entered and they exchanged glances.

"Aaron?"

"I'm sorry Max, I have to go," and he left.

Max continued into the room and looked toward me. "Megan, what . . . ?" He saw the look on my face and immediately stopped.

"Megan?"

"Max . . . I . . ."

"Come here, come sit down. What happened?"

Trying to slow my breathing and return myself to sanity, I started slowly. "I'm not sure. Aaron was upset that I was on television." I turned toward Max, "Did I ruin something? I'm sorry, I didn't know."

He nodded in agreement, "Yes, it was unfortunate that you were on the news, but there's nothing we can do about it now. There was an accident at the zoo? What kind?"

I would have thought he knew. "There was a man at the bottom of the monkey cage . . . dead."

Max shook his head, "The monkey cage? Too bad. That's my favorite exhibit."

My eyebrows furrowed in frustration at his elementary view of the event. "Max? The man in the cage had a red aura."

This got his attention, and his head shot up. "What?"

I recounted with as much detail as possible what I had seen. I paid careful attention to the detail about the dark aura I saw. Max stood and paced around the room listening until I had finished.

"We shouldn't be able to see a red aura around someone who is dead."

I thought about this detail. "Did I mention that it faded out?"

He raised one eyebrow, "No, you managed to leave that out."

"When I walked over and saw him lying there, his aura was still intact, but over the next few seconds it quickly faded away. And then I saw the writing on the wall next to him."

Max thought for a moment before he continued, "And the writing on the wall behind him said?"

"YOU ARE NEXT, in capitals." I didn't know if that last part was important, but judging by the intensity of his look I figured it was better not to leave anything out.

"Megan, if his aura was just fading then that means he was just killed. No one saw anything?"

"Not that I know of, but remember I was going after the dark aura."

He appeared pensive and it seemed like many minutes passed before he finally looked up at me.

"Tomas," Max murmured.

"Tomas," I also heard in my head.

I had to blink and shake my head because I heard both voices simultaneously.

Max looked at me concerned, "What?"

"Nicholai just said Tomas also."

"Are you talking to him now?"

I had to stop and think, as if trying to switch to a different language. *Nicholai?*

"Yes, Megan. I'm here," he answered.

"Yes Max I can hear him."

"Okay, tell him I'm calling him." But as Max reached the phone, it rang. Picking up the receiver he started speaking.

"Nicholai? . . . Yes, I know, this is getting serious fast . . . No I haven't had an opportunity to tell her yet . . . okay . . . let me put you on speaker phone."

Max pressed a button on the phone base and placed the receiver down, "Nicholai?"

"I'm here," came his voice from the speaker on the phone.

"Okay, hold on a minute." Max motioned for me to shut and lock the door.

"Megan," Max began, "We have some disturbing news."

Nicholai continued, "When we left to return home, Tomas mentioned that he needed to run an errand and asked Aleck and me to drive to the airport by ourselves. We questioned this but went ahead. We became very concerned when the second call came one-half hour before we were to get onto the plane. He told us that he was stuck in traffic and would have to take a different flight. Hearing from others that traffic was common in San Francisco, we weren't surprised but still had our doubts."

There was a pause as I looked back and forth between the phone and Max.

"He never made it to Greece," Nicholai's words echoed in my head as they rang out from the phone.

I looked at Max, who was apparently lost in thought, standing with his hands clasped behind his back staring out the window.

"Is he here then? That was definitely him at the zoo?"

Without turning, Max began to speak, "Good question. Aaron and I tried to track him down. We didn't believe it was necessary to bother you yet. We couldn't find him and he disconnected his phone. But . . . well the situation is such now that you may be in danger."

"Why would I be in danger? Because of Tomas?" I asked the question even though I felt it was rhetorical since deep down I knew the answer.

"Remember, Megan," Nicholai said, "anyone can turn from good to bad. It is a choice. A tough one but one that, once that road is chosen, is very difficult to turn back from."

I flashed briefly on my husband's aura but then returned to the conversation. "I don't understand. If you all thought he was bad why did you allow him to continue on as a Senior?"

Max said, "Just because someone is suspected of possible wrongdoing is not reason enough to prosecute. Don't we live by the laws of innocent until proven guilty?"

I found humor in this question, "Aren't we also supposed to live by the law, *Thou shalt not kill?*"

Max smiled, and I heard Nicholai chuckle on the phone and add, "She's sharp, just like her father. Good genes if I do say so myself." Then he continued, "We would have loved to remove him from his position but never had enough proof. As you can see, he has removed himself. No problem on the Seniors panel now . . . except for a vacancy, Max . . . ."

That was clearly a leading question and one which Max seemed to ignore as he continued to stare out the window.

There was a quiet moment in the room while everyone's minds were working.

I cleared my throat, breaking the silence. "So, I have a question. Was 'YOU ARE NEXT' referring to me?" Even though the answer seemed obvious, no one spoke.

"Well?" I prompted.

It was Nicholai who responded first. "I'm not sure. Tomas is a very powerful Aurator. If he had wanted to kill you, it would be feasible to guess that he would have at least tried to. This feels more like a message. Something to be acknowledged somehow."

His last few words trailed off as my attention was beckoned in another direction. Pictures flashed in my mind and shifted as I saw the flowers and the panes of glass. I could clearly identify now the glass dome of the San Francisco landmark, the Conservatory of Flowers. "Could he be making a prediction about the upcoming fight?" I asked.

There was silence. I found myself immersed in visions that surrounded me, blocking out all else in the room. They flipped quickly in front of me, as if I were watching an old silent movie. Images of the zoo and conservatory faded in and out and then spun out of view, only to be replaced by other places and faces I had never seen before. Suddenly the site where the fight was to take place slowed in front of me, so close I could touch it, and then the focus sharpened. I felt as though I were standing there, so close to the flowers I could smell them, and I felt a slight breeze sweep my hair around my shoulders. Out of the corner of my eye, I caught the slightest glimpse of movement among the outlying trees. I squinted for better focus and saw a dark aura moving in and out of the shadows just on the periphery, weaving along an invisible path connecting the massive palm trees that hemmed the skirt of grass around the flower beds.

As I struggled to keep my focus, the dark aura began moving toward me, skimming over and barely brushing against the blades of grass below. My breath caught as the face came into view and broke my concentration. Bringing reality back into focus, I saw that Max was now standing in front of me with anticipation permeating his cautious expression.

"What did you see?" He asked in a concerned voice.

"Megan?" I heard Nicholai on the speaker. I realized from his tone that he hadn't been able to see my thoughts. My voice resounded in the room with a confidence that surprised even me. "Tomas is here and he's organizing. The written message in the monkey's cage was meant for me, but I don't think he set out to kill that man at the zoo . . ."

"Tomas killed him?" Max interrupted.

"Yes."

"Damn him," Nicholai cursed.

"Wait, let me finish. He tried to recruit the man from the zoo, but I don't think he was from this area." I paused, trying to picture the man again. His face . . . alive . . . was one of the images that had flashed in front of me. "He seems a little out of sorts." My head cocked in a perplexed fashion as I stared off into the distance.

Nicholai snapped me out of it, "Megan, is there anything else? He *seems* out of sorts."

"I'm seeing him before he died, though why, I can't seem to get a handle on. Otherwise, there's nothing else."

Nicholai's voice moved from one of concern to a tone of authority. "I'm calling a meeting with all the Seniors. Max, I'll give you a call later. Let me know if anything else comes up."

"Okay, bye," and without breaking his gaze on me, Max clicked off the phone.

23. Connections

I left Max, walked to my car, and drove away. I had an errand to run today. I had decided to take my grandfather's pin that Max had given to me to a jeweler and have it turned into a necklace. I drove to one of my favorite areas of the city, where the street was filled with small specialty shops. Before I had children, I would spend a lot of my free time down here, wandering through the stores, getting a cup of coffee, and frequently spending more money than I should.

Finding parking a block away from my destination was a complete stroke of luck, and I walked toward the shop. I saw the wooden store sign above the door, brown with gold letters inscribed that read "K. Tahati Jewelers." My husband and I had our wedding rings designed and made here. It was a wonderful jewelers and even though I didn't buy jewelry often . . . well, ever . . . I did come to have my ring checked and cleaned every year or so. I passed the display windows and saw the biggest diamond I had ever seen in my life set into a unique, intricately designed setting. Probably a brilliant find for someone who had an extra ten thousand dollars lying around.

I walked through the doors and heard the familiar jingle of the Christmas bells that hung there all year. There were two long counters on either side of the small room with display cases on the wall behind them filled with gold, silver, and various gems that caught the light from the fluorescents above and sparkled. Gretchen stood at the end of the room next to the cash register. She was a tall, slim woman who was always smartly dressed. Probably in her fifties, her brown hair was just starting to gray. It was very becoming on her. Always with a warm smile, her face brightened as I walked toward her.

"Hi Megan, how are you?" I sighed at this. This is just not something you get at the big major retail stores.

"Hi Gretchen, good to see you."

"Is there a problem with your ring? Didn't you just have it cleaned a few months ago?"

"Yes I did, thanks. I'm actually here for something else."

"Great! How's the family?"

I filled her in on the girls and Luke and heard how she and her partner were getting ready for their daughter to go off to college. I opened my purse, pulled out the small box, and handed it to her.

"This pin was my grandfather's but I don't really ever wear pins. I was hoping that Kevin could turn it into a necklace for me." Just then the bells rang and Kevin Tahati, who owned the store and designed and made all the jewelry walked in. He was a very good-looking, easygoing man with a soft-spoken voice, jet black hair that glistened under the lights, and ebony skin that showed absolutely no wrinkles, which was uncommon in a man his age. Likely in his sixties, he always dressed unassumingly for such a successful businessman, in jeans, tennis shoes, and a casual button-up shirt. He owned and operated one of the best jewelers in the San Francisco Bay Area but always had an air of modesty about him.

"Hi Megan, how are you? How's Luke?" Kevin always liked Luke, and they would talk sports when he came in with me.

"Good, thanks. How are you?"

"Oh I'm good, thanks. What's up?" He spoke as he started toward the counter, never breaking eye contact with me.

Gretchen interrupted by holding up the small box. "Megan has a pin she wants to change into a necklace."

Kevin walked behind the counter, setting down his briefcase. "Okay, let's see what we've got here." He opened the box and his expression changed to one of confusion. "Where did you get this?"

I took a quick look at the two standing in front of me. White auras. I didn't think there should be a problem here. "It was my grandfather's."

Kevin studied the pin, removing it from the box and holding it in his hand. Then, as if acknowledging someone speaking, he nodded his head and said, "Okay, my morning is free. I can have it for you in thirty minutes. Okay with you?"

Gretchen looked surprised by this. "But aren't you finishing the Castlers' wedding rings?"

He turned and walked to the back office, which contained all of his equipment. "Yes, but I need to do this first," and he disappeared.

Gretchen turned back toward me with a surprised look that I know must have mirrored my own. "Okay then," she said with a forced and seemingly unsure smile, "half an hour?"

I looked at my watch. That was exactly how much time I had before I needed to be at school for pickup. "Um, okay, sure. I'll go get a cup of coffee and walk around." I turned and left. As I heard the bells jingle behind me, I felt something in the pit of my stomach. I pulled out my phone and dialed Max's number. There was no answer, so I left a message for him to call me back.

I wandered down to the local coffee shop, passing up the chain coffee house that was just across the street. Standing outside with my cup, I started to wonder about Kevin's reaction. There was no red aura so they wouldn't have been able to see mine. They couldn't possibly know anything about what I am. I shook my head and thought that it must be just like other times in my life when I was making something out of nothing.

Switching gears, I began to think about what my presence on television would mean. Would others know about me . . . seek me out? I felt a sudden panic. Would anyone try to hurt my family? I began to wonder if it would be worth it to tell Luke. As I was mulling over this new concern, my phone rang.

"Hello?"

"Hi Megan, it's Gretchen. He's . . . done."

Looking at my watch, I saw that only twenty minutes had passed. "Umm, okay. I'll be right there."

As I walked back in, Kevin met me halfway. "Wow, Kevin, that was quick. I really appreciate it."

He smiled at me as an old friend would to another. "Anything I can do." He then raised his hands up, each holding half of the chain clasp. My grandfather's pin was hanging from a small metal loop that had been added at the top. The charm was shinier than before and it seemed to glow. "Does it meet your approval?" he asked.

I reached out and cupped the form of Asclepius's rod in the palm of my hand. My skin warmed beneath the metal. "Yes, better than I could have imagined. Thank you."

"Turn around and I'll put it on you. I reinforced the charm loop so that there is no chance it will break, and the clasp is the best that I have and . . . should *never* break."

I pulled my hair to the side and saw the necklace come down in front of my face. He pulled the chain around and I heard the clasp click into place. I felt a warmth through my shirt where the metal lay against it. I released my hair and touched the pendant. *I am exactly where I am supposed to be at this moment in time* I thought to myself.

Turning back toward him, I noticed his expression had shifted to one of worry as I spoke. "Thank you for the necklace. What do I owe you?"

The worry lines became a bit more prominent. "Nothing . . . and thank you."

I was caught off guard and nearly speechless. "What?"

But he motioned with his head toward Gretchen in a way that made me realize he did not want to explain further. He repeated, "Thank you . . . for everything."

So confused I could barely speak, I played along. "Okay . . . thank you. Are you sure?" I found myself almost whispering.

"Yes."

I reached out and shook his hand. He held it longer than was comfortable but I didn't pull away. I moved toward the door and waved to Gretchen, who looked confused as well.

"Megan?" Kevin stopped me.

I turned to look toward him, "Yes?"

Then with a knowing smile on his face, he said, "Say hi to Max for me."

I couldn't hide my astonishment as I replied okay. I walked out of the store and toward the car in disbelief when I heard the phone ring.

"Hello?"

"Hi, Megan. Max here. What do you need?"

"Something really strange just happened." I retold my experience in the jewelry store as Max listened. I expected him to be just as confused as I was and to hit me with a barrage of questions, but there were none.

So you had the pin made into a necklace?" Max asked

"Yes, but that wasn't the point of what I just told you. How would Kevin know I knew you?"

"What was the name of the jewelers?"

"K. Tahati."

"I've known him for years. His son is an Aurator who lives in Europe. I met his son years ago after we had seen each other's auras at a medical conference in the city."

"Great, another doctor?"

"A nurse."

"Oh, okay, good."

Max chuckled. "So how does it look?" he asked

"What?"

He spoke slowly as if trying to make a point. "The . . . necklace."

"It's great. It makes a very beautiful necklace." I reached up and touched it.

"Did you feel the warmth when you put it on?" he asked.

"Yeah I did. What's up with that?"

"Power . . . serpodus . . . purpose. It's everything that validates who we are," he explained.

"That's along the lines of what I thought when I put it on."

"Good, then you're paying attention." He spoke with an amused tone.

"Very funny," I scoffed.

"So what are you doing this afternoon?" Max asked as I started my car engine.

Looking at my watch, I realized the time and told him, "Well, I'm off to pick up Abigail." I turned out of my parking spot and headed toward the elementary school.

"Good. If I may be so bold, try to take time to enjoy your girls while they're young because it goes so fast. Plus, in our line of business we don't know what our future holds."

"Max, do most . . . Aurator's families know about them. You know, what they do?" I connected my bluetooth as I drove away, knowing that I did not just ask a simple yes or no question.

"Not initially, a new Aurator usually doesn't understand what's going on enough to explain to their families. However, eventually it becomes necessary to tell your close family. It gets increasingly difficult to keep coming up with new explanations for your frequent absence. At some point you have to trust that if we really are meant to do this then our loved ones will understand."

I entered the carpool lane to pick up my youngest. Luckily I could enjoy the luxury of waiting for just her today because Luke was picking up the other girls. I saw Abigail come out and the teacher nudged her in my direction. "Max, can you hold on one moment?" The car door opened and Abigail climbed in. "Hi honey, good day?" I greeted her.

"Yeah mommy."

"Great, mommy's on the phone okay? Do you have some reading you can start on the way home?"

"Sure."

I then returned to my phone conversation, "Okay, thanks Max. So, can I ask . . . how did Vivian find out?"

"I never planned to tell her, but it became a necessity one night." I could hear him take a breath on the other end and then continued. "First you need to know a little about Vivian. She comes from a very well-to-do family in the city that was very active among the philanthropy circle. My family was, as well, and as much as I hated going to charitable functions it was expected that I attend. I always felt I was meant to do something different than just donate money.

"I was at a large function one night listening to a very pompous speaker tell of all the good he had done when across the room I saw the most unbelievably beautiful woman. Don't get me wrong, there may be more beautiful women in the world to others' eyes, but no one had ever equaled what I was looking at in that moment. While I was looking at her she rolled her eyes at the speaker and I was smitten. When the speech was over, I walked over and asked her to dance. We spoke about making a difference . . . a real difference. We seemed destined for each other."

I pulled into the driveway, and Abi and I went inside. She asked if she could watch television before continuing her homework, and I was so engrossed with Max's story I did the unthinkable and obliged her. After her eyes widened at the unexpected yes, she quickly disappeared into the other room before I could change my mind. I hung my purse on the back of the dining room chair, disconnected the bluetooth so I could hear clearer and continued to listen.

"Several years passed and we were married and eventually had two sons. I had finished my residency and began working on staff at the hospital. My shift usually ended in the middle of the night, and one night while I was leaving the hospital I came across a man with a solid black circle around him. Of course I learned later this was an aura. I was compelled to follow him and suddenly flashed back to what I thought had been a nightmare the week before. My mind connected the two, and my body reacted before I could comprehend what was happening. I completed my first purpose in that moment and got to the car before the pain hit. It was excruciating and I almost went back into the emergency room, but it passed and somehow I knew I was all right. From that day on I saw everyone's auras.

"There were a few more purposes along the way and I eventually met Paul, who stopped me in front of a small shop one day when I was buying a birthday present for Vivian. He had noticed my red aura. He befriended me and taught me about Aurators and what my responsibilities were. He was also the Guardian of the journal which you have been given. His name was Paul Tahati and he was my mentor."

There was a pause and I could only guess some remembrance of sadness. I connected the jeweler's knowledge of us suddenly with more depth.

"Max? How many of us are there in San Francisco?" I asked.

"Hmmm," he pondered, "I don't know exactly. Remember though, except for the Seniors in Greece and us, no one has been formally organized. The Seniors have only been together for around thirty years or so, and that was at the urging of Tomas and . . . well . . . others."

Just then the door opened and my other two girls came in. They saw the television on and looked at me inquisitively, to which I waved that it was okay and they disappeared. It's okay, I thought, double homework tomorrow. I took a moment to mouth, "Where's Dad?" Alex whispered back, "He's working in the garage."

Max cleared his throat. "Anyway, I went off on a tangent. I'm sorry. These purposes went on for some time, but one night in particular was very difficult and I got hurt in the scuffle. It was my own fault really. I fell off a scaffolding. Don't ask how. I came home that night and had some scrapes on my face and arm. Vivian was there and when she asked what happened . . . I . . . well, I thought about lying but I was tired of lying. Not being able to keep it from her anymore, I began to tell her the whole story. She sat on the couch next to me, listening to everything. She made no attempt to interrupt or ask questions. When I was finished, I hung my head and would not make eye contact . . . ashamed. Not for doing what I had done but for being dishonest.

"She got up from the couch at that moment and walked out, shutting the door behind her. I was so scared. I thought for sure she was going to pack, take our two sons, and leave me. Or call a doctor or the police."

I wanted to interrupt him to ask questions but I was sitting on my seat, engrossed in each word he spoke.

"Moments later she reentered the room holding a box. She sat back down on the couch next to me and placed the box on the coffee table. I wondered what was in the box. It looked like an old sewing kit, and for a split second I hoped she didn't have a gun in there."

He chuckled at this.

"Well, needless to say, I'm still here. She unclasped the lid and swung it open. Taking out antiseptic and bandages, she began to clean and cover my abrasions. We still laugh about that box, I'm the doctor in the house and didn't even know there was a first aid kit. She did not speak while she cleaned each wound, and quite frankly I knew better than to say anything. When she was finished she closed the box and sighed. I waited, nervously.

"She said to me, 'Max, you've never given me any reason to distrust you. You are a great husband and father. You have an amazing work ethic and genuinely care about others.'

"Then looking at me she said, 'I believe you. We always agreed we wanted to make a real difference and here's the opportunity.'"

Max paused for a moment, then said, "I was ecstatic, this had gone considerably better than I had anticipated. 'However,' she started again, 'I will not have our sons put into jeopardy. So mark my words, I love you and will stay with you, but the minute our children are in danger I will leave and you will never hear from me again.' I remember this so vividly. Her eyes were intense with no hint of indecision. From then on she knew everything. Everywhere I was going, what I was doing and what I had done. It has made things much easier, but not everyone is as open with their family. You have to make the decision that is right for you, Megan."

"Me?"

"Yes, you. I'm assuming that the reason you asked me this question was not because you are so entranced with my life that you need to know more. Rather, you're gathering information to make a well-informed choice of your own. Am I right?"

I smiled, "Yes, you're right."

"Well, dear, only you will know if it's right or not. If I can help in any other way I will."

I didn't seem to flinch when he called me dear. I thought about this for a moment, took a deep breath, and then took a leap of faith to speak. "Max?"

"Yes?"

"I'm a little curious about my husband's . . . aura."

"What about it?" he asked with interest.

I dropped my voice slightly in case any of the girls were listening in on my conversation, "Well . . . when I married him it was, white . . . sort of, and gold-like, shimmering . . . it seemed to make me feel safe and secure."

Max interrupted, "It's what?! Did you say gold in color? That is . . ."

But I cut him off because that was not my point. "Max, listen to me . . . it's not now . . . it's, well, dark." There was silence on the other end of the line. "Hello? Are you there?"

He cleared his throat to let me know he was still on the line but then said nothing. I waited for what felt like forever until he finally spoke.

"Megan, I think we should talk about this. You are not supposed to be with a dark aura. This can't be good . . . for you. Plus I don't understand why it would . . . change."

He spoke with a tone of authority that I had not heard before. "Max, I thought we had discussed how auras can change based on decisions. Well, I don't know what decisions he could be making that would cause this, but . . . oh I don't know anymore."

I could hear him take a deep breath in, "I'm sorry Megan, you are right, it *can* change. I'm just surprised . . . I . . ." but then he trailed off in a leading fashion and I knew it was my turn to speak.

I wanted to ask more questions about his reaction but decided to table the conversation.

"Max, thanks for everything and for looking out for me. Can we talk about this later?"

"You're welcome. Anything to help you, and yes, we will discuss this later. We will have to." His voice was not encouraging or supportive but rather pacifying.

We said good-bye and hung up. I announced loudly that television time was over and it was time to get homework done. I giggled when I heard the chorus of "Aaawww."

The family had a wonderful night. We laughed over dinner, took a walk before it got dark, and then everyone settled into bed. Even Luke, who had seemed so distant lately, appeared to have a good night.

That night I couldn't sleep. Getting out of bed I walked downstairs. I picked up my phone and dialed Max's number before looking at the clock. Ugh, 12:15 a.m., but it was too late to hang up, the phone was already ringing.

"Hello?" Wow, he answered.

"Max?"

"Hi Megan, what can I do for you?"

"Geez, don't you ever sleep?"

"I'll sleep all I want when I'm dead," he said.

"I've heard that before. Listen, I want to talk to you about Luke and . . . well . . . everything."

"Sure, why don't you come by the house tomorrow, say around ten? We'll see if we can't have another *history* lesson." His voice flitted about as if he knew something I didn't.

"Okay, thanks."

I hung up the phone after our good-byes.

24. Distant

The next morning we all awoke and got ready for the day. Luke was definitely in a foul mood and had announced he wasn't going to work. His aura seemed darker, and I found myself trying not to make eye contact. The girls were thrilled to see both Luke and me taking them to school.

"Daddy?" Trina asked.

"What honey?"

"Are you sick? Why are you not going to work?"

"I'm going in, just later."

Keeping my eyes on the road, I could feel him looking at me from the passenger seat.

After dropping each girl off, we drove back to the house. Once inside, I explained that I had errands to run.

He sneered under his breath, "Always have somewhere to run off to, don't you?"

My heart hurt when I heard his disgusted tone, and I shook my head back and forth slowly. "What Luke? What have I done? Why are you like this? I don't understand."

Losing the battle against the tears that were struggling to break free, I began to cry. I sat down on the couch and put my face in my hands. I let the tears flow. In all the years we've been together, I had never felt as distant from him as I did in this moment. In so many ways I was so strong now, but with this man I felt so vulnerable and fragile. This was foreign, and a very scary place for me to be. My rock, whom I have depended on for years, was crumbling in front of me, and I didn't have any idea how to fix it.

Luke walked over to sit beside me, but as he did I felt a cold front emanating from his aura push against my side and I instinctively pulled away. He responded to my movement and did not attempt to move any closer.

He took a deep breath and began to speak. "I'm sorry for . . . well, I don't know what for. Something is different lately, and, quite frankly I have been blaming you. You seem distant and gone, not here. Even when you're here in the flesh you seem otherwise preoccupied. But the truth is that I seem to be going through something right now. I'm not sure why, but for the first time since we've been together I don't feel connected to you." He paused to see if I would respond.

Looking up finally, I noticed that his aura had a slight shimmer to it. My husband was in there somewhere. I asked him, "What can I do? I don't like us like this."

He shook his head to show he had no answers.

Not wanting to leave things like this, I reached out for him. Pushing past the coolness, I took his hand. He squeezed my hand back, but things were different. "What now?" I asked.

"I don't know," he responded. "You know, other friends have gone through troubled times and they have come out of it just fine. It's just . . ." He turned away as if looking for an escape from the room. He got up, and I watched him pull his fingers through his wavy blonde hair as he walked away from me. He drew in a long breath before he spoke again. "I don't know what's going on. I'm so angry all the time. I've never felt like this and I don't like it but . . . well it's just where I am right now."

"Do we need to go to counseling?" I asked. The husband I used to know would never frown on outside help, but this man? I wasn't sure he'd be up for it.

My breath caught as he turned around briskly and I felt a sharp stab of cold. My instincts to react to this fired up, and I fought to keep my actions under control. I waited and watched as he glared at me for what felt like hours. His face looked angry and pained with words that were struggling to get out and lips that were desperately trying to keep them in. A black aura stretched around what looked like his shimmering gold aura trying to break through the heavy armor. After several moments the scuffle seemed to end as the shimmering gold glimmer of hope slipped away.

He sighed a long sigh, and I knew the conversation was coming to an end. The face that had anger and frustration on it just moments before fell into a flat emotionless facade, covering every emotion he was not willing to entertain. Walking toward the front door he grabbed his jacket, but turned slightly without making eye contact to add one last parting thought. "I don't know how much longer I can feel this way . . . do . . . this." And then he was gone.

25. The Light

A couple of hours had passed since Luke walked out the door. All I knew at this moment was that I needed to change my shirt, which had become saturated with tears. I wish I had an answer for this. What makes someone go so wrong? Was I to blame? Was I doomed to spend the rest of my life with the man who just walked out the door? So many questions and not enough answers.

I jumped at the sound of my cell phone ringing. I raced across the room to grab it. I answered it before checking who was calling, "Luke? Luke?"

There was a brief silence on the other end, and my heart skipped a few beats thinking it was Luke. "No . . . Megan? I'm sorry, this is Max."

Max? I gasped as I looked at the clock which read ten-thirty. "Oh no, Max, I'm so sorry. I'm leaving right now. I'll be right there."

"Megan, take your time," he said with obvious concern in his voice. "Are you okay?"

I took a moment to answer, probably long enough to prove that I wasn't okay. "I'm just running late. I'll be right there."

After hanging up, I rushed to clean myself up and raced out the door. I made it to Max's house in record time, and he was waiting for me at the door. I took a deep breath and told myself to hold it together since this wasn't the right time or place to get into the dilemma that was my marriage.

He reached out for me as I walked into the room and hugged me very close. My walls were crashing down around me, as I struggled to keep control. I opened my mouth to ask him to release me, but what came out instead was a muffled scream buried deep into his argyle sweater vest. The tears came faster than I could have imagined as my body began to shake.

He moved me toward the couch and held me for a while as my frustrations continued to pour out.

Finally the crying slowed and I was able to tell Max about Luke. By the time I had finished the story of his aura shifting, his moods, and the anger that seemed to encompass him, Max and I were sitting apart but he continued to hold my hands. He said nothing and simply listened.

After I finished talking and had a better grasp on my emotions, I asked Max, "What do I do now?"

He reached up to lightly stroke my cheek and said, "Nothing."

He smiled as if reading the confusion on my face. "That's right, Megan, nothing. Not everything in life needs to be fixed. And even if it does, it usually can wait. Give it some time and let Luke work out whatever he is going through. It is not up to you to determine how fast he changes and grows, you just have to determine whether you want to be there to watch him go through the process."

I scoffed. Even if his advice were right, I wanted a fix. Before I could say this, Max interrupted me.

"Megan, this one's not your battle. God, grant me the serenity to accept the things I cannot change, the courage to change the things I can . . . and the wisdom to know the difference."

I didn't want to feel better, but I grew up with this saying in my house since my parents were in Alcoholics Anonymous, and this phrase always gave me a "get out of jail free" feeling. A do-nothing clause for the situations in life when we are at our most hopeless. I nodded at Max, and he leaned to kiss me on the forehead.

"It'll be okay. You'll see." He lifted my face to his, and the look on his face gave me hope.

"Okay Max." Then taking a deep breath I decided to move on. "What did you want to tell me?"

His eyebrows furrowed slightly as he nodded his head up and down. "Tell me about your family, Megan. You have three daughters, correct?"

"Yes, why?"

Max walked over to his desk and started flipping through several papers and old leather-bound books. "Tell me about them? What are they like? Are their auras . . . well . . . white . . . like Luke used to be? Or like he is now?"

I felt slightly defensive at this comment about Luke's aura and that my children, who were good to the core could have anything wrong with them. I decided to explain. "Max, my girls have auras . . . but they are neither white nor black. They are, in fact, gold."

He stopped moving papers around and his head turned and his eyelids raised with a look of inquisitiveness. "I'm sorry, what color?"

"Gold," I stated very matter-of-fact.

There were several moments of silence while he stared at me

"Are you sure? I don't question your instinct on this, but . . . gold?"

"Yes, ever since they were babies each one of them has had a very distinct gold aura."

He had a pained look on his face. "I don't know how to explain this. I have a mathematical equation in front of me that does not add up. Wait a minute." His voice trailed off as he rose from his desk, walked to the other side of his study, and opened a small drawer in a built-in bookshelf. After lifting up a few pages, he pulled out a single sheet of off-white paper wrapped in plastic with what looked like handwritten words on it. Studying it for a moment, he turned to me and took a deep breath before he spoke. "These are words written by another Aurator who was friends with Hippocrates." He held up the single sheet of paper.

I gestured to show that I didn't understand the importance.

He smiled and said, "Listen." He read, "You need to continue to foster the future of our family, and this will be accomplished in the tri-feminine with the secondary gift."

Max's eyes furrowed as he stopped. "Your girls have gold auras? All of them?"

"Yes."

Scratching his head, "I have to admit that this is a bit confusing, but there's something here about a secondary gift. Do any of your girls show any signs of special skills?"

I paused to think about it. "No," I said in a tentative tone, waiting for what was next.

He motioned for me to join him. We walked over to a painting hanging next to his desk. "Have you ever seen this painting before?" Max asked pointing at a reproduction of a painting I had seen many times before of Jesus as a toddler and his mother Mary. I nodded yes.

"Well, what do you notice about the painting?"

I looked at it but came up with nothing and shook my head.

After a moment, Max answered his own question. "Okay, see the halo around both Mary and Jesus?"

I nodded but still didn't understand where he was going with this.

"What if I told you these were auras?"

That got my attention.

Now I could see it differently. Circular gold *auras* were drawn around the heads. I had never considered this possibility, but here I was, staring at a picture of Jesus with an aura—a gold one—and I wondered what it could mean.

Max began again, "Throughout history there have been many paintings of Jesus that had this halo. However . . . they were usually drawn by Aurators and always depicted auras. Sort of changes things, right?"

"Well, it does put a different perspective on those old paintings," I replied

"The word halo, or *halos* in Greek means a light encircling the sun or moon. In other words, a light encircling the whole celestial body . . . aura."

"Wait," I interrupted. "If Jesus was supposed to be of immaculate conception and Aurators were all men, then why did Mary also have the aura?" I was proud of my astute observation and raised one eyebrow at Max.

Max's grin widened with what I could only guess was his amusement at my infantile question. Suddenly I wished I could take it back.

"That's a good question. The history books do depict a woman . . . a virgin . . . getting pregnant with Jesus. So of course, how else could it have happened but by heavenly means. The truth, however, is that in those days they had no means to medically check to see if someone was a virgin. Quite frankly, even today you can get pregnant without . . . well . . . complete . . . um . . . action."

I was surprised and mildly entertained at his sudden embarrassment. He cleared his throat and continued.

"Anyway, my belief, and the belief of all Aurators, is that Jesus was just part of a long bloodline of extraordinary people. However, he seems to have been one of the most powerful and clearly the most famous."

Even though this idea tore apart my religious realities, things were starting to make sense. I was in the right place. The pieces were connecting for me. But what would this mean for my family?

"Hmm," Max said. "I suppose we're going to have to figure this Luke situation out. Give me a minute. I want to make a phone call." He stood and went to the phone and dialed. I heard a ringing echoing in my head and realized he was calling Nicholai.

Fiddling with the spiral cord on his antique phone, Max spoke in the receiver, "Hello? Yes, it's Max." He explained what we had been discussing and then his voice faded out.

My mind wandered to what Max had read to me. Tri-feminine? What did that mean? My maternal instinct fired up when I thought about my daughters being dragged into this kind of madness.

Max hung up the phone and turned toward me. He was just about to speak when someone knocked on his study door. Before he could answer, the door swung open and a tall man with familiar features walked into the room. He was a good-looking man who entered with confidence.

"Hi Dad," he said as entered the room. Then seeing me, he stopped in his tracks. "I'm so sorry. I didn't realize you were with someone. I couldn't find Mom, so I came here." He walked over to Max and they embraced in a hug.

"That's okay. This is my friend Megan." Then motioning back toward his son he made introductions. "Megan, this is my son, Bill."

I stood to meet him as he walked toward me. Now I could see his features more clearly. Salt and pepper hair, which he must have gotten from his mother, but the face was all Max. His aura was bright white . . . just like his mother. We shook hands and then he turned back toward Max.

"I'm sorry to interrupt. We were in the neighborhood, and I just wanted to say hi."

Max's smile shone with the warmth of a proud father as he spoke to him. "No, never a problem. You're welcome anytime. Who are you with?"

"Jeffery's with me."

"Jeffery?" Max exclaimed, almost giddy.

"Yes, he's looking for Grandma to update her on his latest painting."

Max turned toward me. "Come on, I'd like you to meet my grandson."

We all walked out and down the long hallway that led to the kitchen. I had never been to this part of the house. I had just seen the entry and his study. We entered a kitchen that looked like it was straight out of the pages of *Architectural Digest*. The walls were covered by cabinets that were a deep mahogany and reflected the twenty or so meticulously recessed lights sprinkled across the ceiling. There were several black granite countertops that encircled a massive island containing the cooktop and a second sink. The floors looked like Italian tile with hand-painted tiles scattered throughout.

Everything was spotless and shiny and looked brand-new. Vivian was sitting at a small table in a nook next to the kitchen. She walked over to us, stretched her arms wide, and with a large smile she gave me a big hug.

I looked over at the table to the seat next to Vivian's. My breathing stopped. I saw a handsome man in his twenties, their grandson, sitting at the chair. However, I also saw the red aura that encircled him. I took a deep breath and walked forward to greet him. He seemed to sense my odd reaction and looked back and forth at the others before shaking my hand.

We said our pleasantries and Bill began talking with his mother, so Max excused himself and shuffled us back to his study.

Back in his study he shut the door again and turned toward me. "What was that about?"

I looked at him, "What?"

"What happened when you saw my grandson?"

I suddenly wondered if Max could see his aura. "Wait a minute, what color is Jeffery's aura to you?"

Max's forehead wrinkled, "White."

I shook my head, "Max, his aura was red."

His eyes went wide with shock, "What?"

"I swear. That's exactly what I saw. Why didn't you?"

He sat down and stared at the floor mumbling, "I don't understand, how can this be. I don't see it." Then looking up at me, "He didn't seem to notice an aura around anyone. What if he hasn't completed a purpose yet but because of your skills you can see his before?"

"I don't know, Max, but I'm telling you there's no doubt in my mind that he has a red aura."

A smile grew on Max's face and he said with a sense of pride, "Well, it seems I was able to pass it along. I had wondered, but no one's aura ever changed so I figured that it wasn't to be. He's twenty-seven years old. I wonder if he's getting close."

This suddenly was a funny thought to me . . . Max was excited that his grandson was also going to be a killer. Odd that this should be such an acceptable desire for a family member.

Looking at me, Max added, "Well, I guess I missed the obvious when I went to his graduation from his master's program last June. He received his master's in nursing."

"Ahh, smart man," I said.

We said our good-byes and I headed home. My mind couldn't help but wander while driving, and I began to wonder what the future would hold for Luke and me. Was I really to spend my life with someone with a dark aura? I reflected back on that first day we met and I could almost feel the warmth on my skin just as I did on that first day. A smile spread across my face. but as I pulled up to the house I could feel it slip away. I pulled next to Luke's truck in the driveway and saw Luke sitting on the front steps.

I felt a heaviness and sadness in my heart as I looked toward him. He met my gaze with an angry face, one that made me not want to leave the car. I paused for a moment, took a deep breath and then stepped out. As I walked up to meet him, he stood.

"Where have you been?" he asked gruffly.

"I had errands to do. What are you doing home? Work isn't over."

"Well, I came home to talk with you, but you weren't home and you didn't answer your phone. Want to tell me where you've been?" He looked at me with an unchanged angry face that dripped with mistrust.

I did want to tell him, everything. He had reason to doubt me. I had been lying for a while now. This was my chance, I could tell him everything, we could be closer, we could be . . . .

Just then the air around me became colder as I watched his aura grow and darken right before my eyes. I felt sick to my stomach. No! I thought, please no. My eyes filled with tears and I couldn't utter a word. I was frozen.

"I didn't think so." He spoke sharply. "I don't know what you're doing, or who you're doing it with but . . . well . . ."

His voice cut out and I watched his face deepen into a shade of red I'd never seen on him.

"I need to leave. I can't do this right now. I'll see you later," he said.

I watched him walk away, fuming as he stumbled on his way to his truck. I struggled inside my numb self to say something, anything, but nothing escaped my lips.

I watched him drive away and turned to walk up the stairs as I felt the tears flow from my eyes. My body stopped suddenly as if I had hit a brick wall and I spun around in self-defense, but no one was there. I scanned the neighborhood slowly moving from house to house. I couldn't see anything but I felt as if something or someone was there.

I moved to go inside when I felt a sharp stabbing pain to my rib cage, knocking me back several feet. I hit the ground hard and gasped trying to catch the breath that had been knocked out of me. Facing the ground, I tried to get up but felt something pushing me from behind. Struggling against the pressure I suddenly heard someone breathing. I should have been panicked but I was thinking too clearly. Wait. I wasn't feeling any heat or coolness behind me. An Aurator?

A sudden chill started in the center of my back and rippled throughout my body. I could feel my muscles tensing in defense as I reached around with exceptional ease against my attacker. I got ahold of a piece of clothing and twisted so quickly that it surprised even me. Finding myself kneeling in front of another person who was mirroring my own stance, I froze. There in front of me was a man whose brown eyes were wide in surprise. His sandy blonde hair was straight and cut very close to the scalp, a military style. What I noticed the most about him, however, was his red aura. Muddied brown as it was, it was definitely red and seemed to arch over me, hovering in anticipation.

I tried to move backwards but he grabbed me. There were no words spoken as we struggled. Each of my moves countered by his, simulating a rapid dance. He turned me away from him with my arm twisted behind my back. He moved his face to my ear and spoke.

"We saw you on TV. You should have known better. We've been talking about you. You cannot live. But don't worry, once you're gone we'll get rid of your family too so they don't miss you. Although watching your husband and you . . . I doubt he'll miss you." And he exhaled the rest of his breath into my ear.

I could feel the protective nature taking over my body. *No one will hurt my family*, I thought. With a surge of anger I jumped and was able to flip backwards over his head, landing on the ground behind him and out of his grip. I reached up and grasped his head, instantaneously snapping his neck. Feeling the weight of his body pulling on my grip, I let his head slip through my fingers and he dropped to the ground.

The whole event happened so fast that I was stunned. My breathing was still quick as I returned to my defensive mode, looking around. *Protect. Protect.* It was all I could think.

Turning my head slightly, I listened. I could hear the faintest sound from . . . I couldn't tell where. Then I heard a rumbling and realized a car was approaching. I scrambled to move the body as a cool tingling coursed through my veins . . . transformation. An unknown car passed as I heard another sound, this time coming from a group of trees at the end of our block. I moved toward the sound as I saw blackness disappear between the trees. Damn it!

Then turning back to the man I saw the last glimpse of his red aura as it disappeared. Shaking my head in disbelief, I dragged the unknown attacker to the side of the house and rushed to my car, thinking only about my girls. As I drove away, I became more and more anxious not having them near me. If anything happened to them what would I do? I couldn't think about it and accelerated.

I picked up Trina first and then Alex. When I had Abigail I could feel my chest expand as I finally was able to take a deep breath. Feeling thankful to have them, I went back home. I shuffled them safely inside and went to work to get rid of the body.

I called Max and he came over. I took him to where I had left the body. Briefly speaking about what the attacker had said to me, Max nodded as if understanding everything. Without touching the man, Max levitated him in the air and we placed him in the trunk of his car, looking around and wondering how so many people can be so oblivious to what's going on in their neighborhood. It's no wonder so many people get away with murder on a regular basis.

I turned to Max, "Thanks for helping. I wasn't sure what to do with my girls here."

Walking toward me with a fatherly look, he said, "Now dear, I wouldn't want you dirtying your hands. You just kill them and I'll throw out the trash."

He started to turn, then paused before turning back toward me. "Megan, you need to do what's best for you and for your daughters. We'll do our best to help you keep them safe. They know who you are and this may only be the first time you have to deal with such an attack." From his tone I could tell he didn't mean safe only from other Aurators and the Caduceus, but also safe from the darkness growing in my own home.

"I know. Maybe keeping my girls here, where they can find them is the wrong thing." I put my hands up to my face and drew in a deep breath. "What's the right thing to do?" Max reached up and gently brought my hands back down, cradling them in his own.

"Don't worry, you will know. But remember that you are probably the only one who can protect them and that's a tall order. We need you for what you are meant to be, and if something happens to you because of trying to protect your family then all is lost. Just think about it." He smiled a very concerned look at me before getting into his car and driving away.

Just then Luke's car pulled into the driveway and I moved to the side as he walked past me silently and went in the house. From the coldness I felt, I was left wondering why he came back home already.

That night I was alone downstairs while Luke and the girls were sound asleep. I had tried to speak with Luke again that night but he wouldn't engage. I pondered this last thought and decided to get Hippocrates's journal. Maybe there was something in it that could help guide me better.

I went into my closet where I had hidden it in one of my many shoe boxes. It wasn't as mystically placed and magically obtained as Max's hiding place. Still, it seemed fitting for me.

I made a cup of tea and went to the couch. I decided to start at the beginning. I already knew most of it, the story of Asclepius, his birth, so poignant now considering my own birth. As I read of Asclepius's life with his adoptive Centaur father, I began to draw correlations between his life and my own. Hippocrates did an exceptional job of describing the beginning . . . our beginning.

Hippocrates wrote of his first purpose, someone who was attempting to kill the first-born males of all families in his community. He had a painful dream that he wrote about and saw faces of children he knew had died and others who had not yet but that he recognized from the community. This frightened him. He had even helped some of these children with his medicine.

He was walking through his city one night when he saw an ominous aura pass by him. He followed it, pulled by an unseen force. He tried to fight the pull and the urges it was creating. As I read about this, my eyes welled up in empathy. I knew what was happening and what he was about to do. And even though every fiber of our being would tell us it was right . . . there was a piece of us that fought against this weight upon us. But it was undeniable why we were here. We are Aurators and we have a purpose. Our purpose is to remove those most caustic to the world. Our actions do not change the world completely but they may make it a little better, more balanced.

I lay my head down to consider this last thought and drifted off. Sweet dreams. My girls running around in a field of flowers.

I was watching them and turning my face toward the sun to feel the warmth when suddenly the sky turned from bright to dark. I couldn't see my children anywhere. I started yelling for them . . . then screaming. I could feel pain in my heart as if it were being stabbed by sadness.

My eyes blurred as I saw a light in front of me. It was out of focus and I struggled to see it. Slowly the object moved toward me and came into view. At first I thought it was the symbol of Asclepius, a bright white rod with a snake moving up and down it. But as it moved closer and came more into view, I saw the image of a man forming.

As he moved closer I could see his curly hair, hanging in ringlets framing his strong face. His face was strong and rugged with deep thoughtful eyes and a beard that crested around his jawline. The image of the man stopped in front of me, and I could see he was wearing a robe cinched up on one shoulder . . . a toga. His red aura was awe-inspiring as it engulfed the totality of my view, and in one hand he held in front of him the staff adorned by a live moving snake. My breath caught . . . Asclepius.

He smiled at me, but all I could do was stare.

He nodded once at me, and without moving his lips I could hear him. "Megan, my sweet love."

"Asclepius?" But my voice was broken and barely audible.

He nodded in acknowledgement just once.

If I hadn't been in a dream I'm sure I would be hyperventilating right now. But still I asked, "Am I dreaming?"

This time he shrugged his shoulders.

"We are all in a piece of time and have no control over when that time happens. There is always the possibility for different times to wrap over each other and allow those of us who are from what you believe is the past to see forward and you, in your present time, may see your perception of the past. For this brief moment we share the same time and space."

"Why now?" I asked.

His face changed from smiling to serious. "You are the one who is to bring all of us together. Our leader. Now is the time. They are coming soon. They have already attempted one attack on you which thankfully was not successful. The Caduceus is meeting now to discuss their next move to eliminate you." He moved one hand to the side to show another scene just behind him. There was the fight at the Conservatory of Flowers, which I now realized was where my dream had started. Men fought while I stood and watched. Asclepius swept his other arm and I saw the seven pillars of the Greek Asklepion Temple. I saw Nicholai and Aleck fighting others. Then, as soon as it started, he moved his arm again and it disappeared.

"Wait," I held out my hand. "What else is to happen?"

His face looked discouraged. "I cannot influence the course of what will happen, so I can only show you part of what will be. You need to do the rest. But trust in your destiny, it has already been written." His form began to move backwards and blur.

"It is time, Megan. Get Max and Aaron and let Nicholai know. The Caduceus is meeting at the house of flowers right now. They do not know you are coming. Go now."

And he was gone.

I awakened with a start, like when you have the sense of falling in your dream and you are jolted back to awareness. I sat up on the couch breathing heavily. I felt a change coming over me. I could see the fight and the players engaging on the lawn. I saw from the clock that it was late, but I pulled my phone from my pocket and dialed.

"Hello?"

He sounded much too alert for so late at night. This man never sleeps, I thought. "Hello, Max?"

"Hello, Megan. How can I help you?"

Where to start. I paused.

"Megan?"

At the same time I heard Nicholai in my head, saying, "You saw Asclepius? He came to you in a vision? Unbelievable!"

Wait a minute, I told him.

"Max, I had a vision and it was Asclepius. The Caduceus are at the Conservatory of Flowers right now. We have to go. Please call Aaron and meet me there. Tonight is the night. It is the same for Nicholai. Their fight will be at the temple." Thinking for a moment, I added, "Please be careful and don't go out into the open until I get there."

Without any hesitation he responded, "So it shall be. We will be there."

Nicholai, did you hear that?

"Yes, I'm working on it now, trying to get ahold of Aleck and we'll get right over to the temple. Who am I fighting? The Caduceus?"

Yes, they are organizing their opposition here and in Greece. They do not know we are coming, but be careful. I saw bits of the fight and we are evenly matched, although I'm not sure why. This may not be as easy as completing a purpose.

"Understood . . . and Megan?"

Yes.

"Please be careful."

I felt a lump in my throat. *You too . . . please.*

We said our good-byes and I went upstairs to wake Luke and try to explain this madness to him. However, when I walked into our room he was sitting straight up in bed.

"Why are you awake? I thought you were asleep?"

"Can't sleep. Off again?"

"Yes, look I . . . work called . . ."

He put a hand up. "It's okay, I've got some reading to do and, well, have a good night."

I could tell that he was trying to get me to leave. I felt utterly unwanted. A pain grew from my chest and expanded outward to every corner of my body.

"Okay," I finally choked out and turned to leave. Now was not the time for any meaningful conversation. I wasn't sure exactly what I was doing, but whatever it was, I needed to be at the Conservatory of Flowers . . . tonight.

26. Battle

I pulled into a parking spot a distance away from the meeting place according to my agreement with Max. Stepping out of the car, I took a deep breath in as I began to walk toward my destination. I looked up and the stars were on fire, as if ready for something.

I looked around and knew this was the place from my visions. It took a moment before my eyes adjusted to the darkness. As I passed through hundreds of beautifully maintained varieties of flowers, the colors and smells almost took my breath away. The grassy areas on either side of the concrete walkway were meticulously manicured and stretched from the street to wrap around the flower beds. I reached a wide set of stairs leading up to the main building.

The main building . . . unbelievable is the only word to describe it. Architectural masterpiece, in the daytime it was white but in the darkness, all lit up, it let off an eerie blue glow. Stretching out in front of me, rows of windows flanked a grand entrance that beckoned the eyes up toward the majestic dome. I sighed.

I caught my breath. Before my eyes there suddenly flashed a vision of what was to come, here, in front of me. The fight. I could see bits and pieces, broken and disjointed like a book with every other page torn out.

Just then I felt Aaron and Max getting closer. A sense of something was building. I closed my eyes to steady myself. I was definitely on alert. My body was tingling, almost as if I could feel the air move around me.

"Hello Max . . . Aaron." I turned to face them before they emerged from the foliage.

"Whoa. You knew we were here?" Aaron spoke first.

"Yes," I said, but my attention was on our surroundings. "I sensed you coming. I can also sense that the others are almost here."

Max smiled, "I'm so glad you came during my lifetime. I'm not sure exactly what my part is, nor is it important to always know why. I'm just glad to know you and be part of the change coming."

I nodded as a thank you but then felt a sudden pain in my neck as if I had been slapped. I snapped my head around and looked. "They're here . . . somewhere . . . everyone get ready."

Just then two very dark auras move out of the brush, followed by the figures they belonged to.

The first man was a six-foot Adonis-looking creature. Beautiful and deplorable at the same time. He had short brown hair and deep ominous eyes that seemed to bore through me. He was dressed in black from head to toe with a large gold Caduceus hanging on a thick chain around his neck.

The other man was not as tall as the first, with lighter hair that seemed to sweep along his shoulders as he walked. His steps were not as intentional but he was much more graceful. Even in the dark I could see his bright flashes of his green eyes gazing intently into mine as they approached.

My insides burned. My enemies.

They stopped forty feet from us. "Gentlemen," the tallest one started, looking beyond me to address Max and Aaron. "Well, this is a surprise. While I see no need for pleasantries, my name is David and this Jason. We wish no ill toward you. We need only deal with the woman. You may leave now, and you will not be harmed."

I heard movement behind me as Aaron and Max flanked me on either side.

As they moved closer to me, I gasped to see our auras became interwoven, and the color and size grew in intensity and volume. This was the first time I had seen any part of my own aura, and the shock of seeing it combined with Max's and Aaron's gave me a new sense of resolve. Each of the men looked startled as if they were able to see the growing light around us.

Max then took one step forward. I tried to reach for him but he held a hand up.

"We also wish no ill toward you—yet—so you may choose to leave now to avert any unfortunate happenings here," Max said. "However, we will not leave the woman. If you choose to proceed, you will fight us all. You *do* have a choice."

Max's stare intensified as he directed his intentions to the larger of the two men, David, who appeared to be the leader. I looked briefly at Aaron and noticed that he, too, was staring intently but at the shorter man, Jason.

Oddly, it was clear that they had their intended purposes. I had not seen my purpose yet.

I felt a sudden pain inside and something building, almost nauseating. My muscles tingled and tightened. A warmth was growing.

Again David spoke, "Old man, we do not want to hurt you. But if you stay, you will die."

Something wasn't right. How could they be so confident? If they knew we had extra skills as Aurators, then how could mere civilians fight us? I looked back at Max who suddenly stood up straighter, and his aura grew to a size I had never seen before. He then nodded his head, looked back at Aaron, and responded almost nonchalantly, "So be it."

With that, both of the men ran toward us. While Max and Aaron took defensive stances, my body began to shake in anticipation. Aaron ran toward Jason and traded several punches and deflections. In a swift sweeping kick, Aaron knocked Jason off his feet and pinned him to the ground. Jason struggled, and then I saw Aaron get thrown back several feet, crashing to the ground on his back. This display of strength didn't seem possible to me, not considering the red glow that was flowing around Aaron's limbs.

A voice in my head cried out, "Megan? MEGAN? Can you hear me? It's Nicholai. I can hear your thoughts—we're fighting here, too."

Nicholai? You're fighting now? I grabbed the sides of my head trying to hold it together as the pictures of here and elsewhere shifted in and out of focus. Suddenly I could see the fight, not here, but in Greece. I saw it all, Nicholai and Aleck, and in front of them the seven pillars at the Asklepion.

Yes, Nicholai, I can hear you and see some of what's going on. What's happening?

I saw someone run and swing at Nicholai. He stumbled backward to dodge the blow, but stayed upright. Then I saw a man approach him and hurtle a large stone object that shattered into a million pieces when it hit Nicholai. I brought my hands up instinctively to shield against them actually hitting me. But when I moved my hands away I could see shards of stone all around but none of them connected with me.

My heart raced with this conflict between my reality and Nicholai's. I could feel the blood pumping and the heat began raise from within me. I reached for Nicholai who now lay as if unconscious, but I could not touch him. I screamed to wake him but my own sound seemed muffled by a loud crash to my right, as Aaron was being flung into a nearby tree.

I turned my head back from Aaron and saw Nicholai struggling to bring himself back to a standing position as I heard him, "Megan, they are Aurators . . . Aurators who have chosen the other side. We have to fight with all our skills. They are too strong otherwise."

Just then my attention was drawn to my right by a movement, and I saw David jumping several feet in the air. He was aimed to land full force on top of Max. It was in this split second that I saw it. Whenever we connected with them or they fell against anything, their black auras sparked red. It was only a brief flash but it was definitely the Aurator beneath their shadowy aura.

I yelled out a warning, "Max! They are Aurators! We have to use our skills!" Max nodded without looking and raised his arm up to ward off his attacker. When he connected with David, he threw his arm to the side and flung the man twenty feet.

David again got up and ran toward Max, seemingly unbothered.

"You're right Megan!" hollered Max. "Are our auras connected?"

They weren't, so I ran between Max and Aaron. Our auras converged and grew. Just then I saw Aaron grab his attacker with exceptionally more strength than before. I heard the sounds of bones cracking as he contorted and twisted Jason's body.

I was confused for a moment when I realized that I suddenly was looking through Nicholai's eyes again. "Megan, I'm sorry, I don't think we're going to win here. There are only two of us and four of them." I could see that Nicholai was on the ground and another man was running for him.

"NO!" I screamed.

Touch the earth Megan, I heard in my head. I knew enough now to listen to these messages, although I sometimes didn't know who was talking to me—Nicholai, Asclepius, or my own intuition. I felt my body pulled downward in slow motion. I knelt down. I could see movement around me. Greece? I wasn't sure. I put my hand on the ground, closed my eyes and concentrated. I wasn't sure what would happen, but I felt an intense heat radiate from my hand.

I opened each hand to see if what I felt was real. The ground shook and buckled under my touch, then rippled out from my hand and across the land like a pebble landing in a still pond. A shock wave left my body, knocking me backwards.

At that moment I could see the man who was running toward Nicholai. He seemed to mysteriously launch away from Nicholai, and all the dark auras did too.

My vision shifted to two scenes at once, shifting in and out of focus. I saw the effect of the ground rippling as all the Caduceus here . . . and there . . . flew off their feet to land several yards away.

"Megan. Did you do that?"

I think so Nicholai. Are you all right?

"I think so."

Listen . . . if you and Aleck stand close together it increases the abilities you both have exponentially. Do it.

"All right Megan, we . . ."

His voice cut off as I felt someone behind me. I turned but it was too late. He hit me with such enormous force that it sent me into the air and I landed on my side in the grass nearly twenty yards away from where I had been. I looked toward Max and Aaron, who were joined by their auras and fighting David together. Max was flinging him around like a rag doll, dragging him through the surrounding flower beds and slamming him against walls. They couldn't see that I had been attacked.

I tried to scream but he was there again. He grabbed my arms and threw me again, this time in the opposite direction.

"Megan? Are you okay?" I could barely hear Nicholai as I slammed against the ground. Lying on the ground wondering if something was broken, I felt my attacker approach me.

A third man, tall and whose face seemed riddled with hate, sneered at me maliciously, "Neither you, nor anyone else in your family will change life for us."

I looked toward Max and Aaron just as Max flung his attacker into the air and brought him crashing into the glass dome, sending shards of glass everywhere. As glass rained down around the area, I questioned whether I was really the person meant to fix this.

My aggressor pulled out a gun and aimed it at me. I heard a shot but felt nothing. I could see red all around. My breathing sped as if to run away from me.

Thoughts raced through my mind. *My family, my husband, my girls. Protect them at all costs. Guard them.*

A surge of anger electrified my body. "You will not harm my family!" My words surprised me as they came out in an instinctive growl. I noticed that I was lying on a gravel path, and with a speed I had never felt, I grabbed a handful and threw it at his eyes. As his arms instinctively flew up to cover his face, I leapt to my feet and knocked the gun out of his hand. I tackled him to the ground.

Holding him down, I suddenly focused on my hand. There was blood, not his but mine. I looked toward my shoulder that I now realized was throbbing. I had been shot! In spite of all of my newfound strength and feelings of invulnerability, I was in fact not immortal.

I stumbled back, my body felt like ice, and I saw shimmering lights in my periphery. I can't. I can't be this. Not me. I don't want this. I want it to end. For the first time in what felt like a lifetime I wanted to scream and cry, be held and told it would be all right. I didn't want to be responsible. I didn't want . . .

I felt a sharp stab to my gut. My attacker had regained control and was taking advantage of the moment. It was so quick and all I saw was blackness. From behind the curtain of shadows, I struggled to not lose consciousness. A force greater than anything I had felt thus far raged from inside me. I grabbed at whatever was above me, and through the blur I could see the surprise on the face of my target. I felt my muscles expanding and blood rushing to keep up with their need. He struggled to loosen my grip, but my instincts had taken over, and I overpowered him. I suddenly found myself standing upright holding him off the ground. Throwing him behind me, I watched as his body slammed and bent around a stone structure. I walked over to him as I watched him fall several feet down to the ground from the rock wall that formed the walkway in front of the garden area. I moved back over him and he was having trouble breathing, maybe a broken rib. Maybe a lot was broken by now.

He needs to die, I thought.

Keeping one hand above his chest, I was able to keep him pinned as I felt something in the palm of my hand, a throbbing. I pressed down with a force that caused a cracking sound below it. I could feel the throbbing getting stronger and my hand felt as if I was holding something. I tried to wrap my hand around this invisible object and squeeze. That's when I felt it. I was just above his heart. I could feel the roundness of the top part of the heart and the arteries coming off of it. The man below me gasped and clutched at his chest.

My eyes went wide and my breathing quickened as I struggled to maintain my control over the situation. I squeezed my hand and felt his heart battle and shake against my hand.

The man gasped, and then with a final gurgle he stopped moving. He was dead. I felt his heart go limp in defeat under my hand.

Turning slowly I heard Nicholai say, *"We won here, everyone okay there?"*

I looked over and saw Max and Aaron staring at me, eyes wide and jaws open.

Yes, Nicholai, we're all okay.

Just then all of the men screamed out as they fell to the ground in reaction to the transformation. Max and Aaron dropped while clutching their stomachs. Nicholai and Aleck did the same in Greece. Why wasn't I?

Out of the corner of my eye, I saw something move in the bushes. It moved away from us. Tomas? I wasn't sure but I was not going to leave my friends. Whoever it was, I could feel they were already gone.

I felt my body beginning to transition as a quivering chill started in my core. Then electricity shot all over my body, traveling through every muscle and out of my extremities as I felt the familiar feeling of ecstasy warm me from the inside out. I didn't have pain. I didn't fall. This time was different. Shorter.

Max was the first one to rise up. Breathing heavily he walked over. "You okay?"

I took a moment to look myself over. "Yeah, yeah, I think so."

Aaron ran over and grabbed me, wrapping his arms around me. "Are you okay? Oh my God. I wanted to help you when you were on the ground but I . . . I couldn't. If anything had happened." He stopped suddenly and moved away and shifted his weight from one foot to the other uneasily. "Hey, you're bleeding," he observed in a forced nonchalance, averting his eyes from mine.

Max's eyebrows raised as he looked from Aaron to me. "Yes. Megan, are you okay?"

I shook my head at Max to tell him to drop it. Max walked over to me, removed his jacket and wrapped it around my bleeding shoulder. I winced slightly, and he said, "We'll have to fix that up later." Then, walking over to Aaron, he put his arm around his shoulder. Sweeping his other arm out, he said, "Well now, look at the mess we've made."

The comment broke the tension of the fight, and with a sense of relief, we all laughed.

We discussed how to clean up the area and what to do with the three bodies. We noticed that a small tree had fallen nearby, probably due to the earth shaking. Max decided that this would be a good cover-up.

"We should try to make this look as natural as possible." Max held out his hand and Megan was amazed again as he used his gift to pull one man's body out from the wreckage of the Conservatory. He laid him on the ground in front of us. He then reached back up and pulled down a large tree behind the building to make it appear to have crashed the glass dome. It seemed like a stretch but it was the best we had. None of us were sure how this one was going to slip by people.

"Well," said Max, "that earth shaking Megan caused might be a blessing in more ways that we realized. Aaron, check to see if there was an earthquake reported."

Aaron nodded and stepped away to check his phone. Max moved a few more branches to look like they caused the damages in the windows. "Hmmm," he said, "I suppose I'll have to write a check for all of this."

I raised both eyebrows at him, "You have that kind of money?"

"Sure," and he continued his rearrangement of the area.

"So . . ." he started.

"Yes?"

"What was that with Aaron?"

I ducked as another branch flew close to my head. "Hey!"

"Oh, sorry about that."

"Well, I don't know, we were in an argument the other night and then he just . . . got close."

Max stopped and a small tree dropped in front of us that had been in midair moments ago. "What do you mean . . . close?"

"Well, close. Nothing happened."

"Megan?"

"Max, I don't understand. I didn't do anything."

Max motioned to lower my voice. Aaron wasn't that far away.

"Okay, I'm sorry. Listen, it's not that he isn't a nice guy but come on, he's older than me and I'm married to . . . well . . . the only man in the world I can imagine loving. What am I going to do?"

Max continued to move the tree into place as he spoke. "Feelings sometimes get confused when anger, fear, and love cross and lines blur. It sounds like he was angry you were on TV that day . . . that was day this happened, right?"

I nodded yes.

"And he was afraid for you. Plus, on some level, Megan, since we are all connected we have a tight bond. This could be confused with love. I'll talk with him and we'll try to work it out. Don't worry."

Somehow it was calming to speak with him about it, but I also decided it was better to drop the subject.

Just then Aaron walked back over. "There was an earthquake reported but they can't pinpoint the fault line since the epicenter seemed not to be on one."

"That sounds about right," uttered Max.

The three of us stopped and looked around. If I didn't know better I'd say that some natural disaster had occurred here. Brilliant.

"Okay then," Max said. "Aaron, you grab that guy, Megan, that guy, and let's get them to the car before someone shows up here."

We left one of the bodies pinned under a tree and dumped the others in the trunk of Max's car.

Max reached into his back seat and removed a black bag. How cliché, I thought. Opening the bag, he removed suture material and then pulled his jacket from my shoulder. Moving my shirt to the side, he assessed my arm. "Hmm, bullet went straight through. Lucky. A few stitches here and we're all good."

I was curious, "What are you going to do with them?"

"Don't worry, we'll probably put them under a tree or car or something along the way out of the park. It will look natural."

"Okay . . . well . . . that's it?" I stumbled over my words. It felt strange to just leave after this.

"Megan, my dear, go home and see your family." Max cut the last of only four stitches. Hmm, I thought. I had hoped for more stitches.

I watched as Aaron shut the trunk door on top of the men and then looked away.

I sighed, "You're right. I'm dying to see them."

"Go. Go. We've got the other stuff." Then turning, "Okay, Aaron, you ready?"

"Yeah, let's go . . . bye . . . Megan," but he wouldn't look at me.

I waved but he was already in the car.

Getting into my own car, I went home. I drove up to my house, and Luke was standing there waiting for me. He stared at me as if waiting for an explanation. I had no words for him. Stepping next to him, I gave him a quick kiss on the cheek and headed upstairs. He did not press me for conversation, but I could feel him watch me disappear up the staircase. I changed my clothes, flopped on the bed, and without another thought about what had happened, I drifted off to sleep.

27. True Colors

Luke and I sat in silence over breakfast. The girls chatted about different things going on at school. He and I occasionally looked at each other, and I noticed his shadowy aura. I shrugged it off. I don't care today. The news was on in the living room and I froze when I heard the announcer.

In a stunning event of nature there were two earthquakes simultaneously last night. One here and one in Greece, on the island of Kos. Both, however, were not directly on any fault line according to the epicenters. The epicenter for the San Francisco earthquake was in the vicinity of Golden Gate Park and registered a 5.2 on the Richter scale. It was only a few seconds long so the damage was limited to areas near the epicenter.

Not bad, I thought. I wonder if I could get it up to a six. I giggled and when everyone looked at me, I waved my hand as if to indicate that I was crazy. Then I tuned back in to the newscast.

Most of the damage from the temblor was at the Conservatory of Flowers. We have live photos where you can clearly see the destruction that the falling trees caused to this favorite San Francisco tourist attraction. This is going to be a terrible loss and expense to the city. Three fatalities have also been reported, apparently related to the damage and destruction from the quake . . . .

I glanced up and Luke was looking at me with eyebrows raised. I looked at him as if trying to understand what he was thinking. He couldn't know what I had been doing last night so I wondered why he was raising his eyebrows at me. He then gave me a look of disappointment, and I concluded that his look must be in regards to what was going on with us.

He announced to the girls that it was time to get ready to go.

The newscaster's voice broke through again.

We just got news that an anonymous donor has offered the money necessary to put the Conservatory back to its original state. How about that? Now this person is truly an upstanding and generous member of society.

I rolled my eyes and walked into the kitchen with my cereal bowl. I never wanted this, I thought to myself. However, I've never felt normal. Maybe this is my reality. My family is everything to me. Through my recent experiences I have developed a very strong feeling of protection regarding them. I hope that's not because they are doomed to be in harm's way.

Luke walked over to me and his face became serious as his eyes intensified on my own. "I'm worried about our family," he said. I watched his aura lighten and the golden edge return.

"Luke?"

"Yes?" he said, staring at me as if trying to read into my soul. Maybe this was the key . . . the key to his aura.

"Tell me how much you love our girls," I pleaded.

His eyebrows furrowed, obviously confused by my request.

"What do you mean?"

My eyes filled with tears as I begged while I watched the gold rim slipping away.

"Okay, okay. They are everything to me. I love each one. I wake up grateful for another day with them and go to sleep thanking God for every moment of the day."

Then I saw it and gasped. His aura was changing right before my eyes. Warmer, lighter, and . . . gold. He kept speaking about the girls and as he did it continued to change.

My cell phone rang, and Luke stopped talking as he pulled it out of my pocket and opened it for me.

His aura muddied up again as he placed the phone to my ear. I answered, "Hello?"

"Hello Megan. How are you today?"

I was only half listening to Max as Luke walked away from me to the door, where the girls were putting on jackets to leave for school.

I lowered my voice, "Hello Max. I'm good, just tired from very little sleep. Heard the news today?"

"Yes I did, I'm so proud of you. Look at you getting your fifteen minutes of fame."

"Ha ha, very funny. Everything go okay after I left?"

"Sure, fine, fine. I'm actually calling because Vivian and I would like to invite you and the girls over swimming tomorrow."

It had been an unusually warm couple of days in the city, and swimming sounded pretty good. I looked at Luke, "Max has invited us to go swimming, all of us, want to go?"

"Who's Max?" he asked back, seemingly annoyed.

I covered the mouthpiece and mouthed to him so the girls could not hear, "Remember, he told me about my being adopted."

He shrugged his shoulders and mouthed, "He has a pool?"

I shrugged my shoulders in response, "Guess so."

Luke seemed less enthused by the idea, but waved his hands as if to surrender to me to make the decision for the family.

"Okay Max. Sounds great. What time?"

"How about noon?"

"Sure, we'll be there," I said. "Thank you."

Alex was behind us. "Where are we going?"

I hung up the phone. "A friend of mine has a pool and invited us swimming tomorrow."

"Really? Awesome friend. Okay, let's go."

Luke then left with the girls, but not before I got a kiss and a quick "I love you." I watched his aura shifting as he walked away.

I was looking forward to my time alone in my house. I decided to turn the music up loud. Dancing around, I scrubbed and vacuumed. It was a good break for me to escape everything that had been going on.

I stopped dusting as I became distracted with pictures passing through my head of all the people I've encountered. I felt as if I were categorizing them all in my mind in some sort of order. I began to wonder: Were the black auras at the zoo and the Conservatory last night both Tomas? I closed my eyes, searching the pictures in my memories for the answer.

There's no doubt in my mind any more that I will forever have purposes and the uncontrollable need to complete them. In the heat of battle, I can feel my strengths, but when I'm here at home, I start wondering if I have what it takes. I am responsible for bringing our side together. I'm not sure how to accomplish this since most of us are hidden . . . for good reason. If you're purposefully killing people, it's not a good idea to have a very public profile.

I cringed at the next thought, wondering how this would affect my girls.

I had more questions than answers. But for now, I decided to just keep cleaning.

28. Saturation

The girls seemed extra jovial for a Saturday as they hustled and bustled to get their swimming gear together. We headed out and everyone was excited . . . for different reasons. The girls were thrilled to be going swimming, although the day was a bit cooler than expected and they were concerned about being too cold. Luke seemed genuinely happy we were all together, but a little skeptical about meeting new people. And I was just happy to not be killing anyone today.

We drove through the gate to Max's house, and as we continued up the driveway I could hear the girls in the backseat, oohing and aahing as we pulled up to the house. Little Abigail was the first to put her awe into words.

"Mom? I didn't know we knew a rich person."

We all laughed.

When we rang the bell, Vivian opened the door. She welcomed us with a warm smile, clearly happy to see us. Hugging me, she then introduced herself to the girls and Luke, shaking each one of their hands.

After all the hellos, Vivian took us to the backyard toward the pool.

Abigail asked, "Is it going to be cold?"

Vivian smiled, "I don't think so dear. The pool is heated and we're protected from the weather outside." As she finished speaking, she led us through a set of large French doors and into a pool area that was completely enclosed with glass. We could see the steam rising off of the water.

"Well, I guess we won't have to worry about the elements, will we?" Luke spoke up.

"No, now everyone please make yourself comfortable. Can everyone swim? Or does anyone need a life vest?"

"We're good," I replied. "All the girls know how to swim. Thank you."

"Great. Aaron and his wife are here as well. Sofie, his wife, is inside changing, and I believe that Aaron is over with Max at the barbeque."

Ugh, I thought. I didn't know he'd be here.

Luke leaned in when he saw my face and whispered, "Who is Aaron?"

"Another of Max's friends," I answered without looking at him. This was not the time to let Luke jump to the wrong conclusions by reading my face.

I saw Luke nod out of the corner of my eye but did not turn to see the look of concern that I knew was on his face.

Just then I heard a hello from behind us and turned to see a tall woman exiting the house. She looked to be in her mid-fifties but with the figure of someone in her twenties considering how she looked in her bikini. Even Luke's eyes widened slightly at the statuesque beauty. She had auburn hair that was graying around the front and soft, liquid brown eyes. Her face was very inviting as she approached, and we introduced ourselves.

Just then, Aaron stepped around the corner of the house, but his walk stuttered when he saw me. He approached us and attempted to put a smile on his face.

"Hello there, Megan."

"Hi, Aaron." I stood tall showing pride. "This is my family." I looked around but my girls were in Max's pool house changing. I turned awkwardly toward Luke and introduced him to Aaron.

Aaron extended his hand to Luke, who accepted it. As they exchanged greetings, I saw Aaron eyeing Luke's aura, which was tinged with darkness today. Just then I heard the girls come out. I asked them to come over so that I could introduce them as well. One by one I introduced them and then turned to introduce Aaron to them. As he looked at the girls, Aaron's expression changed to one of confusion. I realized that Max hadn't explained their gold auras and this must seem strange to him. I told the girls to go get into the pool so that I could speak with Aaron.

The girls quickly jumped into the pool, and Luke wandered away chatting with Sofie. Once he was out of earshot, Aaron asked abruptly, "Why didn't you say anything . . . about the aura?"

"I'm sorry, I didn't think it was that big of a deal, and I didn't learn about them from Max until just the other day."

Aaron stood straighter and glanced around, "Max knows?"

I paused, not sure why he was so confused by this. "Yes, Max and I have already spoken about their gold auras."

Aaron's eyes narrowed, "Gold?"

I was annoyed now, "Yes, what's the matter?"

He held up a finger and walked around the side of the house. Max came around the corner but not with the welcoming smile that I was expecting. He had a worried expression that deepened every crease on his face. He was searching around for something. Then, just as he walked through the door to the pool area he stopped suddenly.

He wasn't staring at me and I followed his gaze across the tables and chairs, past the diving board, and into the pool. My girls were in the water. I first saw Alex keeping an eye on Abigail in the water.

Then I saw Trina. My breath caught at what I saw. Trina was swimming in the deep end of the pool, diving down to the bottom to retrieve toys. I watched her go down to the bottom and back up to catch her breath.

My legs felt weak suddenly, and I needed to sit down. Luke had walked over to the pool to take towels over to the girls and did not see my reaction. I was grateful for this.

Then I watched as Trina came up to the surface, her aura pushing on the water, causing it to move and shape around her. The other girls' auras did not have the same effect on the water around them.

Max walked over to where I stood with Aaron. "Megan?"

"I didn't know. What?"

Max was shaking his head. "Not here."

We all looked back toward Trina, who was getting out of the water now. The edges of the water lifted out with her, clinging almost as if wanting to stay close to her. She grabbed her towel and came closer, approaching Max.

Max smiled warmly at her, and she reciprocated by holding out her hand to him.

"Hello, sir. My name is Trina. Thank you for letting us come over to swim today."

Max shook her hand. "You can call me Max, and *you* are welcome any time."

"Thank you. It's nice to meet you Max."

She then turned to jump back into the pool and as she did the water around her buckled and moved out of her way, creating space for her.

Vivian walked over and Max whispered something to her. Then he motioned for Aaron and me to follow as he turned toward Luke.

"Luke, can you and Vivian take care of the girls while I steal your wife to talk business?"

Luke nodded in agreement and then shot me a curious look.

Speechless, all I could do was nod.

Max interrupted, "We'll be right back. I'm still trying to get your wife to come work with me."

We walked through, and Aaron shut the doors behind us.

Everyone stood in anticipation, waiting for Max to speak. "Okay, so the water was moving strangely around her, but it was because her aura was pushing it that way."

We all looked at each other more anxiously.

Aaron added, "Only in the water though. As soon as she got out of the water her aura turned gold again. But it was bright in the water, pushing and shoving the water around it. Why was her aura *pink?*"

My chest ached hearing it out loud. I had seen this pink hue in the past and had always attributed it to the red hair.

"Wait. I don't understand. It can't be." I stopped as the reality was slowly setting in.

Max started pacing as Aaron spoke, "And therein lies the problem. Megan was supposed to be the one . . . the woman . . . who was to lead us. There is nothing about another one."

"What does it mean?" I barely got out.

Max was mumbling to himself.

"Max?" I tried to interrupt again.

Max began quoting, "She will carry with her as the descendent the greatest gift of *rebirth, who* will lead us to triumph over all." Max seemed to run out of breath at the end of his statement.

"Oh God, Max—no!" I almost begged. But I knew the answer before he started speaking again.

"I'm sorry, Megan, I believe you are *not* the one to lead us. Trina is."

"*Oh no Megan . . . no, not Trina,*" I heard Nicholai say.

My face fell into my hands as the tears began to fall. "She can't. What have I done by dooming her to this life? Does she even have a choice? What happens to her?"

Aaron and Max looked at each other before Max turned back at me. "We don't know if she knows anything yet, or if she sees anything."

I thought about this for a moment. "I don't think she does because she's never mentioned it. Don't you think she would say something?"

Max's glanced at me to ask, "Did you tell your parents?"

My head dropped in sadness, "No."

There was silence for a while as Max was thinking.

"It is done, Megan. She is to be the one to lead us. You have been given the position of Guardian to protect her and the other girls so that we may again

have peace. Who better to protect her than her mother. There is no one more fierce than a mother."

Nicholai's words rang loudly through my thoughts, and I grabbed at the sides of my head to try and stop what felt like vibrations. I took several deep breaths and when I opened my eyes everyone was looking at me.

Max's face showed he was the only one who knew what had happened.

I cleared my throat. "It is to be. It cannot be undone. Nicholai agrees that Trina is to be the one. I was given the place of Guardian to protect her. I'm assuming the book is helpful now but not nearly as important as Trina . . . and possibly the other girls now, although I'm not sure why yet."

"There is no one more fierce than a mother," Max muttered.

My eyes widened. "What did you say?"

"It is written in Hippocrates's journal after his entry about you . . . or what we thought was you. It didn't make sense to me until now."

Aaron broke in, "Okay, so it is Trina. When? It doesn't make sense because she is so young."

I asked, "So now that we know it's Trina, do we know when?"

"No," sighed Max, "we don't."

We all stood and looked at each other in silence until Max spoke again. "Well, since we are not going to resolve this today, I think we should rejoin our families and try to enjoy what's left of the day. I'm making hamburgers." His smile was infectious, and we laughed with the relief from the tension. We left the room and went back out to the pool.

Luke jumped in to swim with our girls as Aaron and Max stood over the barbecue discussing which hamburgers were rare and which were well done. I watched the girls swimming in the pool and worried for their futures. So carefree right now, laughing about who could swim the farthest holding their breath. What would their future hold? What was to be their destiny?

One thing for sure—I am crystal clear about my destiny. I will protect my daughters. There is no one on earth who I will ever let close enough to hurt them.

I took off my cover-up and joined my family in the pool. My purpose became clear to me as my head broke the water's surface. I am to help each of my girls reach their destiny. Just not today.

CPSIA information can be obtained
at www.ICGtesting.com
Printed in the USA
JSHW081328120423
40227JS00001B/94

9 781669 871385